Life's Surprises

A Novel

SUSAN AMOND TODD

ISBN: 978-1-966343-25-7

Todd. Susan Amond.
Life's Surprises

Edited by: Amy Ashby

Published by Warren Publishing
Charlotte, NC
www.warrenpublishing.net
Printed in the United States

For my daughters,
Elizabeth and Julianne

Chapter 1

As she took the ramp onto Interstate 26 out of Asheville, where she now lived, Rebekah Hayward gazed toward the traffic to her left and merged with ease. Several months ago, she would have been a nervous wreck pulling into traffic like this, but now, she didn't give it a second thought. This rural country girl was easily adapting to city life. In Northern Wisconsin—where she'd lived her entire life prior to her move a few months ago—the only obstacles on the road were the occasional bear, deer, or other critters that lived in the surrounding woods. Most highways were two lanes—one in each direction. All things considered, she was rather proud of how well she was already assimilating to this new city life.

Presently she was on her way to a Charlotte-based restaurant supplier to look at kitchen equipment for the new teahouse and bakery she would soon be opening in Asheville. Her niece Rose and friend Lois had both told Rebekah horror stories about the traffic in Charlotte, so she made sure to program the address of the supplier into both the car navigation system and her phone. Even though she felt fairly confident she wouldn't have trouble finding the place, and was even *more* confident that her sons would laugh if they saw her doubling down on GPS, she wasn't going to take any chances.

The motion of cars going by, the rolling scenery, and the silent passage of time lulled Rebekah's mind into thoughts of three months ago, before she arrived in Asheville for what was supposed to be a short stay. She had been dealing with some major life changes that prompted her to look for her estranged sister Dee. She was quite proud of herself that, after months of digging, she discovered that Dee—and Dee's daughter Rose—had moved to the Asheville area. She decided to make the trek to Asheville after learning that, sadly, Dee had passed away. It was a bright light, however, to discover that Rose, her niece, was still living in the area.

So Rebekah had come to Asheville, North Carolina, to find Rose, and from the moment she met her niece, Rebekah was determined to build a relationship with her. But as is typical of any well-laid plans, the way Rebekah expected to build that relationship and the way it actually transpired were as different as night and day. Rebekah had expected that she would have no problem getting her niece to come back to Milwaukee, where Rebekah had recently moved in with her adult sons, James and Andrew. To her surprise, Rose had no interest in moving to Milwaukee and made it abundantly clear that she thought *Rebekah* should consider living in *Asheville*.

At first Rebekah had discounted the possibility. Why would she want to live *there*? Just the thought of it felt absurd. She had lived her entire life in Wisconsin; in fact, the trip to Asheville was the first time she had left the state in her thirty-six years on Earth. But then Rose helped her to see what a fresh start might look like, and Rebekah realized that perhaps this was the new beginning she had wanted—and needed—all along.

It was shortly thereafter that a unique opportunity presented itself to Rebekah, as if it were meant to be, and without even thinking, she bought a building in downtown Asheville. Her hope with this purchase was to fulfill a desire she'd had in her heart since she was a little girl: to open her own bakery. And hence, her dream was born—or at least it *would* be born soon.

As she cruised down the interstate, Rebekah shook her head and laughed a little, still not able to fully process all that had happened in the past few months but knowing this was where she was being guided. If the past year had taught her anything, it was that sometimes you have to take a chance and follow your heart, not your head. For all of her life, she had accommodated others—parents, family members, husband, kids, employer—and now it was her chance to follow her *own* dream of starting a bakery. She was doing this for herself ... and for Mére. Rebekah's paternal grandmother, Mére, had also wanted to open a bakery, but Rebekah's grandfather, Pére, forbade it because women at that time "just didn't do things like that." Well, thought Rebekah, there was no one left now to forbid Rebekah from doing anything, so she figured she may as well do exactly what she wanted.

Mére had taught Rebekah everything she knew about baking. Many folks said Rebekah was a natural; even her sons had said as much while they filled their mouths and bellies with the various treats she would mix up for them to enjoy after school when they were kids.

Dreams were one thing, but what had finally made the bakery a possibility was when, last year, Rebekah experienced a windfall after playing the lottery. Her—literal—good fortune propelled her into a different world, a world in which she had never even dreamed to live let alone thrive. A world she now knew was her destiny.

It was a sunny day in April, and the sky was a clear Carolina blue, making for a pleasant drive. Rebekah passed an exit for

Lake Lure, a place she would love to visit someday. Rose had mentioned that the movie *Dirty Dancing* was filmed there, which meant nothing to Rebekah who had led a sheltered upbringing in a family where nobody watched TV—except the Green Bay Packers games on Sunday afternoon. This ban on TV had continued into her adult life, including never going to the movies. But the new Rebekah was curious and planned to take a trip to see Lake Lure for herself—after she watched the movie.

Rebekah was grateful that this solo drive to Charlotte had provided her with much-needed time to think about not only the long list of the things she needed to do before opening her business but also the path she had traveled over the past year. It occurred to Rebekah that all of this change had begun *last* April when her father died unexpectedly. It was around that same time when she discovered that the man she thought she had been married to for eighteen years was actually married to someone else. Those were the two major catalysts in the chain reaction that led Rebekah to leave Northern Wisconsin, move to Milwaukee, and then travel to Asheville where she found Rose and her life changed forever. Rebekah smiled as she thought about what her dear friend Tammy back home in Wisconsin would say about this: "When the Universe wants to get you somewhere, it's not always a straight or pleasant trip."

Since Dee's death, Rose had lived with Lois Bender, Dee's longtime friend and employer. Dee had worked in Lois's clothing store and lived with Rose in an apartment above the store until her death. Because of their close relationship, Dee had designated Lois as Rose's guardian in her will. It was devastating for Rebekah to learn she would never see or put her arms around Dee again, but she decided to focus her energy on the great sense of fulfilment she felt over finding—and forming a relationship with—Rose. Rose, now in her early twenties, had quickly become an integral part of Rebekah's life. Getting to know Rose was like having a piece of Dee with her.

Lois Bender and her late husband, George, had run a clothing store in downtown Asheville. After her husband's death, Lois kept up the store as best as she could, but a few months ago, she accepted that she was ready to get out of the business and sell the building. Rebekah, whose life was already at a crossroads, leapt at the opportunity to transform the place into a teahouse and bakery and fulfill her longtime dream.

Suddenly her thoughts were interrupted by the car's navigation as it announced where she should merge. The land had become flatter—not as flat as Wisconsin but a gentle rise and fall in the terrain—with lots of trees. Soon she was merging onto Interstate 85, just approaching the city of Gastonia. The traffic had picked up considerably, making her a little nervous, so she stayed in the right lane and took her time.

Let the other people zoom by, she remembered Andrew had told her one day soon after they had arrived Asheville. *Let's get there safe and sound.*

One thing that helped Rebekah feel more at ease with moving to Asheville and opening the shop was that Andrew had decided to relocate with her. Though they weren't related biologically, Rebekah still thought of Andrew as her son. After all, she had raised Andrew and his older brother James since they were small children. In actuality, they were Ethan's sons from his first wife. *Well, only wife*, Rebekah thought as she shook her head at the absurdity of it.

Rebekah had met and married Ethan when she was just eighteen. At the time, and for nearly two decades thereafter, he claimed that Emily, his first wife, had died in a car accident several years prior. As it turned out, Emily was still in a coma when Ethan left abruptly with his sons after he learned that his in-laws had planned to file for custody of the boys. Ethan changed his and the boys' names and, after a series of moves, took a job as the minister of Rebekah's church. He married Rebekah, and they raised James and Andrew together. Then one day, Emily, having recovered from her temporary amnesia, appeared as if risen from the dead and demanded, in a most unhinged manner, that her husband and—now adult—children return to her, as if she could turn back the hands of time. Rebekah shook her head, wishing she could shake the memory free. The boys were still having a difficult time recognizing Emily as their mother; after all, Rebekah was the only mother they had ever known.

James and Andrew had both graduated from college with accounting degrees, so when Andrew said he was relocating to Asheville to help with the new shop, Rebekah could have jumped for joy. Now if only James would decide to move, she would be a happy woman.

James lived in Milwaukee and was in love with a young lady named Violet who was also an accountant. Oh, how Rebekah wished Andrew could find someone like Violet. Violet was smart, funny, witty, and as cute as can be. Rebekah wondered when James would get down to it and ask the girl to marry him. She chuckled thinking about it. "All in due time," she said aloud to herself.

The traffic was picking up, and it appeared the speed limit was only a suggestion by the way cars were flying by her. Lois had also warned her about the Charlotte drivers, saying, "Most the people around there think they're driving on the Charlotte Motor Speedway. Oh, and when a light turns green, you better count to five or more and look both ways before going through that intersection. I'm not kidding." As she watched the traffic swarm around her, Rebekah decided she'd take Lois's advice.

The navigation chimed in, dictating that she should take the next exit onto Interstate 485. Soon, she was within the Charlotte city limits and could see the skyline with its tall glass-windowed buildings sparkling against the cloudless sky. The city was very pretty and looked like a large island from a distance. She was grateful the appliance supplier she was going to was just off the highway, eliminating the need to drive into "Uptown" Charlotte, as Lois said the locals called it. "Don't say 'Downtown' or everyone will know you're a Yankee for sure," Lois had said with a laugh. Rebekah made a mental note to visit "Uptown" Charlotte one day. Truth be told, Asheville driving was enough for her to tackle right now.

A few miles down the highway, she exited and found the business she was looking for on the left side of the road. After parking and grabbing a folder from the seat next to her, she took a minute to breathe.

This is it. I'm really doing it. I'm opening a bakery. I can do this …. Right?

She had come a long way in a year.

And then she felt a wave of confidence, erasing all the doubt she had been feeling, and knew that Mére, her grandmother, was with her now—as always—guiding her. She couldn't go wrong.

Much to Rebekah's surprise, a few spontaneous tears found their way out of the corners of her eyes. She pulled down the visor above her and, after grabbing a tissue from her purse, looked into the small mirror, making sure she didn't have racoon eyes. Confident her makeup was still in place, she said aloud, "Well, I might as well go in, Mére, and get the ball rolling. The sooner I get this started the sooner I start baking."

She stepped out of the car, took one more deep breath, and entered the lobby of the building where she was greeted by a receptionist who was sitting behind a wood desk with a coffee station next to her.

"Hi, I'm Rebekah Hayward. I have an appointment to look at some equipment for my new bakery," she stated.

"Yes, Ms. Hayward," the woman said pleasantly. "Come right this way. Would you like a cup of coffee?"

"No, thank you," Rebekah replied.

The women walked through the showroom door, and Rebekah smiled as her stomach did a little flip-flop—in a good way.

The showroom was full of stoves, ovens, refrigerators, and other equipment needed to run a professional kitchen. The receptionist pointed to a desk with two chairs.

"Go ahead and have a seat. I'll have a sales rep out in a minute," she said and smiled before turning to depart.

"Thank you," Rebekah acknowledged.

Rebekah opened her folder and pulled out the typed sheet she had created, which listed her kitchen needs. Fortunately, from working as long as she had at Fred's Market and Café back home in Rhinelander, she was more than familiar with many of the appliances she needed and wanted in her bakery kitchen. It also helped that the building she purchased from Lois was a clean slate that she could arrange as she chose. So after she decided what equipment she wanted and took the appropriate measurements, she could plan the layout to exactly the way she wanted it. To be able to design her new kitchen this way was like a dream come true. She knew many new business owners were encumbered with adapting their business to what was already available and was thankful that she had the funds—and the good fortune to have found a building that allowed her to start from scratch.

Rebekah had decided it made sense for her to live in the apartment above the shop where Dee and Rose had lived. She planned to remodel that space too, thinking it might help Rose to feel more comfortable—not so bombarded by memories—when she came to visit. The renovation was coming along well but seemed slow as it always does when you can't wait to move in.

The past several months had been filled with drawing up plans and getting permits for the apartment. Next would be a layout for the bakery and more permits so it could be started as soon as the apartment was complete. She had her fingers crossed for an early fall opening, maybe sooner. She could foresee a lot of work ahead, but it would be fun.

Thanks to Lois, Rebekah had found a good contractor, Harrison Marshall, who seemed to know what he was doing. His father, Douglas, was an acquaintance and personal attorney of Lois and her late husband. Lois had used Harrison over the years for carpentry in the clothing store and in her own home, so Rebekah knew she had someone she could trust.

"Hi, Ms. Hayward?"

Rebekah jumped. The male voice jolted her back.

"I'm sorry if I startled you. My name is Tim. I'm going to help you with your equipment choices."

Rebekah smiled and chuckled slightly. "No problem. I just have a million things going through my mind."

"I'm sure you do." Tim chuckled. "I'm used to that with my customers."

Rebekah handed Tim her list and smiled. "I'm not sure where to begin."

"Lucky for you, I do," Tim responded as he looked over her list. "This list is perfect and just what I need. So … let's get started."

Rebekah took another deep breath and said, "Okay. Yes. Let's begin."

Chapter 2

A s she came down the hallway, Lois Bender could hear laughter coming from the kitchen. She pushed open the swinging door to find Andrew and Rose fixing their breakfast. Lois was so happy to see Rose's transformation since the young woman had discovered her family. It was only natural to want to know where we come from and whom we belong to. Our roots, so to speak.

"All right you two. Are you trying to wake up the whole neighborhood?" Lois proclaimed in her usual matter-of-fact tone.

They both turned and stopped talking, startled by Lois's intrusion.

"Um, no Lois," Andrew started in his standard businesslike manner. "Did we wake you up? I'm sorry."

Lois laughed. "No, my dear, just having a little fun messing with you two. I love to see Rose enjoying herself with someone closer to her age and was actually hoping to get in on whatever monkey business you two were engaging in."

"Oh, we were just laughing about Harrison Marshall, you know the guy who's doing the building remodel," Andrew shared.

"Yes, I recommended him to your mother, and I've known his father, Douglas, for decades." Lois paused to smile, then added,

"Douglas was our attorney, but I haven't had a need to see him, so it's been a while—probably before my husband died, I think. I've seen Harrison, though, when I had him do some minor remodeling to the store and every so often when I needed something fixed around here, but that's been several years ago too, now that I think about it," Lois said and turned to fill her teapot with water.

"Mom keeps coming up with these 'great' ideas that she springs on him, and he looks at her like, *What? You've got to be kidding, lady.* Mom is clueless when it comes to building stuff, you know," Andrew said, and he and Rose chuckled again.

"I have to say, though, Harrison is very diplomatic in his responses and quite the gentleman—he usually takes his hat off as he walks away and scratches his head like this," Rose said, and they all laughed at her imitation.

"So what are you young things up to today?" Lois asked, changing the direction of the conversation as she set the teapot on the stove and switched on the burner.

"I'm headed over to the renovation," Andrew said. "Currently I'm in the process of setting up the accounting system. Since Harrison is trying to get the upstairs apartment finished first before the downstairs demo, I'm working in your old office, Lois."

"I see," Lois said. "I imagine the whole footprint of the place will be changed when Harrison is done."

"And the apartment too. Harrison has quite the imagination for utilizing space and adapting Mom's ideas. It's going to be a cool place when he's done," Andrew said as he took a big bite of an English muffin slathered with strawberry jelly.

"And how about you, missy?" Lois turned to Rose.

"Oh, I'm going for a tour of Asheville-Buncombe Technical Community College this morning," Rose said. "Rebekah—" she hesitated and looked Andrew's way with a smile and a toss of her shoulder-length brown hair, "—and this one here are encouraging me to further my education. Not sure what I want to do, but Andrew says the first two years are filled with the basics, so I have time to decide."

"You do. And a community college is the perfect place to do that," Andrew encouraged.

Rose laughed. "You sound like a parent, not someone in their twenties."

"Having graduated from college, I have a great appreciation for education." Andrew defended himself.

Rose rolled her big brown eyes as Andrew turned to Lois for reinforcement.

"I think that's wonderful, Rose. Your mother would be so proud of you," Lois said with a smile and gave the girl a hug.

"Now you both run along so I can have some quiet time. Go ahead—shoo!" Lois waved her hand in the air, and the young people left, chattering away as they walked out the door.

By this time, the teapot was boiling vigorously, and she removed it from the stove burner to pour the hot water slowly over the tea strainer that held a teaspoonful of loose English breakfast tea.

Nothing like a good cup of tea first thing in the morning, Lois thought as she watched the steam wafting above the cup. While the tea steeped, she went over to a container of scones Rebekah had made and snapped the cover open. *Hmm, lemon*. There were eight of them, and Lois was in heaven. After removing a small plate from the cupboard, she placed one of the scones on it, then thought, *Maybe I'll have another one later*, and smiled to herself.

Her tea now ready, she took the cup and plated scone out to the back patio. It was approaching the end of April, and although from all appearances it looked like it should be warm outside, there was still a morning chill in the air. Lois actually enjoyed the chill—it kind of revived her in the morning.

She decided on a lounge chair that had a small table next to it and situated her tea and scone where she would be able to easily access them after comfortably stretching herself out on the lounge. Once settled in, she took a deep breath of the fresh mountain air and thought about how she was grateful for the day. Now a bite of the scone and a sip of her tea. *Nice.* She took another long sip of tea before she laid her head back and gazed at the clear morning sky, savoring the moment.

Lois's life changed in a way she had never imagined it would after Rebekah Hayward showed up. Actually, things had begun to change a few years earlier when Rebekah's sister Dee showed up, looking for a place to live and work. Dee and Rose had rented the apartment above Lois's store, Bender's Clothier, and Dee took a position working there. Working at the business below their apartment made it easy for Dee to keep an eye on young Rose, and Lois soon became close friends with them. She sighed and shook her head as she remembered the night when Dee passed away unexpectedly from a brain aneurysm, leaving her as Rose's guardian. She raised her eyebrows as she thought, *That right there threw me for a loop.* Raising a teenage girl was not what she had expected at that time in her life. She'd definitely had some doubts about it in the beginning, but Rose turned out to be a blessing.

Lois's husband had passed away about ten years earlier, leaving her alone to run the clothing store. George was the brains behind the business, and Lois was the expert on what would sell and how to display their merchandise. But since she lacked the business sense her husband had embodied, the store had been slowly failing over the years.

Lois reached a point where she didn't know how much longer she could go on with it. After all, she was in her sixties—though most people weren't really sure how old she was, and she sure wasn't going to spill the beans. She was tired and knew in her heart that it was time to close shop, but she refused to give up. After all, the store had been her life for so long. Then one day Rebekah, Dee's sister, showed up and, just like that, bought her building to open a teahouse and bakery. She even offered Lois a job to oversee the teahouse.

Rebekah knew nothing about the art of drinking tea, but Lois certainly did. Lois's mother was English and had instilled much of her British roots into Lois, which included everything about tea. Every Sunday afternoon, her mother had insisted on a formal tea. Lois truly enjoyed it and had tried to pass the tradition on to her own two children—to no avail. They were just not interested. In fact, her children, Geoffrey and Marjorie, were not interested in any aspect of Lois's life. They were both single and career driven. As a result, it had been years since she had seen them and to this day partook in only the occasional phone call. Lois figured they both must have gotten some rogue family gene to be so different than either of their parents. She sighed deeply, gazing blankly just above her teacup before taking another drink. *Such is life*, she thought.

Lois also felt lonely. Yes, she knew she had a house full of people with Rose and now Rebekah and Andrew living with her until the apartment remodel was done, but she was lonely for some companionship—a man's companionship. But where could she find one she could tolerate? That was the difficulty.

Her teacup was almost empty, and the crumbs from the scone lay on the plate. She licked her finger, pressed it on the crumbs, and deposited them in her mouth with a smile before she took the last drink of her tea, laid her auburn-haired head back again, and closed her eyes.

That Rebekah is some girl, she thought. She could bake and cook like no one Lois had ever known. Lois had gained *six pounds* since Rebekah and Andrew moved in with her. It didn't help that Rebekah had Lois and the rest of them taste testing some of her new recipe ideas for the bakery.

She was glad to hear from Andrew that Harrison was doing a good job like she'd told Rebekah he would. It was strange, but for some reason Rebekah seemed a little shy with him. Lois shrugged and softly chuckled. Rebekah would certainly get to know him better during the months it would take to finish the apartment and shop. Maybe the two would become friends …. Or maybe more. Harrison was absolutely charming and, in Lois's opinion, would be perfect for Rebekah.

Lois thought it smart that Rebekah planned to have Harrison gut the entire apartment, changing the whole layout from when Dee had lived there. That would make things easier for Rose, since she no doubt would be visiting them. Lois had enjoyed watching the transformation so far and was eager to stop by again for an update. Harrison had come up with an amazing new layout for Rebekah. *A very talented young man*, Lois thought. After he was done, she might have him come over to her house and give her some ideas on updating a few rooms. Some new furniture might help too. Of course, she'd wait until Rebekah moved out and it was only she and Rose again.

Ah, sweet Rose. Lois was so grateful for the encouragement Andrew and Rebekah had shown Rose to further her education. Rose had become such a beautiful young woman. Slender, petite, with gorgeous thick brown hair and brown eyes like her mom's. She definitely favored Rebekah also. The girl didn't know what she wanted to do, but much of that was just her age. She would figure it out, and in the meantime, they were all there to help steer and encourage her.

Lois was curious about Rebekah's other son, James, and hoped to meet him someday. It sounded like he might be getting married in the next year or so if Rebekah had her way. Lois wished her children were more like Andrew and James, but her kids were just odd, and Lois had nothing in common with them. Now that she'd had this windfall of money after selling the building to Rebekah, she had been thinking of drawing up a new will and leaving everything to Rose. Her children had plenty of money, but Rose needed some security for the future. *Yes, that's a good idea.* She'd call Douglas Marshall and make an appointment for next week.

Lois suddenly remembered she had forgotten to ask Andrew if he was going to be home late that night. She had meant to ask him to remove a heavy box from the trunk of her car. *Shoot.* Now she'd likely have to wait until tomorrow. Andrew had been going out occasionally after work with a girl named Mary Sue Kingston who had worked for Lois at the clothing store. She was a cute girl and obviously smitten with Andrew. You could see it in her eyes. Rebekah offered Mary Sue a job at the new shop after it opened, which was nice since the girl had been displaced by the closing of Lois's store. Rebekah planned to train her in baking as soon as she had her kitchen up and running. *I wonder if Rebekah sees a little of herself in Mary Sue?* Lois thought.

Mary Sue had been born and raised in Royal Pines, North Carolina, a small town probably not dissimilar from the town where Rebekah and her boys grew up. Mary Sue's father was the longtime minister at a church in Royal Pines, which, come to think of it, was another thing Rebekah could relate to. *Mary Sue is perfect for Andrew and would fit in well with the family*, Lois thought and beamed. Time would tell.

Lois closed her eyes and let the sun warm her face for a few minutes. *Time to go in*, she finally decided, not really sure what time it was. Once inside, she saw it was already 9:15. *Might be a good time to call Douglas Marshall's office and make an appointment.* She went into the study and dug around in a drawer where she kept business cards and found Douglas's number. She dialed the office.

"Good morning, Marshall and Associates. How may I help you?" the cheery voice recited on the other line.

"Yes, good morning. My name is Lois Bender. I would like to set up an appointment with Douglas. We've known each other for a long time. I need some help drawing up a new will."

"Certainly," the woman responded. "Now, is this an emergency? Are you going into the hospital or something?"

"Oh, heavens no. Just doing something I've been putting off."

"Great. He's all booked up this week and almost all of the next week …. How about next Tuesday at 11:15?"

"That's perfect. Thank you, and I'll see you next week. Bye."

It's good I'm getting this done, Lois thought as she hung up the phone. *It will be nice to see Douglas again also.*

Since it was still early, she decided to clean up the kitchen and straighten some of the rest of the house. She had never had this luxury during the past several years while running the store alone. And speaking of luxury, she would be meeting two of her friends in Downtown Asheville at Huli Sue's Barbecue and Grill—one of her favorite restaurants—for lunch. After lunch, she'd stop by the store to see how things were progressing before she came home. Lois liked this new way of life. She had never realized how much pressure she was under until now. Rebekah Hayward's entrance into her life had been a gift from God for certain.

Chapter 3

Just because it was Saturday didn't mean Rebekah had the day off. There was so much to do, and Harrison didn't work on Saturdays or Sundays, so it meant she could visit her building alone and assess the renovation work he'd done without anyone looking over her shoulder.

Lucky for her, there was parking behind the shop for about seven average-sized cars, so she wouldn't ever have to search for street parking like some of the other merchants in the area. Plus, the parking lot had enough room to accommodate delivery trucks once she opened for business. For now, though, a construction dumpster took up several of the parking spots.

She unlocked the door, entered, relocked it, and smiled as she enjoyed the silence. Every time she entered that door, a thrill tingled through her body from her head to her toes.

She spun in a circle as she glanced around her future shop. Harrison's guys had it stripped clean, and she couldn't get over how huge the space looked after the demo. All that remained were the beautiful original oak wood floors and the walls that had something called "shiplap" on them, which had made Harrison excited. She remembered the day.

"Oh my gosh," Harrison had said as he took his hat off, ran his fingers through his thick sun-bleached brown hair, and softly chuckled. "I was hoping it was there, and—hot damn—it is. Do you see it? We got us some shiplap."

She felt like an idiot but asked the question anyway, "What's shiplap?"

He chuckled again, then stopped when he realized she wasn't kidding. "Well," he responded, as he replaced his hat and pointed at the wall, "this stuff could save you some money. Shiplap has become quite fashionable. Back in the day it was originally used on wood ships because it was milled with two opposing rabbit joints that would overlap each other, giving a tight seal." He laced his fingers together to demonstrate. "The construction kept the wind and water out. Later, it was adapted to housing construction for the same reason. Some folks used it on the inside walls before there was sheet rock to give them a flat surface to plaster walls and hang wallpaper. I can't give you the exact dates it was used other than a long time ago. It's very sturdy and attractive when finished properly. I suggest we incorporate it in our design."

"Sounds good to me," Rebekah replied. "I love anything that will save me money,"

Harrison smiled and shook his head. "I'm really excited about this," he said—then whistled as he went back to work.

Rebekah let out a sigh as she scanned the downstairs space again. Lois kept telling her she was expecting too much too fast.

When she first decided to use Harrison as a contractor, he told her he had to finish a job already in progress before he started her demo and plans, since they were starting with a blank canvas, but she'd never expected it would take this long. Rebekah had never been involved in a project like this before, though, and had to admit that maybe she *was* expecting too much. Andrew seemed to think everything was progressing nicely.

Up until now, not much was done in the shop area because Harrison had needed to know the sizes of the appliances Rebekah was ordering and where she wanted to place them. Now that she had that out of the way, she hoped he could get the ball rolling. *I'll send him a text about setting up a meeting next week*, she thought as she headed upstairs.

Whenever she went there alone, she walked through the apartment, imagining what her home would be like. She had never owned property or a home before, and it felt pretty cool to think about it.

When she and Andrew first met with Harrison to talk about the renovation, she told him she wanted three bedrooms, two and a half bathrooms, and an open area for the kitchen, dining, and living room in the apartment. She eventually wanted to do some work on the roof patio too, but that would have to wait.

When they met again two weeks later, Rebekah was blown away by the creative layout Harrison presented them with. He really *was* a talented guy. She just had to be patient.

She walked through the door of the room that was to be her bedroom. Her *own* room. The best layout in the room would be to put her bed's headboard against the wall with the shiplap. She laughed. She would never forget shiplap.

As she scanned the skeleton of the bedroom, she imagined the new furniture she would buy and where the pieces would go. Everything would have to be new, given that she didn't own any furniture herself after having lived in a parsonage previously. There, the church had picked out and owned the contents of the house, and she was looking forward to selecting her own things for the first time.

While imagining the way she wanted to furnish her bedroom, a thought she tried to keep out popped into her head. Would she ever love someone again and share that new bed she was buying? After Ethan's revelation, she hadn't thought she could even entertain the idea of being involved with someone again—but now it had been almost a year. She was kind of lonely. Actually, she was lonely for a lot of things, if she was being honest. James; her brothers; her friend Tammy for sure; Wisconsin, snow and all; and, she had to admit—male companionship.

The tears started and she felt angry. She hated Ethan for doing this to her and the boys. The boys hadn't even heard from Ethan since their disastrous post-new year's visit to Canada—where their father and Emily were now living. It sounded like Emily, their birth mother whom Ethan had abandoned, held unrealistic expectations of making up for lost time and figured the boys would be fully on board. But it wasn't the case. Ethan definitely had his hands full with her and, quite frankly, deserved every bit of it. She closed her eyes and shook her head slightly—enough of that! She prayed she would never have to see him again.

Rebekah decided to head back to Lois's but took the long way home, stopping at a bakery that soon would face hers as competition. *You always need to know what the competition is doing*, she thought and smiled.

***

"Rebekah, I didn't hear you come home." It was Lois as she entered the kitchen to find Rebekah with a cup of tea, empty plate, and a white box in front of her that could only be holding some yummy bakery items.

Lois stared, waiting for an invitation that never came, so after a moment, she took it upon herself to peruse the box.

"Oooh a twice-baked chocolate croissant!" Lois said like a kid getting their favorite present for Christmas. "You got this for me, didn't you?"

"Yes, I did," Rebekah said and contained her laugh as Lois sat down next to her.

"I love it when you scope out the competition," Lois said, giddy as she took her first bite. "I've been meaning to talk to you about something. Well, I know you Yankees have some cakes and pastries not familiar to us down here, but we have some delicacies unique to us also. There's one item you *must* have in the bakery, and that's pound cake. Lucky for you, I have the best recipe, but I think every good Southern woman thinks theirs is the best." With that, she jumped up and pulled a recipe box out of a cupboard. "Here you go. But I have to tell you the story behind this first." She handed Rebekah the recipe.

Rebekah looked over the card front and back. The recipe card was handwritten and had random splatters of flour, butter, and vanilla all over it. It was clearly well used—the kind of recipe Rebekah loved the best. At the top of the card, it said Mabel's Pound Cake, and Rebekah noticed it was not in Lois's handwriting.

"So where did you get this, Lois?" Rebekah asked, feeling very curious.

"Well," Lois started, "it comes from more years ago than I want to remember. Now, mind you, I wasn't born and raised in Asheville but in a small Carolina town called Rocky Mount, as was my husband. We were high school sweethearts. My mother didn't want me to marry a local boy but preferred that I go to college and look for a husband who could take me away from small-town life. So I went to the distinguished North Carolina women's school, Meredith College. I received a scholarship. My family was quite proud of me."

"Wow, that's wonderful, Lois. How fortunate for you. I always wondered what would have happened to me if I'd had that opportunity. I guess that's why I want it so much for Rose."

"I want it for Rose also. You're such a dear to want to give that to her," Lois said and patted Rebekah's hand before she continued her story.

"What was good about me going to Meredith and, much to my mother's chagrin, was my husband was in the engineering program at North Carolina State. Our college campuses were next to each other, and we were basically neighbors, so we saw each other all the time. We had dances and such at Meredith that the State guys came to because most of them were looking for a wife, and most of the girls I went to college with were looking for a husband. It's just the way it was back then. We didn't really have much other way to meet someone new and different.

"Well, we had a teacher at Meredith who gave extra credit if we went to her church on Sunday. It was a nice little Methodist church. Everybody in the congregation had the same spot they sat in every Sunday, so I picked an empty place the first Sunday, and there I stayed. It was right next to a couple named Mabel and Rudi Tibbens. They kind of adopted me. Many times, they invited me to their house after church for Sunday dinner. It was nice having a home-cooked meal. Every Sunday I went to their house Mabel served her pound cake that I couldn't get enough of. She always sent me back to the dorm with several slices to share with my friends. Then one day Mabel gave me an envelope and said, 'This is my pound cake recipe. Cherish it because I rarely share it with anyone.'"

"I think I remember that the first time we came over for dinner here we had pound cake for dessert. Was that her recipe?" Rebekah asked.

"Yes, the one and only. I've never given it to anyone, but I think you should have it and make it in your bakery."

Rebekah was touched. This was very important to Lois.

"I will be honored to honor your friend this way. And it will be Mabel's Pound Cake on the menu."

Lois grabbed a tissue and dabbed at the corners of her eyes. Rebekah got up and hugged her.

"So did you keep up with Mabel?" Rebekah asked.

"No. Like a typical kid I graduated and made my way in life, never turning back. I should have looked them up and regret it."

"Well, I'll be happy to configure this so we can make a bunch of them at the same time—and you never know. Someday someone will come in the shop and say, 'I knew a Mabel who made the best pound cake, just like this one.'"

The women laughed as Lois peeked into the white bakery box again, exclaiming, "Oooh, a lemon scone. Did you get this for me too?" She looked up at Rebekah. "Let me fix a cup of tea. Can I fix you another one?" She began to fill the teapot with water.

"Sure, why not." Rebekah laughed and drained her cup before she went over and placed it on the cupboard next to the stove, then sat back down in her chair.

She watched as Lois finished filling the pot and placed it on the stove. It was amazing how her life had turned. She closed her eyes and thought, *I am so grateful for all I have!* A warm feeling came over her, and she just smiled.

Chapter 4

As Lois walked down the hallway to the kitchen, she caught a glimpse of Rebekah standing in the foyer by the front door.

"Morning, Lois. Got anything special going on today?" Rebekah greeted her as she slipped a lightweight jacket on.

"Good morning. Nothing special. Maybe run a few errands." Today was her meeting with Douglas Marshall about her new will, but she wanted to keep that to herself.

"That's great. Andrew and I are meeting Harrison this morning about the teahouse renovation. I'm waiting for him. You know I wake up in the morning and can't believe I'm actually fulfilling a dream I've had, all thanks to you," Rebekah said and gave Lois a hug.

"My dear, I just happened to have an old building that you took off my hands. You are the catalyst making it happen. The visionary." Lois waved her right hand in an arc motion.

"I guess we were both in the right place at the right time. Wonder what's taking Andrew so long. Hey, before I go, I want to ask you something about tea."

Lois looked at the clock. It was 9 a.m. Her appointment at Douglas Marshall's attorney office was at 11:15, so she had some time before she had to get ready.

"What do you want to talk about?" Lois asked.

"I'd like to have a little education about tea, and you're the expert. I wonder if you could just give me the basics as we go along." Rebekah smiled.

"Of course. It would be my pleasure." Lois placed her hand on Rebekah's shoulder. "Once Harrison finishes the apartment and starts the teahouse, I plan on beginning my research to see what kind of product is available for us in the area of tea. I'll keep you in the loop on every aspect. How's that?"

Andrew breezed down the hallway. "Let's go, Mom. Morning, Lois," he said and headed straight out the door.

"That sounds great, Lois," Rebekah said as she began to follow Andrew. "Hey, why don't you come by today and see the place when you're running your errands? A lot's happened since you've last been there."

"Yes, I think I will. Probably in the afternoon."

"Okay, see you later." Rebekah smiled and headed out the door.

Lois entered the kitchen, thinking she was happy no one was home to ask any specific questions about where she was going. After a light breakfast, she got dressed and left the house at 10:45 for Marshall and Associates.

***

"Hello, my name is Lois Bender—here to see Mr. Marshall," she said to the receptionist.

"Mrs. Bender, Mr. Marshall will be out to get you shortly," the receptionist said and motioned to some chairs where Lois took a seat.

A few minutes later, Douglas appeared at the door. "Step back here to my office."

Lois hadn't seen Douglas in several years, but he still was the tall, dark, handsome man she remembered. The wrinkles around his brown eyes and the touches of gray at his temples and peppered through his dark hair added to his distinguished look. *Not bad for a guy in his sixties*, she thought.

Once they were seated in his office, Douglas continued. "It's been a long time since I've seen you—several years before George passed away, I believe. I always liked George. He was such a nice fella. So what have you been doing with yourself? I hope all is okay?" he asked.

"Thank you, yes. I tried to keep the clothing store going but just didn't have the same desire after George was gone, so I recently sold the building. How is your wife, Nancy?"

"I'm sad to say she passed away three years ago."

"Oh, I'm sorry. I didn't know. I wish I had."

"Well, there was no way of you knowing. George and I were golfing buddies, so you only would have found out through him, actually."

"Yes, you're right," Lois responded, feeling a momentary sadness about how life changes so quickly.

"So I see you need a new will," Douglas said, getting down to business. "Tell me about it."

"Well, my selling the building is what has prompted me to come here today. I've amassed a good little nest egg, and I don't want to leave it to my son and daughter. Both of them are very well-off, and I'll be honest, I never hear from them. They're both single with no children of their own, and at the ages they are now, I don't think it will ever happen. They definitely don't need my money, so I would prefer to leave it to someone who does," Lois explained, then paused as she contemplated her next words. "A young woman I became very close to, like a daughter, passed away and, to my surprise, assigned me guardian of her teenage daughter. That teenager is now a young woman and, just like her mother, has become like a daughter to me. I want to make sure her future is secure, so I want to leave her my money and need to change my will to reflect it. Can you help me with this?"

Douglas paused in contemplation for a long moment before proceeding. "Many times children will contest a will like this, feeling it is their right to the money and thinking maybe their mom or dad wasn't in their right mind or was coerced. I suggest you inform them both of your decision in writing and ask them for a response in writing stating that they understand your wishes."

"I can do that," Lois responded. She wasn't concerned that her children would contest the will; they were both very well situated and would likely find her money a mere pittance.

"Then yes, I can help you. I'll have to take a look at your current will and ask you a few questions if that's okay?" Douglas asked.

"Go right ahead, Douglas."

He paused and looked up at Lois. "And one other thing—please call me Doug," he said as he tipped his head down slightly. He held a gentle eye contact with her as he chuckled a bit.

"Doug it is," Lois responded and gave him a friendly smile back, batting her eyes.

The next thirty minutes or so, the two were all business as they went over the previous will and the papers Lois had brought with her.

"Now that we have the business part over …" Doug started with a big grin, then glanced down at his watch. "Ah! You know, it's lunchtime. If you don't have somewhere else to run off to … would you do me the pleasure of joining me for lunch?"

Lois was surprised to feel a little flush rising as she beamed and accepted his offer. "Sure, Doug. I would be happy to join you."

"There's a nice little unknown restaurant around the corner I go to all the time. We can walk to it if that sounds okay."

"I think that sounds lovely." Lois loved discovering new little places in Asheville.

"Let me inform my receptionist that I'm leaving. I'll be right back." Doug headed out the door.

As Lois watched him leave the office, she felt an excitement welling up inside her. She hadn't gone to lunch with a man like this in … well, not since her husband had passed away. How nice of him to ask her. She giggled to herself and had a little lift in her step as he led the way.

They exited through the back door of the office building and set out on an old well-worn, uneven sidewalk to a restaurant that Doug told Lois only locals knew about. When they arrived, it seemed like everyone working there knew Doug by name, which Lois found charming. A couple of the guys working there asked Doug if he would introduce his girlfriend to them, which made Doug blush and laugh as he waved them off.

Doug informed Lois he didn't have a client until two, so they didn't need to feel rushed. They had a nice, leisurely lunch and Lois soon learned they had much in common. They both loved going to nice restaurants, enjoyed the arts in Asheville, and were interested in traveling. And they both enjoyed cooking—Doug being more of a grill master, while Lois enjoyed cooking indoors, preferably pasta, seafood, and chicken with a gourmet flare she had cultivated over the years.

"Lois," Doug started, as they were enjoying a dessert of homemade pecan pie, "I was …" he hesitated a bit and started again. "I was wondering if you would like to do this again sometime?"

Lois again felt a slight flush on her neck and cheeks. "I would love to, Doug," she said and let out an almost girlish laugh. She had never imagined her trip to have her will revised would turn out like this.

"I have your number at the office, but let me give you this so you'll know it's me who's calling," Doug said and pulled out a business card, jotting his cell phone number down on the back before handing it to Lois. "That's my personal phone number." He gave her a wink. "This has been a pleasure," he added and took her hand as his warm brown eyes looked into hers.

"I couldn't agree more," Lois responded with a blush and a flirtatious smile.

***

Rebekah, Andrew, and Harrison were looking over the empty space that would soon be the bakery and teahouse.

"I came across this large roll of paper," Andrew explained as he held it up to show Harrison. "I thought we could cut pieces to the size of the new appliances you've ordered, Mom. You can move them around in the area you want for the kitchen to see how it all fits."

"What a great idea, Andrew," Harrison said, clearly impressed. "Could save a lot of time trying to figure out if things will flow correctly."

"That's for sure," Rebekah chimed in.

Harrison turned to Rebekah. "This son of yours is not a normal kid in his twenties. I hope you know that."

"Oh, I do," Rebekah replied with a laugh. "And his brother is not much different. I'm a blessed woman," she said and gave Andrew a little peck on the cheek.

"Aww shucks, Mom." Andrew looked down and twisted his right foot, feigning embarrassment.

They all laughed.

"Now back to business," Andrew said, suddenly serious. He looked at his mom and then at Harrison for a moment as he regrouped. "I think the best spot for the kitchen and the bakery case is to the right when you walk in the door. In the back we want to have a space for storage and Mom's cake room, which will be used in the future. Also, I would like to see a party room in the back that can be rented out. It could bring in extra revenue for us. Oh! And don't forget a decent-size office for me." He smiled.

Harrison nodded as he wrote everything down. "You're not asking for anything crazy, so let me get back with you all and share my ideas."

Just then, a smiling Lois walked in. "Hello," she said and nodded from one to the next. "Three of my favorite people."

"Well, hey, Lois. Hope you're doing well," Harrison greeted her.

"Thank you. I am doing well, and I've come by to see how your transformation upstairs is going. These two keep talking about it, so I wanted to see myself."

"Prepare to be amazed," Andrew stated.

"I would love to stay for the tour, but I have to run to another job I have in progress," Harrison explained.

"Thank you for coming by, Harrison," Rebekah said, still in disbelief that they were finally at this point. "I can't wait to see what you come up with. See you in a couple days."

Harrison nodded a friendly goodbye and left.

"Ready to go upstairs?" Rebekah asked Lois.

"Lead the way," Lois replied.

Just then Rebekah's phone rang.

"Listen, you two. It's my brother Steve, and I better see what he wants. My brothers don't call often. Andrew you can show Lois around while I take this, can't you?"

"Sure, Mom. C'mon Lois," he patted his mom's shoulder as he and Lois went up the stairs.

"Hi, Steve," Rebekah answered.

"Hi, Rebekah, hope you're doing okay. We sure do miss you."

"I miss you guys also. How are you doing?"

"I might as well get right to the point. We're real worried about Mom. She doesn't seem to be getting much better. I never thought Mom and Dad got along that well and that she would even miss him, but she seems lost. Doesn't eat much either. We invite her to our houses for supper and stuff, but she won't come. She never leaves the house."

"I hate to hear that. What does the doctor say?" Rebekah asked.

"He thinks she's depressed and has given her some medication, but I don't think it's making any difference. She does look forward to the lady who comes in during the week and is interactive with her, but there's just something missing."

"What can I do to help, Steve?" Rebekah responded with concern.

"I'm glad you asked. We were all thinking maybe if you came for a visit with your boys and well—" Steve hesitated, "—Rose."

Rose. Rebekah wasn't sure of that. Rose had her own issues in that area and still needed to process the deep anger she felt about how their mom and dad—her grandparents—had cruelly treated her mother when they found out Dee was pregnant with her.

"The boys and I will be happy to come, but … I don't know about Rose, Steve," Rebekah said reluctantly. "Rose has a lot of anger towards Mom and Dad and, really, all of us. I mean, think about it. They threw Dee out of the house when she was pregnant with Rose without a single concern for what would happen to them. No one did anything to help. And Rose lived through all of that with her mom." Rebekah paused and sighed. "It wasn't an easy life. It makes me angry too, honestly, but I'm not the one it happened to. Rose is a young woman without her mom now, and she feels it's her job to defend her mom's memory."

"You're right. I get it. But can you talk to her? See if she will come. If not, will you come anyway?" Steve asked.

"Yes, of course I will. Let me get back to you with the particulars, okay?"

"Sure. I look forward to your call," he said, and after chitchatting a bit longer, they said goodbye.

Rebekah found Andrew in the temporary space he was using as his office.

"Has Lois left?" she asked.

"Yep. What did Uncle Steve want?" Rebekah was distracted, still considering all that she and Steve had discussed, so Andrew repeated himself. "Mom, what did Uncle Steve want?"

"I'll tell you on the way home." Rebekah shook her head, feeling a hurt bubbling up inside her that she thought she'd had under control—the pain of her sister's absence. She would always miss Dee.

Andrew spent the rest of the day going over numbers on his computer, and Rebekah worked on her kitchen layout until around 4:30 when they decided to call it a day.

On the way home, Andrew asked Rebekah if she was ready to tell him what Steve wanted.

"It appears Grandma isn't doing well, and he wants us to come visit. James too."

"We can do that." Andrew went along. "When do you want to go?"

"Soon," she said and then hesitated a moment. "He … he asked if Rose could come also." Rebekah looked at her son blankly as he steered them down the road.

"Geez, I'm not sure about that one. I guess you'll have to ask her," Andrew responded, keeping his eyes on the road. "Or if you want, I can."

"I appreciate the offer, but I feel I have to do that. I'm just trying to figure out the best way to broach the subject."

"Mom, just ask. And if she comes to me after you talk to her, I'll back you up," Andrew said and placed his hand over his mom's.

"Thank you, son," she said, and they rode in silence the rest of the way home.

Chapter 5

t 5:30 a.m., after parking their car in long-term parking at the Charlotte Douglas International Airport, they wheeled their suitcases over to a glass-enclosed area to wait for the shuttle bus that would take them to the airport terminal. They would then check their bags, go through security, find their gate, and wait for their flight to be called for Milwaukee Mitchell International Airport. The whole process was making Rebekah's head spin. She could never have done this alone.

Andrew had thought it a good idea to stay at a Charlotte hotel near the airport the night before, making it easier to catch their 8:00 a.m. flight. Rebekah agreed since they had to check in at the airport long ahead of time, and Asheville was about two and a half hours away. This was her second time in the Charlotte area, and thus far, neither trip had afforded her any time to see the city. She made a mental note to plan a visit sometime.

Rebekah wheeled her new suitcase over to a bench, sat down, and closed her eyes as she mulled over the past several days. She had spent a lot of time talking with Harrison about the apartment remodel since there were so many decisions to be made for the next stage. The apartment would be done soon, he said, and then he would get started on the space below. It would all be finished before she knew it. In the meantime, she had asked him not to hesitate in calling her while she was gone or to even FaceTime if need be.

Waiting for the shuttle gave Rebekah time to think about the conversation she'd had with Rose about joining them in Wisconsin. She had spoken with Rose the same day she received the news from Steve about their mother's decline. Supper was over, and Lois had gone to watch television in her room, so Rebekah told Andrew to go find something to do while she spoke with Rose privately.

She caught her niece as she was heading to her room. "Hey, Rose, can you sit down here with me a little while? How about we have one of those brownies I made the other day?"

When they were comfortably seated and munching away on brownies, Rose laughed before licking a crumb from her lips and taking a drink of milk. "You've got me spoiled, Rebekah."

"I'm glad you feel that way. There's something I want to talk to you about that I knew would come up one day. I received a call from my brother Steve today, and it appears my mom, your grandmother, is not doing well. Last year after my dad died, she fell apart, and she has gone downhill ever since. Steve seems to think I need to come home, and I think I should also." Rebekah looked down to her hands and then straight into Rose's eyes, which were sharply focused on hers. For a short moment, it was as if Dee were sitting right in front of her. Rebekah hesitated a moment and took a deep breath before she could continue, "I would love for you to come with me."

Rose remained wide-eyed and silent as Rebekah continued.

"When I moved to Milwaukee, I believed you and your mom were probably still living there or close by and hoped I would eventually find you. Before I left for Milwaukee, I thought I would take a chance and see if my mom had any information about Dee she may have kept to herself that could prove helpful for me. I found out your grandmother had seen you once—which she was happy to tell me about that day when I confronted her. She had to sneak out to see you at a park while my dad was away on business. I have remembered exactly what she said about you because it was so touching. 'The baby looked just like her name—Rose. I held that sweet thing to my chest and smelled the top of her head, not wanting to ever let go. I'll never forget the smell of that baby's head; it was like heaven.'

"She also told me how it broke her heart to say goodbye to you both that day. Dee had said she would try to get together another time, but it never happened. Mom told me with great regret that she wished she had stood up to Dad the night he told Dee to leave. She never forgave herself for not doing so."

Rose still said nothing but maintained a steady stare, so Rebekah continued.

"When Mom told me about that day in the park, I told her you and Dee had moved to Milwaukee, and since I was moving there, I was going to find you and your mom and bring you home. Mom wanted to tell Dee she was sorry and was eager to finally know where all her children were.

"That day I saw a side of my mom I never had before, and it just about broke my heart. I realized then that she lived in a different world than me, and I wasn't going to judge her anymore for things she had done or said to me in the past. The day I left for Milwaukee, Mom hugged me and said, 'Find Dee and bring her to me.' And I promised I would."

Rebekah paused and took a deep breath before she continued. Rose's expression remained stoic, her stare intense and unfaltering.

"Will you please think about coming with us?"

The two women sat there for what seemed like forever before Rose spoke.

"I don't want to see those people—ever," Rose responded emphatically. "What they did to my mom was cruel, and I can never forgive them." Her voice broke a bit as she uttered the last few words, and her once stoic eyes became glassy.

"But Rose, it wasn't my brothers' fault, or mine—or even my mom's. My dad was the driving force behind abandoning your mother."

"I don't care. I hate them all for letting it happen and not standing up for her." Rose's jaw quivered for a moment, and then the dam broke and the tears fell. She ran to her room, sobbing heavily.

Andrew heard the raised voices and went to see if Rebekah was okay.

"Hey, Mom. Didn't sound like things went too well with Rose."

"No." Rebekah sighed as she stared down at her hands. "I'm going to bed. See you in the morning." She stood and patted Andrew on the shoulder, then headed down the hall to her room.

All night Rebekah was restless with a million things—past and present—running through her head. She had finally fallen asleep when she heard a knock on her bedroom door. She opened her eyes and immediately squinted; to her surprise, it was already early morning, and light spilled in through the blinds. She stood and opened the door to find Rose standing there, still in her pajamas, her eyes slightly swollen. It was obvious to Rebekah she hadn't slept well either.

"Can I come in?" Rose asked.

Rebekah opened the door wide without uttering a word, and Rose came in and walked to the window. The girl kept her back to Rebekah a few seconds before she turned around and spoke.

"I've been thinking about our conversation all night," Rose said. "I think … I'm really not sure what I think." Rose sat down on Rebekah's bed, hung her head and, with a little waver to her voice, wiped away a tear as she continued. "To be honest … I've spent a good part of my life hating all of you, and I still have a lot of anger inside me. I'm sorry I flipped out on you last night …. But I couldn't help it. I know things were different back when Mom first found out she was pregnant with me, but still …." She sighed as her tears once again caught up to her.

Rebekah sat down next to Rose and silently took her hand as she let her niece continue to vent.

"I'm also kind of apprehensive, to be honest. I'm concerned I might not fit in. You all have known each other your whole life, and now here I am. The odd misfit relative."

"Oh, Rose, you will fit in. I think you'll be surprised how quickly you'll become a part of them, just as you have become a part of Andrew and me," Rebekah countered.

"Well, yes. You have overwhelmed me with your love and kindness," Rose replied as a tear escaped and rolled down her cheek.

"Then be prepared for more of the same from the rest of the family …. *Your* family. They already love you and cannot wait to meet you." Rebekah went to Rose and enclosed the girl in her arms. "Please come with us. You'll get to meet my son James also. It will be like having another brother."

"Hey, Rebekah, I see the bus coming."

Rose's voice, and a squeeze of her hand, pulled Rebekah back to the present. Rebekah stood and grabbed the handle of her suitcase.

"We better come out here to the curb," Rose said.

Rebekah looked at the girl and smiled. She was so grateful Rose had changed her mind and decided to come. "Oh," Rebekah muttered, and she felt a little flutter in her stomach as the shuttle rolled to a stop in front of them. *Go away! Stop that!* she told herself and drew in a quick breath.

Rose must have sensed her apprehension because she smiled and gave Rebekah's hand one more quick squeeze.

Andrew lifted his mother's suitcase onto the shuttle and then gave her a hand up. Rebekah deferred to the two young people and followed their lead into the airport, on to check-in, and through security. She had never seen so much human activity in one place before. There were people everywhere—all in a hurry. As she studied them, she couldn't help but wonder, *Where did all these people come from, and where are they all going?*

When they made it to the gate area for their flight, they found it crowded, but fortunately, Rose spotted three seats together and quickly claimed them so they could sit together. Andrew stood up to peek at the sign listing their flight information and noted that it was still on schedule and set to board soon. After just a few minutes, they started calling seating sections to board, everyone settled in, and the pilot announced they were ready for takeoff. Rebekah had decided they should fly first class, so she and Rose were on one side of the plane—Rose insisting Rebekah take the window seat—and Andrew was in the aisle seat on the other side.

It all happened so fast. Soon the plane was shooting off like a rocket into the blue sky at an angle that forced Rebekah to cling to her seat. But once they reached altitude and the plane leveled off, it amazed her that she felt as if she were sitting comfortably anywhere but thousands of feet above the Earth.

"Well, this is it, Mom." Andrew subtly leaned across the aisle and grinned at his mom. "Another milestone in the life of Rebekah Hayward. The sky is literally the limit," he proclaimed and winked at her. "What will you do next?"

"Stop that, Andrew. You're embarrassing me," she said and laughed.

"I thought that's what children were for, Mom," her quick-witted son told her. "Right, Rose?"

"Don't drag me into this," Rose said, muffling a laugh.

"I'm sure after James meets you, he'll agree that you might as well be the sister we never had." Andrew raised his eyebrows and laughed.

"Lucky me," Rose countered with a dry laugh and a shake of her head as she settled back in her seat and closed her eyes.

Andrew let out a gentle sigh and leaned back in his seat, allowing the steady hum and rumble of the plane lull him into a state of relaxation. His thoughts wandered to his conversation with Rose the night his mom had spoken to her about coming to Wisconsin. Rebekah had told him to let her handle things, but from what he'd overheard, it seemed that her efforts had gone nowhere. He felt he had nothing to lose in speaking to Rose himself—and there was no reason for Mom to even know.

Andrew waited about fifteen minutes to make sure his mother was settled in bed. Plus, he figured he would give Rose some time to calm down. He padded down the hall quietly and softly knocked on Rose's bedroom door.

"Hey," she said as she opened the door, wiping a few remaining tears from her eyes with her sleeve. "I guess you heard."

"Um, it was kind of hard not to. Sorry." He walked in and sat at the foot of Rose's bed, and she closed the door. "You want to talk?"

"Nothing more to talk about as far as I'm concerned." She plopped herself down next to him, her jaw set with stubbornness.

Andrew shifted a bit to look at Rose, and she turned her face away. Even when she was obstinate like this, he found something endearing about her. Something he had grown to … like.

"I think you should come with us," he said gently. "You're missing out on getting to know these people. Our grandpa was the one who caused all the trouble with your mom and the one who called all the shots. Grandma, well ... she's old-school for sure, and let me tell you, she had her ornery moments. Remember, she raised six kids. But ... she was pretty subservient to Grandpa, and she could occasionally be a pushover for James and me too if we played it right. She took care of us when we were small so Mom could work. She's a good person, Rose, and now that Grandpa's gone, you wouldn't have to face him." Andrew took Rose's chin in his left hand and gently turned her face toward his. He scanned her face for a moment before he continued. "C'mon, Rose. I want to show you what it's like in Wisconsin instead of just telling you." He raised his right hand. "I duly promise to protect you from any unkindness you may encounter—which will be none, by the way. Our uncles are all great guys, and Grandma is not so bad really. Please come with us?" He flashed her a goofy pout followed by a grin. "Please?"

Rose showed a hint of a smile that she'd tried to hold back.

"And, hey ... you'll get to meet James and Violet and hear all the crazy stories about what a nerdy kid I was. It would be worth it just for that. I understand your apprehension, but I'll be there to protect you. I promise. This is your family, and remember, we're not all perfect and—" he paused for dramatics, "—neither are you. What do you say?"

Rose gave Andrew a blank look. "I thought I was perfect," she said, imitating Andrew's faux pout.

"Huh, in your dreams sweetheart," he scoffed, causing them both to laugh.

Rose sighed. "I guess I can sleep on it," she said and gave an ever-so-slight smile.

Just then Andrew felt a wave of tenderness come over him. He looked into Rose's beautiful brown eyes—warm, inviting—and on impulse, he leaned forward, hesitating a moment, closed his eyes, and then kissed her tenderly, full on the lips. Once their lips met, he didn't want to stop, and to his surprise, Rose didn't seem to either as she responded in kind and wrapped her arms around his neck.

After a few moments, Andrew leaned back and opened his eyes to see Rose gazing up at him. "I … oh geez, I don't know what came over me. I'm sorry."

"Why?" Rose answered in a soft, breathy tone.

"I mean …" Andrew didn't know what to say.

"You're thinking because Rebekah and my mom were sisters that we're related," Rose responded. "But we're not *really*—and I'm happy we're not," she said and smiled, slowly taking Andrew's hand in hers.

"True … I guess we're not, are we?" Andrew paused for a long while as the two just stared at each other. "Well, right now, I think we need to just focus on this trip. I don't want to give Mom anything more to be concerned about at the moment."

"Yes, I guess maybe you're right," Rose agreed.

"I'm going to my room. For now, I want you to think about coming with us, okay?" Andrew stood and Rose followed suit, stepping in close to him.

"Yeah—sure," Rose responded. "Good night," she said and leaned forward, looking up into his eyes.

Andrew hesitated for just a moment, then put his arms around Rose. He had wanted to do this so many times. As she melted into him, he kissed her again. His whole body shuddered. He could have stayed there all night.

A *ding* from the airplane speakers interrupted Andrew's thoughts, and he opened his eyes to glance across the aisle. There Rose sat—eyes closed, peaceful, beautiful. Something stirred within him. *Stop,* he told himself and fixed his gaze at the seat in front of him. He was so happy Rose had decided to join him and his mother on this trip, but now *he* felt a bit apprehensive. He still didn't know what had come over him the other night, and Rose hadn't said another word about it. Could there really be something between them? Rose was right; they weren't *actually* related. Rebekah was his mother in word and thought only. She had adopted him and James when they were little, but any legality to the adoption had become null and void after Emily, their birth mom, showed up. Truth be told, Rose felt more like a friend than a cousin—and now something more. He couldn't stop thinking about her and how desperately he wished he could kiss her again, but he didn't want to put any more on his mom's plate. Andrew sighed. He would let things be—for now—and see what might evolve.

***

Before they knew it, they were nearly at their destination. Rebekah looked out the window as they approached Milwaukee, descending over Lake Michigan. The lake was huge, and Rebekah was mesmerized by the white caps on the waves. To her, it looked more like an ocean. Soon there was a clear vision of the shoreline, and the city of Milwaukee grew closer and closer until they were once again on land. *I did it!* Rebekah thought. *What a great way to get where you want to be.* She was already happy she had made this trip.

After retrieving their luggage, they headed off to the car rental desk. Although James had a car, she wasn't sure how long James and Violet could stay at her mom's. And, to be fair, she wasn't completely sure what she was walking into. She felt it best to have her own set of wheels just in case.

Andrew was worth his weight in gold the way he took charge. *He will make some lucky woman a good husband one day*, Rebekah thought as he opened the car door for her. She couldn't wait for James to meet Rose so she could finally have the three most important people in her life all together.

"How are you doing, Rose?" Rebekah asked when they got into the car. It had been a long day, but soon they would be at James's place. Rose seemed to be holding up well.

Rose responded with a forced smile. "I'm doing great, thanks. Looking forward to the next several days." She paused before adding, "Okay, I'm a little nervous."

Rebekah put her arm around the girl's shoulders and smiled. "All will be just fine. Trust me."

"I do, but the anticipation is messing with my mind."

"I'm a little anxious myself, so know you're not alone," Rebekah said, giving her niece a peck on the cheek

Rebekah was determined it was going to be a good week for them.

***

The next day, James suggested Rebekah and Rose ride with him and Violet on their trip to Northern Wisconsin and Andrew drive by himself.

"It will give me an opportunity to have Mom to myself and get to know Rose better," James suggested.

"Well, I guess that will be okay," Andrew agreed. "I can play my music and sing along without anybody telling me to stop." He laughed and gave his brother a little punch on the arm.

"Oh, and you can trust me, we would definitely be telling you to stop." James laughed and raised his eyebrows.

Rebekah loved the brotherly banter she had grown so accustomed to and missed.

They left around 9:00 a.m. for their almost four-hour trip.

"Hey, I want to stop in Cecil at that diner we always ate at when we drove home from college," Andrew told them as they walked to the cars. "They have the best homemade pies—no offense, Mom, but they are as good as yours," Andrew said apologetically.

"No offense taken. In fact, I would love to try them. You never know where a good idea will come from. Every bakery needs to have their specialty, and I've decided I'm going to offer some of the baked goods from up here to the people down in Asheville," Rebekah confided.

"That's really a great idea, Mom," James said, "and something you're really good at."

"Thanks, son."

Around 1:15, both cars pulled into the driveway of the house where Rebekah had grown up. She always thought it a large well-kept house, but today, it looked rather small, sad, and dreary as she surveyed the dwelling with different eyes.

"Well, here we are," she said and turned to Rose with a smile. "All will be fine, sweetheart."

"This is the first time I'm meeting all of them also, Rose," Violet piped in. "We can start our own support group. C'mon," she said as she linked arms with Rose.

"You two are funny," James said. "This one here has been a nervous wreck about meeting our family," he said, tossing his head toward Violet and then speaking to her. "Now you should be prepared for some teasing, Violet, and anything my uncles tell you about me as a kid is probably a fabrication."

"Oh, is that so?" Violet said with disbelief in her voice. "I'll be the judge of that."

They all had a little laugh before heading to the house—a much-needed stress reliever for each of them. As they started walking up the driveway, Andrew arrived, shut off the rental car's engine, and ran up to join them.

"Hey let's go in," Andrew said. "Does grandma know we're coming? I mean, I don't want to scare her."

"I see Ben's car around back; I think we're fine. I told Steve about what time we'd arrive, so I'm sure that's why Ben's here." Rebekah had no sooner said this when Ben came out the front door.

"Hey, you guys. Hope you had a good trip." Ben came straight up to Rebekah, wrapped his arms around her, and gave her a big bear hug that lifted her off the ground. "God, I miss you."

Rebekah felt her eyes start to water and chuckled.

"Aww stop that now or you'll get me going," Ben said and wiped his eyes across the sleeve of his shirt.

He next looked to the two young women. "Now who's who here?"

James stepped in. "Uncle Ben, this is my girlfriend Violet, and this is our cousin—and your niece—Rose."

Ben shook Violet's hand, stepped back, and shook his head. "I can't believe he hooked himself a beauty like you. Are you sure about this? My brothers and I got some good stories to tell you."

Violet looked to James and raised her eyebrows.

"I told you," James said, extending both hands.

Ben laughed again, but as he turned to Rose, his demeanor quickly changed. Tears quickly pooled at the bottoms of his eyes, one spilling its way over.

"So you're our Dee's little girl," he said, placing his hands on Rose's shoulders at an arm's length and studying her face. "Welcome to the family. We're so happy to finally meet you and have you be a part of us."

Rose could only manage a timid smile and quiet thank you.

That did it for Rebekah. She let the tears fall. Rose *had* to know how welcome and loved she was at this point.

"Sorry to get everyone emotional here," Ben apologized and chuckled as he again wiped his eyes on his sleeve. "Mom's napping right now, but we've prepared her for your visit. Myself, Jake, Tom, and Steve told her about Dee's passing when you first told us, Rebekah. We didn't go into details, but the first thing she asked was, 'What about the baby?' We told her the baby is a grown woman now, and we hope someday she will visit us. She seemed confused by that. We just do the best we can."

"And you've done wonderful," Rebekah said.

They brought all their bags in and settled in to their rooms. Rebekah was in her old room, and Ben put James and Andrew in a room together and Violet and Rose together. Even though Mom was out of it, James and Violet would never get away with rooming together in that house.

According to Ben, their mom usually slept for several hours every afternoon—until about 3 p.m. The plan was to settle in and then head over to Jake's house at 4:30. Since it was Saturday, the family auto repair business closed at 2 p.m. Ben no longer worked for the family business since moving to Green Bay after his divorce the previous year. And now, because he worked Monday through Friday, he was able to meet with them earlier than the rest. Ben had recently married a lovely woman named Mary Lou, but to keep family peace around his mother, he never brought her to family get-togethers. His divorce was a sore subject with his mother.

"You guys get settled in and rest a bit before we go over to Jake's," Ben said. "We're doing a potluck thing tonight like we used to do all the time. Mom will like that. Jake has a fancy grill and has done some barbecue for supper, and everyone else is bringing something to have with it. He's obsessed with his grill. You have to tell him the barbecue is as good as what you have had down South or he might cry." Ben chuckled.

Rebekah smiled. It was just like old times. She had missed it.

Chapter 6

After getting settled in their rooms, they gathered in the living room and visited with Ben until their mother, Ruth, was heard moving around upstairs.

"Well, you ready to go see Mom?" Ben inquired.

"Yes, I believe so," Rebekah said, wondering what she would say to her mother. She didn't want to confuse her if she was having trouble with her memory. It was best not to worry and play it by ear.

Rebekah and Ben headed up the stairs and found Ruth in her room, sitting in a chair.

"Mom, I'm so happy to see you," Rebekah said.

Ruth looked so frail, as if a big wind could have blown her away like a leaf. She stood up and held her arms out for a hug. "Oh, Rebekah. They told me you would be here."

As Rebekah embraced her mother's slight frame, she could tell something had changed. Ruth had never been this happy to see Rebekah before. "Yes, I took my first flight ever to come see you today. You know I moved away from Milwaukee?"

Rebekah guided her mom back to the chair and sat on the edge of the bed, facing her.

"Yes, I know, but I don't understand why you have to live so far away." Ruth's face was more wrinkled, and she looked puzzled. "Are you doing well? Are you working? Your brothers told me you're living in North Carolina now of all places. That's ridiculous when you have a perfectly good place to live here. I don't understand."

Now she was sounding like the mom Rebekah knew. Rebekah started, "Remember I told you when I moved to Milwaukee, I was going to look for Dee, and you were all for that? I did, and well, it took me to Asheville, North Carolina. Dee had worked with a law firm in Milwaukee and was so good at the job, she moved up in the company and was promoted a few times. She moved all over the country and ended up in California."

"For Pete's sake! Why would she want to do that? Did she drag that little baby with her? Is she here with you?" her mom questioned.

"Let me continue with my story, Mom." Rebekah looked briefly at Ben who had sat next to her on the bed. He nodded and gave her an encouraging smile. "She got married in California to a man who turned out to be very bad, and she ran away from him to Asheville so he couldn't find her and Rose. She ended up working in a clothing store for a wonderful woman named Lois who became like family to her, and—this is where it gets sad."

Rebekah paused for a moment, not wanting to continue but knowing her mom needed to hear the full story from her. She wanted to make sure her brothers hadn't missed anything.

"Dee died, Mom. From a brain aneurism. Lois and Dee had become very close, so Lois took care of Rose. Rose is now a beautiful young woman."

Ruth got up from her chair and walked to the window, looking out. Rebekah was afraid maybe she had given her mom too much information all at once.

"Yes, they told me about Dee," Ruth said, keeping her back to Rebekah. "So what you're saying is you found Rose. I honestly didn't think I would ever see either of them again. I'm sad about Dee …." Her voice quivered, and she paused for a few seconds. "So sad. I should have stood up to your dad. I'll never forgive myself for not doing that, but even more, I don't think I've ever forgiven your dad for throwing her out like he did. I never felt the same about him or our marriage after he sent Dee away. It angers me that he died and I never got to tell him that I felt he was wrong."

As she listened to her mother, it was like a light came on for Rebekah. That's why she had become so mean, especially to Rebekah. Ruth had kept her own regrets inside for all those years and let them fester to the point that she had no joy left in her life. The repressed anger had destroyed any happiness. Rebekah's heart ached at the realization. How could any of them have known? Rebekah got up from where she was sitting and went to her mom, who was still gazing out the window. She wrapped an arm around the old woman's shoulders, feeling bones where Rebekah remembered there were once strong muscles from all the hard work Ruth had done around the house raising six kids.

"I didn't know that, Mom. I wish I'd known. You could have counted on me for support," Rebekah said, her voice tender.

"You were just a child when it happened, Rebekah, and then you had your own life with Ethan."

Ruth was right. *And* Rebekah had her own set of problems with Ethan.

Ruth kept her gaze on the window.

"Well, the story continues, Mom. When I found out Rose was still in Asheville, Andrew and I drove down there so we could meet her and let her know she had family. She wasn't very receptive to us at first, but we won her over. I convinced her that she needed to meet her family. In fact—she came here with us. She's sitting downstairs in your living room."

"What?" At last, Ruth turned to Rebekah, wide-eyed. "She's here with you?"

Rebekah nodded.

"Well, what are we doing up here?" Ruth headed to the door then abruptly stopped. "Let me stop in the bathroom and comb my hair first. I can't meet her with bedhead," Ruth added and briskly headed out of her room to the bathroom.

After they'd heard the door close, Rebekah turned to smile and blink several times at her brother who hadn't uttered a word since they came upstairs. "That went well, I think, don't you? You sure were quiet."

"You were doing just fine without any help from me. Besides, I've learned the female species is much better in these situations. You guys rule." He smiled sheepishly and gave his sister a high five, which she returned.

After a few minutes, Ruth came out of the bathroom. Ben took her gently by the arm and guided her down to the living room with Rebekah trailing just behind.

The kids immediately stood up when they saw Ruth enter the room.

"Mom," Rebekah said, wrapping an arm around her mother's shoulders as she fought back tears, "I want you to meet your granddaughter, Rose."

Ruth walked over to her granddaughter, as if in a trance, and touched the side of Rose's cheek with her hand.

Rose beamed as she leaned forward to give her grandmother a kiss on the cheek.

"You remind me of Rebekah when she was your age. I held you once when you were a tiny baby. So sweet. I didn't want to give you back to your mom. I love babies," Ruth shared.

"Yes, Rebekah told me … Grandma. I'm so happy to be able to meet everyone. I had no idea I was related to so many people. I … I always thought I was alone." A single tear rolled down Rose's cheek, which she quickly wiped away.

"Oh, and there are a lot more of us, for sure," Ben interjected. "In fact, at about four fifteen we're going to head over to Jake's so we can all visit and have some barbecue."

"Oh, that should be fun. I love his barbecue," Ruth proclaimed with a smile.

"Mom, we have someone else for you to meet. This is Violet, James's girlfriend," Rebekah said. She didn't want poor Violet to be lost in all that was going on.

"Girlfriend? How wonderful! When did this happen? Why haven't you brought her up here before?" Ruth scolded and took Violet's hand in hers.

This was not the mother Rebekah had known, but she liked the change. They all sat and visited until it was time to leave for Jake's house.

***

Rebekah was overwhelmed by the hugs and kisses she received from her family. Her brother, Tom, had just gotten a new high-tech camera, so she was sure the event would be well-documented.

James endured the teasing about having a girlfriend none of them knew about and then came the always anticipated question: "When are you two getting married?" Rebekah listened intently for James's answer; she had wanted to ask the same question but didn't want to pressure him. Both James and Violet blushed but never really answered.

Andrew was interrogated next by Rebekah's brothers. "What about you? Where's your girlfriend?"

"Well, for your information, I have been going out with someone," Andrew quickly responded and gave Rose a quick glance. "Her name is Mary Sue, and it's only been a few months. Nothing serious." He threw up his hands defensively, lest anybody start asking about marriage. "Back off you guys!" Andrew shot a glance back at Rose who was laughing.

"Mary Sue?" Jake said in a Southern drawl. "I do *declare!* I think you may become a Southerner, dear Andrew."

They all laughed.

"Well, yes, she is a Southern girl. But what else is there going to be in North Carolina?" Andrew raised his hands, palms up. "They sure do have some beauties down there though. *Southern Belles,* I believe they call them." He gave a big smile and a look toward Rose. Fortunately, no one noticed.

Rebekah looked around and noticed that everyone, even her mother, was laughing. She'd been amazed at her mom's behavior throughout the evening and knew she'd done the right thing in coming to visit.

Eventually, Rebekah's four brothers pulled her aside to talk.

"Rebekah, your visit has certainly had an effect on Mom," Tom, her oldest brother, said. He lived the closest to Ruth and had been caring for her.

"I know," Ben said. "We had such a nice visit before we came over. Mom seemed so happy. You were the perfect medicine."

"Personally, I think *Rose* was the perfect medicine," Rebekah said and looked over at their mom who was in an absorbed conversation with her granddaughter, both smiling ear to ear. "So tell me more about Mom's health."

"I went to her last doctor's appointment with her when I was home a few weeks ago," Ben started, "and the doctor said she had high blood pressure and some atrial fibrillation of her heart. It's probably not much different than what was wrong with Dad, it's just he would never go to the doctor. He also said she suffered from depression, but you would never know it by looking at her today."

"So what is the doctor doing to help her?" Rebekah queried.

"Medication, basically," he responded with a lift of his shoulders. "Diet change, although she doesn't eat much anymore. She hasn't been cooking much at all, so we bring stuff to her, which is good because then we can control her diet."

"One of us usually takes her to the grocery store once a week to get a few things, but we have meals in the freezer that she can either microwave or heat in the oven," Steve added.

"Wow, I'm so proud of the four of you," Rebekah said, shaking her head. "I feel guilty, but yet I feel led to North Carolina and Rose. She has no one but Lois—the woman Dee worked for. They became as close as family."

"It's okay, Rebekah. Your job is to be there for Rose. She's a nice young woman, for sure, considering all she's been through," Tom said and put his hand on Rebekah's shoulder.

"Well, let me tell you, she was not that happy to meet me at first. Felt we all had deserted her mom. But Andrew stepped in and won her over for me. Then she almost didn't come here with us on this trip, but she—thank goodness—changed her mind. She's a different person now, and she knows she has a place where she belongs. She's even going to college this fall. I'd like to believe we've had an effect on her life." Rebekah took in a deep breath and exhaled as she turned and looked at Rose who was still chatting with her grandma and newfound relatives.

"Rebekah," Steve said with a smile and softness in his eyes, "you have always had an effect on all of us just with your presence—since the day you were born."

Rebekah teared up and was unable to speak. She felt so overwhelmed with love from these four guys she was privileged to call her brothers.

"I have a question," Steve said, scratching at his chin.

Rebekah's stomach fluttered as she anticipated his question.

"How in the world is it that you're opening a business in Asheville, North Carolina? Where did you get the money?"

Rebekah chuckled softly. This was the question she had been dreading but knew was coming. The last thing she wanted was for her family to find out about the lottery money she had won—not that they would ask her for any. She just felt it might change their relationship if they knew how wealthy she was.

"We've all been wondering that, sis," her oldest brother Tom added. "We know how expensive it is to run the family auto business, so how are you running this place you're opening?"

Rebekah took a deep breath. "Well … as I mentioned before, Lois Bender was the woman Dee worked for in Asheville. She basically gave Dee and Rose refuge after they were forced to change their identity. Lois became Rose's guardian after Dee passed. She owned a clothing store that was not doing well. So, for Rose's sake, I decided to stay in Asheville, and I'm opening a bakery and teahouse in Lois's soon-to-be-renovated building. Lois is an expert in all things tea, and I'm an expert at baking. It seemed like a perfect idea. I've always wanted my own bakery, and now I'm getting it. There's also an apartment above the building—where Dee and Rose lived. We're remodeling it so Andrew and I can live there. I eventually want to buy a house, and the apartment will be rented out. Andrew is doing all the accounting for us. I really love Asheville, and I hope you all will come visit." She exhaled and then smiled as she looked from one brother to the next.

"Still, it's got to cost a lot of money to do what you're doing. Did you get any money from Ethan?" Tom pressed for more information.

Rebekah shook her head and pursed her lips like she'd just eaten a lemon. "Uh, no. That would be the last place I'd go for money. Just rest assured we have it all under control. I appreciate your concern, but we have a good business plan thanks to Andrew." Rebekah wanted to change the subject.

"Did you try to get Rose to move back here with you?" Ben asked.

Phew. "Yes, I did, but she wouldn't budge. Every time I suggested she move here, she came back with, 'Why don't you just move to Asheville?' And honestly, guys, after what happened with Ethan, I would never come back here to live—too many bad feelings. I probably would have lived in Milwaukee, but Rose could not be convinced. That girl needs someone, and I know that someone is me."

Ben came to Rebekah and kissed the top of her head. "I agree, little sis. It is you. We all need you, but she needs you the most."

"Rebekah, we wish you great success, and I'm putting Asheville on my list of places to visit," Tom said, and their brothers nodded.

"Since Ethan's name came up ... have you heard from him at all, or have the boys heard anything?" Ben asked.

"Yes, we've been wondering. It's like he fell off the Earth," Jake chimed in.

"I have heard nothing and hope I never will," Rebekah said with great finality and raised a hand as if to signal a stop. "He's in

Canada somewhere as far as I know. The boys might know more, but they never share information pertaining to him, because they know I've closed that chapter. They did go visit Ethan and Emily a few months ago, but according to Andrew, it went bad. I don't think there's a plan to go back again. Ask the boys about it."

"Will do," Ben replied.

"How long do we have the pleasure of your visit?" Steve asked.

"We'll be here until Thursday morning when we go back to Milwaukee to spend a few days, then we'll fly back to Asheville on Sunday. Got to get back to the shop renovation and set up. I'm thinking the apartment will be done fairly soon after we get back. It's all rather exciting." Rebekah smiled.

"That's just great. I can already tell this visit from you is going to be good for Mom—and for us also. So happy to have you home," Tom said, and the other brothers all agreed. "Let's go back to the others. Don't want them to think we're talking about them," Tom said and chuckled.

Rebekah gave him a quick hug and then walked back to the rest of the family, so happy to be there.

Chapter 7

They hadn't even been gone twenty-four hours when Lois already began to miss Rebekah, Andrew, and Rose. It was Sunday morning and so quiet. Rose was a beautiful addition to her mundane life, but now Rebekah and Andrew had completed it. Lois was a blessed woman and grateful beyond words for *this* gift.

Lois fixed her usual morning cup of tea—a new yummy one she had discovered called Paris—and opened a plastic container with some apple muffins Rebekah had made before she left for Wisconsin, placing one on a plate and grabbing a fork, knife, and napkin. She was raised that it was more ladylike to eat muffins with a fork then stuffing them in her mouth. Her mother was English *and* a Southerner—what other proper way could there be to eat a muffin?

Lois headed out to the patio. She situated herself in the lounge chair with a small table next to it. Her yard had always been her favorite place to indulge in reflections of life.

Speaking of reflections … it was certainly interesting how Doug Marshall had become a part of her life after her visit to his office. Handsome, professional, and a gentleman, as well as in her age range … and available. What more could she ask for?

But yet she found she was ... she wasn't sure ... maybe hesitant ... maybe a little *un*sure? Lois sighed. Although it hadn't yet been a full week since she was at Doug's office, he had called her several times just to say hi and see how she was, wondering when they might be able to see each other again. That felt pretty exciting for a sixty-something woman. Kind of like being courted.

She shook her head. She was so silly .... But then an idea came to her. She had the house all to herself for the next week, so why not invite Doug over for dinner the next time he called? She felt it was too forward for her to call him, but she knew he would call her. Now what should she make for him?

She was deep in thought, planning her dinner with Doug, when her phone rang and startled her. She had forgotten she placed it in her pocket. It was Rose.

"Hello, Rose dear, how are you? I've been missing and thinking about you."

"Hi, Lois. It's not too early to call, is it?" Rose asked.

"Why, no. I've been up for a bit. I am still in my jammies though." Lois chuckled. "And I'm on the patio, enjoying a cup of tea and one of Rebekah's muffins. Please tell her I said, 'Thank you.'"

"I'll be sure to. I wanted to check up on you. You know, make sure all is okay?"

"Why, of course I am. Missing you all, but still enjoying the solitude." *How sweet of the girl to be concerned*, Lois thought. "Now tell me about the trip and how things are going."

"Well, it's very different here. Even though the land is so flat, it's very wooded—makes me feel more at home. Everyone talks funny, but I'm already getting used to it." She chuckled. "Rebekah's brothers—my uncles—are very nice guys. Tom is the oldest, then there's Jake, Ben, and Steve. We went to Rebekah's brother Jake's house yesterday for a cookout. I met lots of extended family, and to be honest, I don't remember all their names, but everyone couldn't have been nicer. I met so many relatives I didn't know I had. Andrew says he's going to show me around this week. Rebekah's son James and his girlfriend Violet are nice also. I think we're going back to Milwaukee Thursday to stay at James and Violet's house and see some sites around there before we come back on Sunday."

"I'm so happy you're having a good time. What about your grandmother?" Lois was most curious about how things were with Ruth since she had heard some *stories* about the woman from Rebekah.

"It's kind of sad. I feel like my grandmother is ... broken down. Rebekah had a talk with me before we went to Uncle Jake's last night. She thinks her mother never came to terms with my mom leaving and that she wasn't in agreement with Rebekah's father. He's the one who really turned his back on my mom, and Rebekah thinks my coming to visit is helping Grandma come to peace about the whole situation. I think she's right. Grandma has been nothing but loving and kind to me."

"Dear, I'm so happy to hear that. Sounds like you're becoming a very important member of that family," Lois said.

"Yeah, maybe. You know ... I really didn't want to come here at first, but I feel a part of these people. It was always just me and Mom, and then me and you. Still wrapping my head around all these people—but in a good way."

Lois smiled. Rose sounded so happy.

"Grandma has some health problems Rebekah told me about. Something with her heart and high blood pressure. She also said depression, but I don't see that. Maybe because of all the activity right now she's happier. Could be a possibility," Rose speculated.

"Darling, you would lift anyone's spirits. You lift mine all the time." Lois felt her smile spread from her lips to her heart. "So what are you and your newfound family doing today?" she asked.

"I'm not sure exactly, but Andrew and James said they want to go fishing, travel the trails around here on ATVs, show me the family auto shop, go to Rhinelander—which is the largest town close by—and all sorts of things I can't remember. Then, like I said earlier, we're going back to Milwaukee Thursday before we fly home to Asheville on Sunday, so I'm pretty sure I'll be busy and have a great time." Rose paused for a quick breath and then asked, "What about you? What are you going to do while we're gone?"

"Oh, me? Well, now that the frost is past, I think I'll get some flowers planted and just putz around the house."

"Just what you like to do—and in peace and quiet too. Don't get too used to it," Rose said.

"Never, my child. Now go have fun with your family. That has a nice sound, doesn't it?"

Lois heard a little inhale and exhale before Rose said, "Yes, it sure does."

"See you in a week. Bye-bye."

"Bye," Rose responded and hung up.

Lois looked up to the sky, placed her phone on the table next to her, and thought, *What a relief.* She only wished Dee were still there to share in the moment with her daughter. She was sure Rebekah and Rose were wishing the same.

Lois figured it was time to go in and get ready for the day. She was going over to the local plant nursery to look around for something colorful and pretty to put in the backyard flower gardens, but first she needed to get some laundry going, make her bed, and clean up the kitchen. To her surprise, however, it was already a little after ten o'clock, and knowing the nursery was already open, she figured she would head on over and do the rest of the housework when she came back.

Just as she was grabbing her purse to go, her phone rang and she saw it was Doug. She felt a little tickle in her chest.

"Good morning, Lois," Doug greeted her.

"Well, good morning, Doug. What a nice surprise. Having a good day so far?"

"Why yes, and it's even better now that I'm talking to you."

"You make me blush, Doug. To what do I owe the pleasure?"

"I was wondering if I could convince you to go to dinner with me this evening. I know all your boarders—" He chuckled a little at his comment before continuing, "—are up in Wisconsin, so I thought you may enjoy some company."

"As a matter of fact, I would," Lois responded. "But how about I have you over here to my house instead for dinner and cook you something delicious?"

"Wow, even better," Doug responded.

"Wonderful, let's say you come around 6:30. I'll let you bring the wine. How does that sound?" Lois was getting good at this dating thing.

"Red or white?" Doug countered.

"Let's say red," she responded. "I'm going to do something Italian. I hope you like that?"

"I love Italian," Doug confirmed.

"Wonderful. Make sure you bring your appetite. Until then," Lois said cheerily.

"Until then," Doug repeated and hung up.

Lois decided to add a stop at the grocery store to her outing. She knew exactly what she would cook and quickly made a list before departing.

***

It was just before six, and Lois was in the kitchen putting the finishing touches on her chicken Parmesan for dinner. While the chicken slowly simmered in the sauce, she went into the dining room to set the table. She wasn't going to go really formal with her mother's English China but instead used her casual, plain white Mikasa pattern. Of course, she would use her silver flatware and crystal glasses though. She opted for the woven steel-blue placemats and added some sunshine-yellow cloth napkins, which complimented the colors of the flowers she arranged in the crystal vase she set in the middle of her cherry dining room table. After stepping back for a good look, she smiled.

This is so much fun, she thought and giggled.

Lois went back to the kitchen to check the chicken Parmesan and to get her pot ready for the angel hair pasta, which she would serve the entrée over. A salad was already dressed and ready in the refrigerator, and the rolls were going in the oven to slowly warm until she was ready to pop them in the bread basket lined with one of the same yellow napkins she used with the place settings. She planned on plating the dinner in the kitchen and then presenting the dish. Much easier with what she was serving, she figured. And she had picked up a tiramisu at the grocery store for dessert— Rebekah didn't have to know about that.

She checked the clock. It was 6:29. Lois removed her apron and walked into the hallway, stopping at the large mirror above the hall table to primp a little. She didn't look too bad in the three-quarter-sleeved pastel-patterned shift she was wearing. As she was arranging her hair a bit, the front doorbell rang.

She opened the door, and there stood Doug with a bottle of wine and a bouquet of the prettiest pink sweetheart roses in his hands. He was dressed nicely in a pair of navy dress pants, a crisp navy-and-white-striped button-down shirt, and Bass Weejuns on his feet. *Very handsome.*

"Doug, welcome to my home. Please come in," Lois said in an inviting tone. "I'm so happy we could get together tonight"

"Me too. I just called to chat, and I'm getting a homecooked dinner out of it."

They both laughed.

"These are for you," Doug said and handed the roses to Lois.

"Why thank you, Doug. They are absolutely lovely. Pink roses are my favorite." Lois smiled demurely. "Come in the kitchen with me, and I'll put these in a vase. Dinner is actually ready, so how about you uncork the wine and I'll get the plates ready?" Lois suggested.

"Sounds like a plan," Doug responded.

They entered the dining room—Lois with the plates and Doug with the opened wine bottle.

"Go ahead and fill our glasses, and I'll return with the rest," Lois directed.

When she returned, he was still standing, waiting for her before he sat down. He came over and pulled her chair out. *What a gentleman*, she thought. *I love it!*

Dinner was very enjoyable. The conversation flowed, and the evening was full of laughs and smiles as they got to know each other better.

"I hope you like tiramisu," Lois said when they were finished with their meal.

"Um, I just happen to love it," Doug responded.

"Me too," said Lois. "Let me take these plates in the kitchen, and I'll bring it out. Better yet, let's have dessert in the living room where I put the lovely flowers you brought me. I can look at those beautiful pink roses then. What do you think?"

"Sounds great, but I insist on helping you clear the table and clean up," Doug said and raised his hand in case Lois gave him any dispute. "I insist, so don't even try to argue. This meal was fabulous, and it's my way of saying thank you to the cook."

"Well, if you put it that way, how can I refuse?" Lois said and smiled. "We can clean up and then have dessert."

Doug seemed to know his way around the kitchen, and soon they were in the living room, sitting next to each other on the sofa with their plated tiramisu.

When they had finished, Doug put his plate on the coffee table in front of them and then took Lois's plate from her and set it down carefully next to his before taking her hand.

"Lois, I've been yearning to find someone whose company I enjoy. I know this may seem fast to you, but face it, we're at a time in our lives where we need to take advantage of every moment. I enjoy your company and would like to take you out on a regular basis—see what develops. I hope you feel the same," he said with a heartfelt look on his face that Lois thought made him look younger.

"Why Doug, I'm flattered. Even though I have a house full of people right now, I too have longed for someone special I could spend time with. I have to say I've looked forward to every phone call from you over the last week, and when you agreed to come over for dinner, well—I was excited. Yes, let's see where it goes."

"My thoughts exactly," Doug agreed. "It's getting late, and I have to work tomorrow. Let me help you finish cleaning up the kitchen before I go. I insist."

So Doug helped Lois finish cleaning the kitchen. He reminded her that he was a "grill guy" and suggested she come over for dinner Saturday, since he worked all that week.

"I think it would be great," Lois responded, "and I insist on bringing dessert."

"It's a deal," Doug agreed. "Do you like pulled pork?"

"I do."

"Great. Bring your appetite. I'll probably send you home with leftovers," he said.

"For my 'boarders'?" Lois responded, laughing at herself.

"Yes." Doug chuckled. "For your boarders."

The kitchen was clean, and it was approaching ten o'clock. The end of a pleasant evening.

"Thank you so much for dinner and your company. You are a wonderful cook and hostess."

"Thank you, Doug. I have enjoyed your company also. Looking forward to Saturday."

"Oh, and I forgot! I have your new will done. Call and make an appointment to stop by this week. It should only take a minute but will give me a chance to see you. By the way, it's on the house." He put up his hand as he had earlier. "I insist."

She walked him to the door, and he leaned over to give her the most passionate kiss she thought she had ever had. Neither uttered a word. The kiss said it all.

After closing the door and hearing Doug's car pull out of the driveway, she dreamily went up to bed—happier than she had felt in a very long time.

Chapter 8

Rebekah was so happy they had decided to go to Wisconsin for a visit. Her mother continued to be uncharacteristically pleasant and was excited to see James and Andrew—but especially Rose, which was understandable. Plus, Rose appeared to genuinely enjoy her grandmother's company, which was even better.

It was already Tuesday. James and Violet had a day planned for just the two of them so he could show Violet all his favorite spots from when he was growing up in the area. Rebekah found it kind of sweet. While the two lovebirds were away, Andrew suggested Rose might like to take ATVs around the area trails through the forest, which seemed to be a cool thing to do according to Rose. That left Rebekah free to do what she wanted, which was to drive over to Rhinelander and Fred's Market and Café to see her old pal and coworker, Tammy.

Highway 8, which Rebekah had driven to work for twenty-plus years, hadn't changed a bit. She enjoyed the time alone as it gave her an opportunity to reflect on the visit with her family.

She was very impressed with her brothers. They had really stepped up with taking care of Mom. Had Rebekah stayed and lived with Ruth as her brothers originally suggested, she would have been doing everything. Oh, they would have helped out here and there, but caring for her mom would have been *her* main duty.

Rebekah was now more certain than ever that she had been led to Asheville—first for Rose, but second, for herself. There was definitely a visible spiritual hand in the course of her life since her discovery of Ethan's past. There had to be. Or … maybe all these wonderful twists and turns could be a sign that Dee was looking out for her. Yes! Why hadn't she thought of this earlier? She knew that this was her time to spread her wings, and she was going to make a new, wonderful life for herself. Whenever she shared the plans of her new teahouse with someone, she could feel a wave of excitement coursing through her from head to toe. There was no doubt she would succeed and realize every happiness.

She smiled as she thought about this and observed the budding greenery and flowers that grew beside the road at this time of the year. There were patches of purple and white wood violets, the Wisconsin state flower, here and there along the roadside as well as some marsh marigolds. Then out of the corner of her eye, she caught some trilliums to her excitement. They were her favorite wild flower. Yes, spring was definitely her favorite time of the year.

Fred's Market, the place where she had worked since she was sixteen years old, looked the same. Instead of parking her car in the designated employee area where she always had been required to park, she pulled the car into a spot by the front door and chuckled to herself as she got out of her vehicle.

Inside was much the same. She stopped by the front to say hi to Fred who was manning the customer service desk as always.

"Well, look who's here," Fred announced. "I'll be darned. Rebekah, I was just thinking of you the other day, and here you are. I'm either psychic or psycho!" Fred laughed at his own joke.

"Good to see you, Fred." Rebekah faked a little laugh at his joke and extended her arms for a hug.

"You want your job back, don't you? You're hired; just say the word," Fred said, sounding completely serious.

"Fred, I can't tell you how much that means to me, but I'm just home for a visit. I live in Asheville, North Carolina, now, and I kind of like it. Thanks to all the experience I got here, I'm opening up my own little bakery." She didn't go into elaborate details about the teahouse, which she knew would prompt questions from Fred, since she wanted to spend her time there with Tammy.

"The door is always open to you here, Rebekah." Fred put his hand over his heart.

"I'm going to sneak over to the bakery and surprise Tammy," Rebekah said, then had an idea. "Oh, but first, let me buy some scratch-offs for old times' sake? How about that one, two of that one, and three of that one," Rebekah said, pointing out the tickets she wanted. She planned to give them to Tammy.

"Will do," Fred said and handed her the tickets.

She made her way back to the bakery and deli area and saw Tammy's five-foot-six frame with her back to Rebekah, speaking to another employee.

"Excuse me, can I get some help?" Rebekah said to Tammy's back.

Tammy whipped around, and a look of shock spread across her face for a moment before she broke down into tears.

Rebekah felt tears of her own begin to well up as she smiled at her best friend. Tammy hadn't changed a bit. Same curly bleach-blonde hair, blue eyes, and big, happy smile.

"Oh my God have I missed you, girl! What are you doing here? Look at you! Beautiful as ever!" Tammy expounded. "Why didn't you tell me you were coming?" she said and threw her arms around Rebekah, smothering her in the kind of love only Tammy could give.

When Rebekah came up for air, she said, "I thought it would be fun to surprise you. Can we sit down and visit for a few minutes?"

"Of course," Tammy said. She turned and gave some orders to the employee she had been talking to before she led Rebekah to a table.

"I can't believe it," Tammy said enthusiastically as she sat down. "Wait till I tell Spencer and the kids tonight. So you here for just a visit?"

"Yes, and I got you a present, Tammy. Bought them as I came in. Old times' sake." Rebekah handed Tammy the scratch-offs. "I'm sure North Carolina has scratch-offs, but I haven't played any since I got there."

"Oh, I love it, Rebekah! You're something else."

The sound of Tammy's beautiful laugh rang in Rebekah's ears. God, she had missed it.

"The bakery looks great," Rebekah said and turned her head to survey it. "Are things going good here?"

"They are, but of course not as good as it was when you were here." Tammy put her hand up before Rebekah could protest. "You are missed. Customers ask about you all the time when they come in. No one can decorate cakes like you is all I have to say."

"It just takes practice and time. I don't know how many cakes I'll be doing at this new place in Asheville at first. It's a bakery and teahouse, so it will be more pastries and sandwiches, I think, at least starting out. Lois, who previously had a clothing store in the building, knows everything about tea, so I just have to concentrate on the bakery. Once the ovens are in and I have a working kitchen, I'm going to start practicing more on French pastries. But I think it would be nice to incorporate bakery items we enjoy here in Wisconsin since it's what I know. I'm so lucky Andrew has decided to relocate to Asheville with me. He's going to be my business manager, keeping the books along with any accounting we need, and Dee's daughter, Rose, will work there also while she attends college. It's all fallen together nicely. Just the new start I needed."

"It sure is, sweetie, it sure is," Tammy said and took Rebekah's hand. "Maybe you'll even meet someone and find love again. I would love that for you."

Rebekah gave a little chuckle before she responded. "Maybe someday, but that is the least of my concerns right now." She quickly changed the subject. "I don't think I told you this, but Andrew and I are temporarily living with Lois at her house. There's an apartment above my new bakery and teahouse where Dee and Rose used to live when they were in Asheville. Right now, it's getting a much-needed remodel so Andrew and I can live there. It shouldn't be too long after we get back before it's done. I'm excited about having a place of my own."

"I bet you are." Tammy smiled.

"My goal is to buy a house eventually. Then I will really have a place of my own."

"Either of those boys found them a girl to marry yet?" Tammy inquired.

"Andrew is dating a girl named Mary Sue, but he just started taking her out, so not sure what to expect."

"Well, that's a Southern girl's name if I ever heard one," Tammy said, nodding her head with a soft chuckle and a smile on her face.

"James, on the other hand, has been dating and living with Violet for a while. I'm wondering what's taking him so long to ask her to marry him. They've both been out of college long enough and have good jobs. They live together for Pete's sake. Andrew and I think he may ask her by the end of the year. I don't pry into his love life." She chuckled and rolled her eyes a bit. "I'm just the mom."

"Know whatcha mean. I've got two of mine married now and two to go. My youngest will graduate from high school next year. I'm glad I had my kids young."

"Yes, I'm glad mine came into my life when I was young too," Rebekah agreed and chuckled.

"Speaking of that, do the boys have much contact with their dad?" Tammy asked.

"As far as I can tell, no. They bring his name up as little as possible—if ever—and it's obvious they have minimal interest in him since they are so dedicated to me. I couldn't ask for anything better than my relationship with them. They are *my* boys." Rebekah's eyes teared up just a bit.

"Yes, they are," Tammy said and hesitated before she teared up herself.

Rebekah could tell something was on Tammy's mind. "What is it, Tammy?"

"Well, Spencer is having some problems. His energy is low, and he just doesn't feel good—hasn't felt like himself for a while. He's got a doctor appointment in two weeks, so we'll know then. Trying not to think about it," she said and gave Rebekah one of those beautiful Tammy smiles.

Just then one of the bakery employees came over to their table to tell Tammy they needed her help, so Tammy got up and said she'd be right back, leaving Rebekah alone at the table.

Rebekah looked around at the bakery where she had spent so much of her life and then thought about her new bakery in Asheville. She was a fortunate woman, there was no doubt.

Her thoughts were suddenly interrupted when she heard a familiar voice.

"Rebekah?" It was Michael, Fred's son, who ran the deli and was the store's assistant manager.

"Michael! Hi. How are you?" Rebekah stood up to greet him cheerily. "I hope you're doing well?"

"I am, thank you. Have you moved back?" Michael asked with a tone of surprise.

"Oh, no," she said, shaking her head. "Just home for a visit. I'm living in Asheville, North Carolina, now." She wanted to keep it simple. Way back when she was just a girl, before she married Ethan, Tammy had always insisted that Michael had a "thing" for Rebekah. In Rebekah's mind they were just friends and coworkers, but Tammy thought Michael might still feel differently.

"Yes, I heard you moved somewhere after you went to Milwaukee, but I didn't know it was North Carolina. Don't know too much about that state, but I bet you don't get any snow," he said and chuckled.

"Actually, it does get snow, and I've experienced it firsthand. Just doesn't last long," Rebekah responded.

Michael looked at the table she was standing next to and asked, "Can we sit down and talk a minute, or are you in a hurry?"

"No, I was just talking to Tammy, and she had to take care of some bakery business. Have a seat." She pointed to the chair opposite her, and they both sat down.

"We sure do miss you around here," Michael started. "You brought a certain spirit to the place, always so kind and sweet. I felt bad about what you had to go through with that husband of yours. Do you think you'll ever move back here?" he finally questioned.

"I'm fairly certain I won't." Maybe he did like her. He had never married, and she found that odd. "I'm actually opening a bakery in

Asheville, where I'm living. It's a very long story how I got there, and I don't care to go through it right now, but I'm there to stay. I needed a clean slate after Ethan, and that's what I'm getting."

"Well, I can understand." He paused for several seconds before proceeding. "I think I can trust you with a secret. You have to swear you'll keep it to yourself." He looked her straight in the eyes waiting for her response.

"Why yes, of course, Michael." Now she was curious.

He looked from one side to the other making sure no one was around. "Dad has sold his name and the store to someone who wants to open several places just like ours. They said our store is very unique. They're going to open them in Wisconsin, Minnesota, and Michigan to start out with. Dad is making a *fortune* on this deal. Who would have ever thought when he opened his dinky little first store it would come to this? They're going to let us keep running this one. No one knows but Dad and me."

"It sounds good, Michael, but are you happy about it?" Rebekah asked.

Michael hesitated. "I guess I am because Dad is. It's just there will be a day I'm sure they will no longer want either of us involved. That's how it usually goes with that kind of stuff. Dad has been thinking about retiring, so it works for him. I always thought I would inherit the place, but Dad says the money is something he can't ignore. Eventually I will have to get some other kind of job. Time will tell."

"That is big news. I hope it all works out well for you," she said and smiled.

And then Michael's demeaner changed. "Rebekah, I was wondering if I could take you out to dinner while you're here. Maybe we could talk more. I've always thought highly of you since we were teenagers working in the store—or maybe you'd feel more comfortable going to lunch? What do you say?"

"Honestly, Michael, I really need to spend time with my family for the days I'm here. The reason I came home right now is because my mom isn't doing well, and I want to devote most of my visit to spending time with her. It was sweet of you to ask though." And she really meant it. Michael had been a nice kid and was now a nice man. "How about some other time when I come home to visit?"

"Sure, Rebekah. I'd like that."

Out of the corner of her eye, Rebekah saw Tammy working her way back to the table. Michael must have seen her also because he stood up.

"I see you found our visitor. We really miss you here, Rebekah. Don't we, Michael?" Tammy said and raised her eyebrows when Michael turned his head from her to Rebekah.

"Yeah, we do." Michael smiled, and his blue eyes twinkled at Rebekah. She thought she might enjoy going to dinner with him, but not this time. Maybe next time.

"Well as they say in the South … Y'all, I've got to go!" Rebekah said with her best Southern drawl, and they all chuckled.

On her drive home, she thought about how happy she was to be in Asheville now. It was interesting what Michael had told her about the store and its name being sold. It wasn't always a good thing when something like that happened, and she only wished the best for Michael. He really was a nice man. They did have some differences when she was running the bakery, which should be expected, but they had never held a grudge and always worked well together. This part of her life was over though. After what had happened with Ethan, she could never live back up there comfortably.

***

Later that evening, Rebekah received a call from Tammy.

"Rebekah, you'll never believe it. Those scratch-offs you gave me are big winners! One of them was $5,000, one was $1,000, another $3,000, and finally two were $500. That's $10,000 total! I've never seen anything like it before. I have to split this with you at least. I can't keep it all."

"Tammy, it's all yours. I gave them to you," Rebekah said, elated to hear the news.

"No, no, no! I have to give you some. I insist." Tammy's voice was very determined.

"And I insist you keep it …. Tell you what. After taxes, put half of it away so you can come visit me sometime. How does that sound? Should be enough for a couple of visits. I think that's the best idea."

"Well, that is a good idea, I guess." Tammy was seeing the light. "Okay, that's what I'll do. I wish I would have had you buying tickets for me all those years before you left! Darn it all. I could be rich."

Rebekah laughed and said goodbye to her friend. Apparently, she hadn't lost her touch with lottery tickets. Maybe she would start buying tickets in North Carolina when she got back.

Chapter 9

When Rebekah came down to breakfast Wednesday morning, she found Andrew and Rose sitting patiently at the kitchen table with plates and silverware set in front of them and her mother at the stove.

"Hi, Mom. Are you making breakfast?" Rebekah inquired in a slightly surprised voice.

When Ruth spun around, spatula in hand, Rebekah saw her mom was wearing the same floral apron Rebekah had seen her wear so many times over the years, and she had her favorite cast iron pan on the stove burner. The smell of bacon permeated the air as it spitted and sputtered in the pan.

"Just making these two some breakfast. Going to fry their eggs in bacon grease when I'm done here, and I've got the waffle iron warming up over there." Ruth pointed to the adjacent cupboard. "Rebekah, do you think you can pour some batter in the waffle iron for me when you see the red light go out? Thank you," she added and turned back to the stove.

"It's so nice of you to make this for us, Grandma. I don't think I've ever had quite as big a breakfast as this before," Andrew said and gave a quick side-glance to his mother.

Rose chimed in, looking to Rebekah, her brown eyes opened wide. "I *know* I've never had one like this before."

Rebekah asked Andrew, "Where's your brother and Violet?"

"I don't know. They came through here about thirty minutes ago and headed out for a walk."

"Hmm," Rebekah raised her eyebrows as she went to work on the waffles.

The breakfast was delicious and brought back old memories of Sunday mornings when Ruth would make the family a full breakfast before church. Once Ethan and the boys had come into her life, Rebekah marveled at the way her mom was always able to do the breakfast so smoothly.

"I made enough bacon for James and Violet and can make their eggs and waffles when they come back." Ruth had no sooner said this when in walked the two lovebirds, grinning from ear to ear.

"Well, hi you two," Rebekah said. "Where did you head off to so early? We started eating breakfast without you, but Grandma is ready to rustle you up some eggs, and I'll get your waffles started."

"I took Violet down to the lake for a little walk," James responded.

"So early? Have you had more than enough of us? I don't think we're that bad," Rebekah teased with a smile.

Just then Violet extended her left hand to reveal a beautiful oval-shaped diamond ring on her finger. Rebekah turned to James, who at that moment looked more like a man than a child, ready and eager for this next chapter of his life.

"I just asked Violet to marry me, and she said yes!" James said, almost like he couldn't believe it.

When did he grow up? Rebekah began to tear up, realizing at that very moment, her life had taken another wonderful new direction. She took a breath and gained enough composure to say, "Oh my goodness, congratulations, you two! I couldn't be happier. Now come here and let me hug you both! Violet, welcome to our family."

Andrew stood up, looked at James, and said, "It's about time, bro." He wrapped his big brother in a bear hug before turning to Violet who opened her arms for an embrace. Before hugging her, he paused and stared for a moment, his eyebrows knitted with concern. "Are you sure?" he asked, and they all laughed.

"I've never been surer of anything," Violet responded and looked at James with love in her eyes.

Ruth put down the tongs she had been using to turn the bacon and gave Violet a hug. "So happy to have you joining our family, dear."

Next was Rose. "I'm so happy you'll be part of this family. We can be like sisters. I always secretly wished for a sister."

Violet hugged her back, then responded, "Me too, and thank goodness! I only have brothers." The young women hugged again and laughed.

"Mom," Rebekah said, turning to Ruth, "your wonderful breakfast is now a celebration!"

"When we get done with breakfast we're going to call my parents," Violet shared. Glowing, she turned to James who gave her a little peck on the lips.

"You know what? Uncle Jake is having a cookout again tonight for us. I'm baking you kids an engagement cake so we can all celebrate," Rebekah added.

"Oh, Rebekah, you don't have to do that," Violet exclaimed. "It's our last full day here."

"Nonsense, I'm making James's favorite chocolate cake, and I bet Rose will help me."

Rose smiled and gave her a thumbs up.

***

The cookout-turned-engagement celebration was a nice finale to their visit. Everybody was interested in the happy couple's plans for the future. James and Violet hoped to be married in Milwaukee before the end of the year.

Thursday morning arrived too quickly, and everyone found it hard to say goodbye. Thankfully, Rebekah's brothers all promised they would visit sometime.

For Rebekah, saying goodbye to her mom was the hardest. Even though their visit seemed to have uplifted her mom's spirits, Ruth was still in poor health, and Rebekah wondered when—or if—she would see her again.

More than anything, Rebekah was happy her mom and Rose had been able to meet and get to know each other. This visit was so important for Rose to learn she was connected to others who loved her, and for Ruth to see the woman that little baby from years ago had blossomed into. Rebekah knew Dee was looking down at them and smiling.

After a tearful goodbye, they were on their way back to Milwaukee with promises of doing this again soon.

***

Friday, they spent the day shopping, eating, and showing Rose around Milwaukee. Rebekah wanted to visit some bakeries for inspiration—and of course buy something yummy at each one. It reminded her of when Tammy had come to visit her own mom who lived in Milwaukee after Rebekah moved there and the two ate their way through the city as they canvased the bakeries.

In the evening, they went to a favorite tavern of James and Violet's for a fish dinner and a beer or two—even Rebekah.

After hearing the good news of the engagement, Violet's parents had invited all of them over for a dinner party on Saturday. Rebekah was so happy she would finally be meeting Violet's parents. From what James had told her, they sounded like great people.

And again, Rebekah baked one of her signature cakes for the party—a vanilla cake with raspberry filling and white chocolate frosting. *A bride-like cake*, Rebekah thought.

Violet's parents, Betty and Jerry Wolfman, lived in a beautiful home. They had invited many friends and family, including Violet's uncle and private investigator, Bobby Becker, whom Rebekah had employed last year to help her find Dee. It was nice to catch up with him and share the twist and turns she had gone through that finally led her to Rose. He had been right in ultimately surmising that, since there was no trace of Dee, she had either left the country or changed her name; the latter turned out to be true.

The evening was lovely. After meeting Betty and Jerry, Rebekah knew why Violet was such a nice person. Betty told Rebekah she would be in touch about the wedding—especially when it came to the food and cake. Rebekah told Betty she would love to be a part of the wedding plans in any way she could.

After they got back to James's place, Rebekah had a thought. She wondered if James had called Ethan to tell him the good news. Truth be told, Rebekah dreaded the thought of him and Emily being at the wedding and thought it possible that they may not come at all. She decided to ask James when they were alone for a few minutes.

"Sweetheart, I was wondering if you called your dad to tell him about your engagement?"

"Geez, Mom, I forgot about that. I guess I need to," he responded.

"Yes, you do, son. He will be happy to get the news, I'm sure. You can do it tomorrow after we leave," she said, then hesitated.

James picked up on it.

"What is it, Mom?"

"Well, I want your dad to know as little about me as possible. He's probably going to know I'm living in Asheville since Andrew is there with me, but if it comes up, the story I'm sticking to is that Lois closed her clothing store and asked if I would open a teahouse and bakery in its place because she had been so fond of Dee and Rose, and she wanted me to be in Rose's life. It's okay if he knows Dee passed away—but nothing more. I know maybe I'm being silly, but I want to keep all this between us. Not even the rest of our family knows everything."

James looked at Rebekah and took both of her hands in his so they were facing each other. He looked into her eyes for a few seconds before he spoke.

"Mom, I totally get it, and so does Andrew. We've talked about it and are in agreement. I guess Lois knows about the lottery and Dad?"

"Lois doesn't know everything, but she does know more than most. I don't talk a lot about your dad and my history with anybody, but she knows more than the basics. And no, I didn't tell her about the lottery. If I dwell on the past, I'll never move on. It's just the way I am."

"Okay, I get it. So it's you, me, and Andrew—and that's the way it will stay. And you're right, Dad's probably going to already know you've moved, and you have to work at something, but the rest is between us. Even if he asks, I'll avoid saying anything. Okay?"

Rebekah looked at her son. How nice it was to have him and Andrew in her life. There was no way she could do any of this without them.

"You're right, son. I need to put it out of my mind. That will be easier when I get back to Asheville because it will be full steam ahead with the shop. You know I've only received one call from

Harrison, the contractor we're using, about a paint color for the apartment while I've been gone. Makes me a little nervous about what I might see when I get back. Maybe you and Violet can plan to come for the grand opening of the teahouse and bakery," she suggested with excitement in her voice.

"I would love to if we can. When do you think it will be?" James asked.

"Well, I'm wanting to open as early in September as I can. Harrison is focusing on the apartment now so we can let Lois have her house back, but honestly, I think she likes having us there. She's such a nice woman. We'll see plenty of her and Rose leading up to and after the opening of the shop. Both will be working there," she shared.

"I thought the opening might be earlier," James stated.

"Well, according to Harrison, we need to add more plumbing and electrical connections for the appliances. What's there now is older and probably won't pass code anymore. It's all stuff you don't see but needs to be tended to, or so he tells me. It's the expensive stuff, actually," Rebekah scoffed and raised her eyebrows. "I'm not going to rush him, because I want it done right the first time."

"Understandable," James agreed.

"Andrew said you're taking us to the airport tomorrow?"

"Yes, I thought we'd leave about ten fifteen if you think that's good."

"I think it should be fine." Rebekah smiled.

"Mom, make sure you let us know as soon as you have an opening date for the shop so Violet and I can see about coming there. Can't wait to check out Asheville. Andrew and Rose talk so much about it."

"It's a lovely place," she said and wrapped her arms around James. "I love you so much, son."

"And I love you, Mom."

Chapter 10

Rebekah opened one eye and looked around the room. There it was. Through a side crack where the blinds met the window poured a small strip of sun, shining right in her eyes. She turned her head ever so slightly to escape the invasion. She felt so comfy and had no desire to get out of bed or move but still wondered what time it was.

Their flight out of Milwaukee had been delayed the day before, and when they finally arrived at the Charlotte airport, they still had to wait for their luggage, which seemed to take forever. Then they had to jump on the shuttle so they could get their car from the long-term parking lot before finally heading back to Asheville. Once on the road, Andrew brought up the fact that they hadn't eaten all day—except for the pack of cookies given to them on the plane—and claimed he was starving. Rose and Rebekah agreed, so they stopped at a barbecue restaurant, resulting in getting them home around 9:45 p.m. After bringing everything into the house, unpacking a little, briefly talking with Lois, and getting a snack, it was after 11:30 before Rebekah was wound down enough to go to bed.

So much for lying in bed for a while; she needed to use the bathroom. When she was done, she decided to go ahead and crawl back into bed but once situated soon realized it wasn't as cozy as it had been when she first woke up—and then she glanced at the clock. 10:05. It had been a very long time since she'd slept that late, so she dragged herself out of bed, found her robe, and headed to the kitchen. It was very quiet, and Rebekah found Lois sitting alone at the kitchen table with a cup of tea, engrossed in a book.

"Well, good morning. I bet you didn't even miss us, did you?" Rebekah asked.

Lois looked up at Rebekah over her reading glasses. "You're up!" she declared with surprise. "Why yes, of course I missed you all." She pointed to the teakettle on the stovetop. "The kettle should still be rather warm, so stick it on the burner for a bit to reheat it, then fix yourself a cup of tea and join me." She then closed the book and set it aside on the table. "I want to hear more about your trip."

Rebekah did as Lois asked and sat down next to her while she waited for the kettle to boil.

"First, how did you like flying?"

"Well, I think it's great, especially when your flight's on time."

"Oh yes dear, it's unfortunate your flight was so late. I think it's become quite common lately from what I hear. Flying didn't make you nervous or sick though, did it?"

"No. I actually like the fact that you can get somewhere so quickly. I had a window seat, which I really enjoyed. I loved peeking out the window and seeing how the land changed from the mountains here to the flat farmland up in Wisconsin. I'm looking forward to my next trip, wherever I decide to go," Rebekah shared.

"That's wonderful. I haven't been anywhere in a long time, and you make me want to go someplace." Lois took a long sip of her tea before she continued. "The store prevented me from doing many things, but now I'm free to do whatever I want, aren't I?" She looked curiously at the tea inside of her cup, and before Rebekah could respond, she continued, "I just found this wonderful black tea and peach blend. Absolutely yummy. I've been trying some new teas with anticipation of the teahouse. Go ahead and try it," she said and pointed to a tin next to the teapot, which had started boiling on the stove.

Rebekah got up, fixed her tea, and came back to the table, waiting for it to steep and then cool slightly before she tried it.

"You *should* go somewhere, Lois, now that you don't have the clothing store holding you back. Any special place you might have in mind?"

Lois was thoughtful. "No, not at the moment, but something could strike my fancy. Maybe I'll go to Wisconsin with you sometime. Meet your family."

"I would love that. It's a different world from here, but I would love to share it with you," Rebekah said, and she meant it. "So what did you do while we were gone? I hope you weren't too terribly lonely."

"Oh, the first day I missed all the activity but then decided it was a good opportunity for me to get some flowers planted and do a little yard work. You'll have to go take a look later." Lois paused to take a sip of tea and the doorbell rang.

"Let me get that, Lois. You look so content and comfortable. I'll be right back," Rebekah volunteered.

Rebekah looked out the side window and saw a man holding a bouquet of flowers at the door.

As she opened the door, the man said, "Hi, are you Lois Bender?"

"No, but this is her home. She's here. Do I need to get her?"

"No ma'am, just sign here," he said, handing her a clipboard with a shipping receipt on it.

Rebekah thanked him and took the massive bouquet into the kitchen. The flowers were beautiful, all different and brightly colored, like a spring garden.

"This is for you," she said curiously and set the vase on the table in front of Lois.

Lois stayed silent, her face not showing any emotion.

"I wonder who they could they be from?" Rebekah asked when Lois made no effort to reach for the attached card. Her curiosity only grew as she observed Lois's stoic expression. "There's an envelope stuck in here." She pulled it out of the arrangement and handed it to Lois.

"They are beautiful" was all Lois said as she surveyed the flowers, stubbornly set the note upon the table, and continued to sip her tea.

"Lois! Open the envelope and see who they're from!" Rebekah was beside herself with curiosity. The flowers *were* beautiful and not your run-of-the-mill bouquet from the grocery store. Whoever sent these had spent some money on them.

"I will later. I don't feel like it right now," Lois said, then slipped the envelope in her pocket. She quietly sipped her tea and went back to reading her book so she could avoid eye contact with Rebekah.

After a few awkward moments, they heard movement down the hallway. Rose and Andrew walked into the kitchen, talking a mile a minute—until they both spotted the flowers on the table.

"Wow," Rose said. "Where did these come from, and who are they for?"

Lois stood quickly, picked up the vase, and headed to the door. "They were sent to me, and I don't know who from," she said, obviously annoyed, and left the room.

"Whoa," Andrew said. "I think we hit a nerve."

"Ya think?" Rose said as she popped an English muffin in the toaster. "I've never seen her like that before. There must be more to this story."

"Yes, I agree. But let's just leave it. She'll tell us in her own time," Rebekah said, even though she was dying to know who they'd come from. She decided to change the subject. "What's on your agendas today?"

"I'm going over to the shop sometime in the afternoon to see what's up, you know, what I need to tend to, check in with Harrison. I'm just not in any big hurry though. Yesterday was tiring," Andrew said.

"I have to work this afternoon at Biltmore," Rose said. "How about you, Rebekah?"

"I'm heading off to the shop also as soon as I get dressed to check on things, and I think I'll stop by the grocery store for a few items before I come home. If either of you want anything, jot it down on the paper over there. I was thinking of some kind of pasta for tonight. Does that sound good?"

"Yeah, it does," Andrew responded.

"I'll be home late, so just save me some please," Rose said.

"Hey Rose, why don't you keep Lois busy so I can sneak into her room and find the card that came with the flowers? I wonder who sent them," Andrew connived. "Maybe she has a secret admirer?"

"I don't know if you should do that—unless you think you'd enjoy sleeping on a blow-up mattress in your office after Lois finds out what you did." Rose gave Andrew a toothy grin before she sat down at the table with a bowl of cereal.

Rebekah had begun to head out of the kitchen but stopped and turned back to Andrew. "Listen to Rose." Then she wagged a finger and looked sternly from Andrew to Rose. "And don't harass

Lois about the flowers. I mean it. It was a nice surprise for her, and she will share it with us when she's ready."

"Yes, ma'am," Andrew said with an exaggerated pout that made Rose snicker.

Rebekah shook her head and laughed as she left the room, but she couldn't help thinking, *Who* are *those flowers from?*

***

The back of the building didn't look any different than when she had left. It was still a construction site, and off to one side sat dumpsters filled with wood, insulation, wires, and various discarded building products. Although it had only been a week since she last saw it, she felt like it had been longer and couldn't wait to see what had happened inside while she was gone.

Harrison's truck was outside. This was a good sign since she knew she would be able to get an update from him. Hopefully there wouldn't be any—*We found X, so before we can continue, I have to tear the whole thing up, and it will cost Y amount of dollars*—updates.

Just then, Harrison—dressed in a plaid shirt, bibbed denim overalls, and his favorite navy-blue ball cap with a pencil tucked behind his ear—walked out the back door, threw a piece of scrap wood in the dumpster, and waved to her. She got out of her car.

"Hey, welcome back. The place is still standing," he said, taking his hat off and waving it toward the building.

"Yes, that's good," she said and laughed. "Can't wait to see what you've been up to while we've been gone."

"Well, let's go upstairs so you can find out."

He was smiling. Another good sign.

"So is everything good with your family back in Wisconsin?" Harrison asked as they headed up the stairs.

"Actually, better than I thought. My mom wasn't doing too well, but it seems our visit perked her up. She does have some health problems to deal with that aren't going away, but I feel like we improved her mood."

"I'm sure you did perk her up, Rebekah. You're just that kind of person."

He stopped right next to her, and she realized how tall he was. *Must be over six feet*, she thought. He gave her a warm smile and a quick wink.

Rebekah felt her cheeks flush and looked down at her feet. She wasn't sure how to respond. "I ... thank you," she said, meeting his soft brown eyes for just a second.

When they reached the top of the stairs, Harrison said, "You know I met your sister, Dee, when I did some work for Lois here several years ago—not long after she first arrived in Asheville."

"You met Dee?" Rebekah was so surprised. "It never occurred to me that you might have met her, but I guess if you did work for Lois, you sure would have." She hesitated for a moment and looked down and back up before she spoke. "This may sound silly, but what was she like?"

"I saw her maybe three or four times. She pretty much kept to herself, but was always friendly. Now Rose was another story. Very animated would be a good description of her—even today. Dee—well I knew her as Sarah—and you look very much alike, you know. Even your mannerisms. No doubt in my mind that you would have been related in some way."

"This may seem like a silly question, but did she seem happy? It's something I've always wondered, especially now since I can't ask her myself." Rebekah hoped she didn't sound desperate.

He must have sensed her insecurity, so he took a deep breath and smiled before he continued in a gentle tone, "As far as I could tell, she seemed happy and content. It was obvious she and Lois got on very well, and Rose was a normal, happy child. My conversations with her were mostly about general things, nothing deep, but she always came across as a happy and pleasant individual."

Harrison smiled at Rebekah who just stared at him for a few seconds and took a deep breath before she responded.

"Thank you for telling me that, Harrison. You have no idea what that means to me. I idolized my sister, and my world was devastated when she left. There wasn't a day I didn't think of her." Rebekah's eyes started to tear up slightly.

"Why sure," he said and lifted both hands with an open palm gesture. "Again, I didn't know her well, but we did talk, and I could tell she was a fine person—just like you." Harrison smiled and glanced down for a moment before he looked up and changed the subject to what was at hand. "So what do you say we take a look at your apartment? I think you're going to be happy." When he opened the door at the top, he said with flair, "Ta-da!"

Rebekah couldn't believe it. In just a week while they were gone, Harrison had finished the apartment. It looked like a home—it *was* her home.

"I'm speechless. It's absolutely beautiful. How did you get so much done?" Rebekah questioned.

"Well—" he took his hat off and ran his fingers through his sun-bleached brown hair, "—it's amazing what you can do when the people who contract you aren't around."

They both laughed.

The kitchen, dining area, and living space was all open, making the apartment look huge. The three bedrooms were on the sides of the open area, two on one side and a larger bedroom on the other side along with a little half bath on the end.

Harrison led her to the two smaller bedrooms first. They were identical in size and shared a full bathroom with just a shower between them. Next was the larger bedroom. That was Rebekah's room. As she walked in, the first thing Rebekah noticed was the shiplap on the wall where she planned on putting the headboard of her bed. There was plenty of room for a dresser and even a small desk. The door on the far wall led to a spacious bathroom and adjoining closet. Rebekah was speechless.

"Harrison, this is amazing. I have to let it all sink in. It's beautiful." She turned around and around, admiring the space.

"I'm happy you're so pleased. Still waiting for some of the inspections yet before you can move in, but I wanted you to see it as soon as you got back from your trip. I have to tell you I'm kind of proud of what I did here. Was like putting a puzzle together to utilize the space, but I always love a challenge." He was beaming, his eyes shining at her with pride.

"I can't wait till Andrew sees it. He was just getting up and going when I left, so he'll be by later," Rebekah told him.

"Now what I need you to do is go over it with a fine-tooth comb for things that might be wrong or that you want done differently. While you do that, I'm going to get started on some preliminary stuff for the space below. I've been looking it over while you were gone and did some minor work and got some quotes. I think one day this week you, Andrew, and I need to sit down and talk. Maybe tomorrow do you think? I'm running over to my other job sites this afternoon and have to stop by my dad's later, so I can't do it today."

"Tomorrow sounds good," Rebekah agreed. "Maybe about ten-thirty? Will that work?"

"Actually, that should be fine," he said.

"Everything okay with your dad? Hope he's well."

"Oh, he's fine, especially now that he's been seeing Lois. He's like a new man." Harrison chuckled and then saw the look on Rebekah's face. "You knew they were seeing each other, didn't you?" he asked, rather unsure, and then realized by the look on Rebekah's face that she definitely had not.

"No, I had no idea." Rebekah's surprise turned into a smile on her face. "But when she got a bouquet of flowers today and didn't want to look at the card in front of me, I figured there must be *someone* special in her life. I'm guessing it's your dad who sent them?"

"Yep, probably is. I see it as a good thing, don't you?" Harrison asked.

Rebekah laughed softly. "Definitely. I'm just surprised and wondering why she didn't want me to know, that's all."

"It's a new thing for both of them. It just started a couple weeks ago, I think, and she's probably getting used to it. We'll keep it between us for now, how's that? Please don't tell her I told you, okay?" he pleaded.

"I won't." Rebekah laughed. "It's our secret," she added, and when she looked at Harrison's face, he had that same warm look in his eyes she had seen earlier but never truly noticed before. She lingered for a few awkward seconds until Harrison spoke.

"Ah, well ..." he stammered for a moment as if he had lost his train of thought. "I've given you some homework. Get Andrew to give the place the once-over with you, and let's say that after all the final inspections, your move-in will be around the second weekend in May. Now, I've got to run and check on my guys at another project."

"It looks great, Harrison. I'm so excited. I better start ordering my furniture this week now that I've seen how this all looks. Lois has a few pieces she wants to give me, but I have nothing of my own. I lived in a parsonage before, and—" Rebekah caught herself before she said anything else. *Too much information.*

"I know. Andrew told me."

I wonder what else Andrew may have told him? Rebekah thought.

"Thank you for all the work," she said. "I'll get my pad of paper in the car to write things down and start looking everything over myself till Andrew gets here. I'm sure it's perfect and you won't have to do a thing, but anyway …." She was starting to ramble. *Be quiet.*

"One more thing. While you were gone, someone moved some wood and equipment around outside. Might have been some kids goofing around or someone else wanting to steal stuff to sell. I'm making sure I keep everything locked up inside from now on, and I'm thinking about putting up a camera in the back. A little vandalism happens at job sites occasionally—could have been a onetime incidence. Should be fine, but wanted to give you a heads-up. Let me know if you see anything suspicious."

"Okay. I'm glad they didn't take anything," Rebekah said.

"Me too. Whoever it was has no business back here—at least no business that leads to something good. I have a friend on the police force who I talked to about it and asked him and the other folks who police this area to take a run back here when they come by. That should take care of it."

"Okay. I'll let Andrew know too." She looked around her new apartment again. "You know, this is really amazing. Thank you so much, Harrison. Can't wait to see your ideas for the shop."

"This was a fun project." He pointed toward the floor. "I'm looking forward to working downstairs too."

"Me too. It's my dream," she said and smiled at Harrison.

"Well, see you tomorrow." He put his cap back on and gave her a smile and a wave before heading out the door and down the stairs. Rebekah chuckled as she remembered how she'd first met Harrison at the end of January. She had just dropped Andrew off at the airport to go back to Wisconsin so he could pack up their things to make their permanent move down there. Lois had, unknown to Rebekah, given Harrison a key to the building so he could look it over in anticipation of the apartment and shop remodel. She hadn't even known he was there until she heard the toilet flush and out he came, buckling his pants. Scared her half to death.

She walked to the window that overlooked the alleyway behind the building, and just as he had been that first night they met, Harrison was standing by his truck, looking up at her. He waved, jumped in his truck, and left.

"Hmm," she said to herself.

Chapter 11

Around 6:30, Harrison smiled to himself as he drove over to his dad's house to pick him up for dinner. Both men stayed busy with work and didn't get together like this enough. His dad was at a point in his life and career where he could easily retire, but Harrison believed he kept working because he wouldn't know what to do with his time otherwise. After Harrison's mom died, Dad's only interests seemed to be work and golf. Before then, Mom had been the social one who was always planning and coordinating things for them to do.

And now, his dad was dating Lois Bender. Harrison laughed to himself. Like a couple of high school kids. Lois was a great person, and Harrison really couldn't be happier for his dad. Maybe she could even get him to retire, or at least semi-retire, and go on some trips with her. Dad had been so excited, he couldn't wait to call and let Harrison know he was seeing Lois, even though they had only been on a few dates.

I guess when you get to be their age you know what you want, he thought. *And when it shows up, you go for it.*

Harrison really wished he could find someone to share his own life with. He had never been married but wanted to be. When he was in his late twenties, he had been hopelessly in love with a woman who turned out to be more in love with his best friend, Gary. Now, at age forty-two, there just didn't seem to be anyone he was interested in.

Well, that wasn't all true.

He would love to ask Rebekah Hayward out but wouldn't, and for two good reasons. First, because he was doing a job for her and didn't believe in mixing business with pleasure, and second, because Andrew had told him the story about how and why he and Rebekah had ended up moving to Asheville. There was no way Rebekah was ready for a relationship after what she had been through, and maybe she'd never be ready. He liked Andrew a lot and felt a friendship starting—even though he was old enough to be Andrew's father. The kid had great business sense, and Harrison had always respected that in a man.

It angered Harrison to hear how Andrew's dad had lied and falsely married Rebekah when he was still married to someone else. *And the guy was a minister to boot? Unbelievable.* Poor Andrew and his brother James, having to face something like that. Plus, Andrew had said their birth mom was a bit of a nutjob, and they had only visited her earlier that year out of respect. As far as they were concerned, Rebekah was their mom. She had raised them as if they were her own children, and it absolutely showed in their relationship.

Harrison liked Rebekah from the first time he saw her that night in the old apartment he was now renovating. Lois had given him a key so he could pop in, look things over, and see if he wanted the job. So that's what he did. And while he was there, he figured he might as well test the plumbing by using the bathroom. When he finished and came walking out—there was Rebekah. Rightly so, he scared the heck out of her. Thank God she didn't have mace—or something worse. Now that he thought about it, the whole situation was kind of funny—though it wasn't at the time, even if he'd tried to make light of it. He'd felt sure Rebekah wouldn't want him to do the project after that incident, but thankfully, she came around. He was glad and kind of took it as a sign that maybe there *was* someone out there for him. And, just maybe, when the timing was right, he could ask her out. Meanwhile, he was just happy to be remodeling her new home and business so he could be in her life. Hopefully Rebekah would be happy too.

He wouldn't be able to start on the teahouse and bakery until around the first week of May. The project was bigger than the apartment renovation, so he had to finish another big job before he'd have enough guys available to start on it. He didn't want to spread himself too thin. From experience, he learned he could keep three or four jobs going at one time depending on the size. Rebekah's project was the equivalent of two *big* jobs since he had to add a lot of plumbing, gas, and electrical work for the kitchen. He didn't mind, though, because it meant he was able to see Rebekah more. He liked her and would love to get to know her better—and especially for her to get to know *him*.

He pulled into his dad's driveway, parked, and walked to the front door. Kind of convenient that his dad had a thing for Lois, since she was such good friends with Rebekah. He smiled to himself thinking about his dad having a girlfriend. Lois would certainly bring a new spark into his life, no doubt. She was a fun woman.

"Hey, Dad. I'm here and I'm starving. Are you ready to go?"

***

All day long Lois thought about the flowers Doug had sent—and her resulting schoolgirl dramatics when Rebekah and the kids had pressed her for information. She chuckled to herself, thinking about the looks on their faces. She had to admit that the whole situation *was* kind of funny, but it hadn't felt that way at the time. She sighed. The flowers were beautiful, and she was very touched by Doug's thoughtfulness. She didn't know why she wanted to keep her relationship with him to herself a little longer. Maybe she was being silly.

And then there was the sweet card he had sent with the flowers. It read: *Thank you for a glorious week. I can't remember the last time I had this much fun. My Love, Doug.*

She did like Doug. She just hadn't expected that he would send her flowers and sign his card that way—*My Love, Doug*. Still, she had to admit, she couldn't stop thinking about him, how sweet he had been, and when would she see him again so she could personally thank him for his thoughtfulness. This past week *had* been wonderful. They were together just about every day for lunch or dinner, and a couple of nights he had come over to watch a movie. Lois hadn't felt that happy in years. Was she falling in love? At this time in her life? She giggled.

In fact, the more she thought about it, she realized it was time to tell Rebekah, Andrew, and Rose that she was seeing Doug. She'd share the news over dinner tonight.

***

"Lois, I'm home." It was Rebekah calling from the kitchen, lugging several grocery bags that she plopped on the table. She had left the shop in the early afternoon not long after Andrew had arrived and spent the rest of the day running errands.

"I'm in the living room," Lois called to Rebekah.

Rebekah came in and sat in a chair next to her.

"So everything looking good over at the renovation?" Lois asked.

"Oh my, yes. The apartment is basically finished! Harrison has done a fabulous job with the amount of space he had to work with. Wait till you see it. Sounds like we'll be able to move in about two weeks from now, as long as all the inspections pass. I'm so excited. Thank you for suggesting him. Can't wait to get started on the shop downstairs now."

"That's just wonderful, dear. And what will I do without you and Andrew here? You have become a part of my life," Lois responded rather sadly.

"We will still be a part of your life! And Rose is still here with you, Lois. We have to make sure that girl gets through college. I think it will take both of us and Andrew to keep her focused," Rebekah stated.

"I do think once she gets into college life and learning something she has interest in, she'll be like a dog with a bone. She's a smart, capable girl just like her mom—and her aunt, I think."

"Oh, well thank you, Lois," Rebekah responded, looking at her hands. "I've really never done anything other than baking."

"I beg to differ, my dear. Look at where you are now. You don't give yourself enough credit! In one year, you've become a different person, the person I believe you *really* are. Not much different than what Dee did." Lois stood up and shuffled toward the door. "I need to run out back and turn the sprinkler off. Planted some flowers today and put the sprinkler on them for a bit. Don't want to drown them!"

Lois left and Rebekah was alone.

Rebekah looked down at her hands again. *Am I really a different person?* She hadn't thought much about what she was doing. After all, opening a bakery was her dream and what she thought she s*hould* be doing. In reality, the bakery and tea shop had become far bigger than any dream she'd ever had. She'd always thought she would just open a little local bakery somewhere in Wisconsin—not far from where she used to live. She'd imagined Tammy would come work with her, and then she would continue her life as it always was. Now she realized that where she had ultimately landed was completely different, and as a result, she *had* changed. How could she not have with all that had happened? *Life can sure send you in some interesting directions*, she thought and took a slow breath—in and out.

She knew she couldn't have undertaken what she was doing without all the support she had from so many, and she was grateful. Andrew, Lois, Rose, James, her family in Wisconsin—even Harrison. Harrison seemed so excited and proud of how the apartment had turned out, and he had become a good friend to both Rebekah and Andrew. Rebekah smiled and shook her head. *Lord knows Andrew could use a strong male figure like Harrison in his life*, she thought. And well, so could she if she were being honest.

Rebekah got up and headed to the kitchen to put away the groceries and start the pasta dish she had promised the kids she would make. It was already getting late—about 6:30. After her meeting with Harrison, she had been so excited about the apartment, she decided to do a little furniture shopping that afternoon before she came home, and like it always seemed to, the afternoon had gotten away from her. It was time-consuming looking at all the beautiful pieces of furniture, but it was exciting to imagine what they would look like in her own place. She knew the look she wanted—homey and comfortable but still well put-together. She had seen a sofa today she liked, and a kitchen table and chairs too.

As she was pulling some pots out of the cupboard to start cooking, Lois came back in the house.

"The flowers look happy in their new garden home. I was just going to ask you what you wanted to do for dinner. I was thinking takeout instead of cooking." Lois laughed. "Why don't we do that?"

"You don't have to convince me," Rebekah responded with a chuckle. "Since I told the kids pasta, let's order from the Italian place we like."

"Sounds like a plan. How about you call and order what you want and I pay for it? We can maybe have Andrew pick it up on his way home."

"Great idea, Lois. Speaking of Andrew—" Rebekah looked at her watch, "—he's usually home by now. I wonder if he's maybe going out with Mary Sue tonight since we've been out of town? I maybe better give him a call." She pushed his number on her phone. "Hey, just wondering when you might be coming home? … Yeah, I kind of figured that. … No problem, sweetheart. See you later. Say hi to Mary Sue."

Rebekah hung up and shrugged her shoulders. "Yep. He's with Mary Sue. They're going out to eat. I should have figured that. How about we go to the Italian restaurant to eat and bring something home for Rose since she's working late?"

"Let me go comb my hair, put on a little lipstick, and grab my handbag," Lois responded. She was always ready to go out to eat.

"I'll be waiting in the car," Rebekah said.

***

"Son, I feel like we should be doing this more often." Doug sat back in his chair as their server grabbed his now-empty plate. "That was one great steak."

"I agree, Dad. This place definitely needs to be added to our list of favorites I would say," Harrison said and sat back as well.

Doug had suggested they try the steak house in Biltmore Village, and it did not disappoint.

"I know you're a busy man, but we only have each other, and it means a lot to me when we can get together like this." Doug smiled at his son.

"Well, I don't know about only having each other, Dad," Harrison countered. "What about your new woman?"

Doug instantly turned red, and Harrison laughed.

"I heard she received a huge bouquet of flowers today. You wouldn't know anything about that by chance?" Harrison continued to tease.

Doug looked surprised. "How do *you* know about that? I guess I have no secrets."

"Rebekah mentioned today that Lois had received a beautiful bouquet of flowers, and I assumed it was you. Don't worry, your secret is safe," Harrison said, respecting Rebekah's wish to not let on that he had spilled the beans.

"Well, yes. It was me. We had a wonderful week together. I just wanted her to know how much I enjoy her company, that's all."

"Hey, I'm just joking with you. I'm kind of jealous, if you want the truth. I'd love someone special to send flowers to. Lois is a wonderful woman. Enjoy every moment. Maybe we can get you to at least semiretire now that you have someone to do things with," Harrison suggested, having spent the past few years trying to convince his dad until he was blue in the face that he should just retire already. Doug had always countered that he didn't know what he would do with his time. But now that Doug had Lois, Harrison wondered if his dad would reconsider so he could slow down and enjoy this part of his life.

"Honestly, I think I may if things keep going as they are. I would like to do some of the things your mom and I talked about doing but never got a chance to," Doug said, staring at the flame of the candle on their table. He paused awhile before looking at his son.

"Go for it, Dad." Harrison placed a hand over his dad's and gave it a squeeze. This was what Harrison had been hoping to hear. "Mom would want you to be happy."

Doug looked back at the candle flame and then turned to his son again, this time blinking his eyes and slowly nodding his head.

"Now that you've got a girlfriend, your schedule is going to become tighter, Dad," Harrison teased, trying to lighten the mood.

"Stop it, son. You know I always have time for you. We can do lunch also," Doug suggested as they pulled in his driveway. "How about coming in for a little brandy to cap off the night?"

Harrison looked at his watch. It was already nine o'clock. "How about a beer for me?"

"Got that too," Doug said and laughed.

The men had just sat down when Harrison's phone rang and he saw it was Rebekah.

"It's Rebekah. I better answer—sorry." Stepping aside, he answered the call. "Hey, what's up, Rebekah? … Are you serious? I'll be right there."

"What happened?" Doug asked, immediately thinking of Lois.

"Rebekah got a call from the police. I noticed someone had been messing with my supplies and things around the jobsite, so I asked the police to make a pass in the back of Rebekah's building when they were in the area. Tonight, they noticed when they went by that the back door had been broken into. Turns out someone went in with spray paint and did some major damage to the new apartment. I've got to go and meet her there."

"Of course you do, son. Give me a call later and let me know what's going on."

"I will, Dad," he said and raced out the door.

***

When Rebekah arrived at the building, she spotted an officer waiting in his car. As she and Lois got out of her car, he approached them.

"Are you the owner of the building, ma'am?" the officer inquired.

"Yes, officer, I am. I'm Rebekah Hayward, and this is my friend Lois Bender. Do you need some ID?" Rebekah fumbled through her purse.

"No, ma'am. I've been by here before and have seen your car. I'm also a friend of Harrison. I'm Officer Brooks. Harrison asked if me and some of the other officers could swing by occasionally, and I'm sorry to have found this."

Just then, Harrison pulled into the lot and jumped out of his truck.

"Hey, Sam." Harrison shook the officer's hand. "Thanks so much for stopping by. So what happened?"

"Hey, Harrison. Was just starting to tell Miss Hayward and Miss Bender what was going on. I came to check on things like you asked me to, and saw the back door open and no cars, so I called for some backup and went in. The downstairs looked fine, but the second floor had been vandalized with spray paint."

Harrison shook his head and said, "Seriously? I guess it could have been worse."

"Yes, it sure could have. I've gone through the rest of the building, and I didn't see anything else suspicious," Sam reported.

Rebekah looked at Lois who shook her head, speechless.

"Most of the paint was random spraying in red and black, but on one wall, they wrote *Get Out* in big black letters. It appears someone doesn't want you here, Miss Hayward. Can you think of who it might be?"

Rebekah, Lois, and Harrison looked at each other, puzzled. Rebekah didn't know anyone other than Lois and Harrison in Asheville. Then she thought, *Could it be Ethan?* From what little she had heard from the boys, their dad was not in a good situation with Emily. She knew Ethan would have run away with her if she had been agreeable, but do this? No.

Or would he?

"Officer Brooks, please call me Rebekah. I can't imagine anyone who would do this. I don't think I've lived here long enough to make someone dislike me."

"Maybe someone from your past?" Sam continued.

"Sam, Rebekah is one of the kindest, most good-hearted people I've ever met," Harrison chimed in and waved his hand at the building. "The thought of someone singling her out to do something like that is absurd. No one would purposely want to hurt her. It's got to be someone who hangs out around here and likes to cause trouble."

"Well maybe one of our city street cameras picked something up," Officer Brooks suggested. "Why don't we let the ladies go on home, and after you secure the door to the building, Harrison, you and I can go down to the station and see what we can find. Then if we need to speak to the ladies, we can do so tomorrow. Those of us who patrol this area know most of the regular troublemakers, so it could be that simple." Officer Brooks turned to the ladies. "I'm so sorry about this, Rebekah."

"Thank you. I hope we can find out who it is so it doesn't happen to someone else."

"Since Harrison is the contractor, and it has impacted his job, will it be okay with you for us to use him to fill out the report while we're at the station?" the officer asked.

"Sure, that's fine. Are you sure you don't mind?" Rebekah turned to Harrison.

"Not at all. You and Lois go home. I'll call or text you if we find anything out."

"First, I would like to see the damage for myself if you don't mind," Rebekah said to Officer Brooks.

"As would I," Harrison agreed.

"Of course," Officer Brooks responded and led the way. "Just don't touch anything—including the railing, walls, and door knobs."

The apartment looked just as Officer Brooks had described. Red and black paint sprayed everywhere in every room with *Get Out* in large black letters on the long living room wall.

"I've seen enough," Rebekah said shortly after she gave the place a quick look around. She shook her head slowly before heading out. Once outside, she turned to Officer Brooks and thanked him.

"Well, hope you ladies have a blessed rest of your evening," Officer Brooks said, looking from Rebekah to Lois before walking them back to Rebekah's car.

Rebekah and Lois climbed in and silently buckled their seat belts. After a moment, Rebekah spoke. "I guess I should feel grateful it wasn't a fire. How nice of Harrison to take charge." She started the car.

"Yes, how nice of him indeed. That was a pretty passionate speech he made about you too—especially since he's 'just your contractor,'" Lois said. "There isn't something you might want to tell me, is there?"

Rebekah was glad it was dark in the car because she could feel a flush going up her neck. It annoyed her that Lois had chosen to focus on a relationship between her and Harrison while she was so worried about her new home. She decided instead to turn the table on Lois. "I have no secrets, Lois, but what about you? You've been holding out on me. Where did those flowers come from?"

"Well, I was actually going to tell you tonight, but all this came up." Lois paused for about five seconds then took a little breath before she continued, "I think I'm falling in love with Harrison's father, Doug. He's someone I've known for years and is an attorney, so I made an appointment to have a new will drawn up, and well, he asked me to lunch, and the rest is now history. We have been spending a lot of time together, and I am *very* fond of him. So now you know." Lois raised her hands and shoulders in a shrug, then let them drop to her lap before she took a breath in and out.

"Lois, I think it's wonderful!" Rebekah smiled. "I'm happy for you." She leaned over and put her hand on top of Lois's.

"It *is* wonderful," Lois replied. After a few moments of silence, she changed the subject back to the vandalism. "So do you have any idea who could have done this?"

Rebekah hesitated briefly. "No, no idea." She thought again of Ethan but reasoned that Ethan wouldn't do something like this. It wasn't in his nature …. *Was it? No, he wouldn't do it.* But then she realized there was someone who just might. *Emily would do something like this.* According to what Andrew and James had told her, and Rebekah's past experiences with Emily, it seemed that the woman was mentally unstable. Still, Rebekah was not going to jump to conclusions or accusations. She would wait and see what the police came up with and not mention Emily's name. Not yet.

Chapter 12

The next morning after Andrew got up, Rebekah told him what had taken place the night before. Poor Rose had been concerned when, strangely, she found no one at home after work. Rebekah and Lois were able to explain everything to her after they arrived home, and then, exhausted, they all headed to bed before Andrew came home.

"I can't believe someone would do this, Mom," Andrew said as he fixed himself a cup of coffee and English muffin. "I mean why? It's just mean and destructive."

"I agree, son. I'm looking forward to talking to Harrison today. He left me a text late last night after I went to sleep. Apparently, they have an image of a person of interest. Not sure who it is at this point."

"I'm going over to the shop after I grab some breakfast. I'm anxious to see the damage. You take your time. Hopefully Harrison has more news for us."

"Yes, I still can't believe it. I'll see you later, son. Closer to noon," Rebekah responded.

***

At ten o'clock, Harrison showed up at Lois's house. "Hey, talked to Sam this morning, and he texted me an image of someone who was behind your shop last night. It's some man I don't recognize," he told Rebekah when she answered the door.

"Come on in the kitchen. Would you like some coffee?" Rebekah was somewhat relieved. "Can he be identified?" She motioned for Harrison to sit down and poured him a cup of coffee.

"Not yet. He didn't match any mug shots on file, but they're still searching."

"Have you caught the person yet?" Lois asked as she joined them in the kitchen.

"No, but Sam texted me an image of him this morning," Harrison shared. "I was just getting ready to show Rebekah."

"Let me see too." Lois moved over to look at Harrison's phone and the picture. She took in a deep breath when she saw it. "I think I know him."

"*What?*" Harrison said with surprise.

"Yes, well, it's not that I *know* him. I have no idea what his name is. I never took his information when he tried to give it to me because, honestly, I didn't want to talk to him. He's that awful man who pestered me about selling my building to him. Things weren't going good for me in the clothing business, and I wasn't sure what I wanted to do. He came in politely a couple of times, but then one day he came in very threatening. I was quite upset, so I talked to Rebekah about it." Lois turned to look at Rebekah before continuing. "And it was at that point she said she wanted to buy the building from me."

"So if you saw him again, say, walking on the street, do you think you would possibly recognize him again?" Harrison asked.

"Oh, I think I would," Lois scoffed.

Harrison stood up, turning his back to the women, and silently paced around the room with a contemplative look on his face. "Hmm. We have to find out his name, and then I'll file a restraining order on him. I would love to get this guy in court and question him. Tear him up."

"Well, isn't that something we would have to get your dad to do?" Rebekah asked.

"What? No …. Oh, right, I guess you didn't know. I have a law degree, and I kind of practice law a little on the side. Dad insisted I go to law school because he wanted me to follow in his footsteps, but building stuff is more who I am. I still practice law occasionally though. I help out my fellow contractors here in town when they have problems or need advice, and I volunteer at a senior center once a month. It keeps my license active."

Rebekah was speechless.

"Anyway," Harrison went on and turned to Lois, "I want you to think who this guy might be. Anything that comes to mind. I'll pass this info on to Sam. Maybe some of the other building owners on the block have had the same experience with him and might know who he is. This is a great lead, Lois." Harrison headed toward the door. "Well, I've got to get going. Sorry to have to tell you this, Rebekah, but since I have to get my painters back in your place, we may have to bump your move-in date back. I can promise when they're done, though, you'll never know what happened." He gave her a big reassuring smile.

"Thank you, Harrison." Rebekah stood up to see him out. "You've gone above and beyond the normal contractor, and I appreciate it."

"Well, you see, Rebekah," Harrison said, his brown eyes twinkling as he put on his cap to leave. "I'm not your normal contractor," he added with a wink and walked out the door.

***

While driving to the shop later, close to noon, Rebekah mulled over everything Harrison had shared that morning. Her biggest fear was that this incident was just the beginning of something more. Before she left, Lois had told her she might visit some of the other stores on the block that afternoon and ask what they might know about the identity of the man they suspected had vandalized the apartment.

Then Rebekah thought about Harrison and the fact that he also had a law degree. He even helped other contractors and volunteered his time. The man was full of surprises. *And* he was humble; had this incident not come up, she probably would have never known. She had to admit, she was impressed. She felt both fortunate and grateful that he was doing her project.

When she arrived at the shop, Andrew immediately asked her to fill him in on any progress about the vandalism. She told him she would, but first she wanted to go upstairs and see the apartment again. Looking around in daylight, Rebekah was even more saddened by the mess. *How can someone be so cruel?* she thought as she and Andrew walked back downstairs to sit down in his office and talk.

"I just can't understand why someone would do this to us," Rebekah said. "Harrison came by Lois's with a picture of the suspect this morning, and Lois thinks she may recognize the guy as someone who approached her about buying the building just prior to the time I purchased it," Rebekah shared.

"Well, that's interesting," Andrew said with a puzzled look on his face.

"I thought so also. She doesn't know his name since she asked him to leave before he could give her the particulars and told him she wasn't interested. We wondered if any other building owners around here had the same experience, so she said she's going to speak with a few other shop owners she knows this afternoon."

"That sounds like a good idea," Andrew said and nodded as he went back to his computer.

"Oh, and guess what else I found out? Harrison has a law degree! He certainly is full of surprises, isn't he? Who would have guessed that? I'm certainly impressed, and he's so unassuming about it."

"Oh yeah, he told me that when he first started our project. He's a pretty smart guy. He actually helped me with a couple things I had to file for the state that I was confused about. Made it really easy for me."

"Really? How nice of him. Why didn't you ever mention it to me?"

Andrew looked up blankly from his computer. "I don't know. Just never came up. Hey, now that the apartment is almost done, I want to go over some figures with you and talk about how we're going to furnish the shop. You know, plan out how much money we may have to spend. Don't want any surprises."

"Sure," she said, happy for the diversion. She instantly recalled how she'd pictured her bakery from the time she had told Mére she was going to open one someday. "It may sound over the top—" she hesitated a moment, "—but I want a crystal chandelier hanging in the entrance—one you can't miss. The tables and chairs I would like to be a mismatch of different styles and sizes. Not new, but kind of vintage looking."

"Sounds good. You can probably get a lot of the décor at flea markets and antique stores. Sounds like a job for you and Lois, huh? You and I can visit some of the lighting stores in the area and maybe take a few pictures to show Harrison what you want. He can let us know the maximum size we should look at. How about the color of the place?" Andrew was down to business this morning, which was good since Rebekah didn't know where to start, and it took her mind off the situation from the night before.

Andrew and Rebekah spent the rest of the afternoon reviewing how much they had spent and his estimation of costs to come. According to Andrew, they were within his anticipated budget. Rebekah felt relieved to hear it. She did have a good amount of money from her lottery winnings still, but she didn't want to spend it all on her business. She wanted to have some saved for the future. Andrew was certainly taking good care of his mom and her money.

Around two o'clock in the afternoon, Officer Brooks showed up.

"Hope you all are doing well today after what transpired last night. Harrison gave me the information from Miss Bender, and I have an officer going to visit some of the buildings on the street tomorrow to collect information from anyone who may recognize the guy in the picture. Hopefully someone will have a name of the man—or maybe even a business card," Officer Brooks reassured them.

Andrew asked, "Can I see the picture?"

Officer Brooks handed Andrew a print out.

Andrew looked down and then up again. "No, I've never seen him around here. So what can we do to find out who he is or why he wants the buildings?"

Officer Brooks shook his head. "You all don't need to worry about figuring anything out. I'm on the job." He threw his right hand up in a stop position. "I have an idea what's going on, but I need to do a little more investigating. All you all have to do is live your life like normal and call me immediately if this guy shows up here. Here's my number." He handed Andrew a card. "Your mom already has it, but I want you to have it also."

Andrew took the card and another studied look at the picture before handing it back to Officer Brooks, saying, "I got it. Thank you." He shook the officer's hand.

"I'll be back in touch when I have more to tell you. Have a safe and enjoyable rest of your day," Officer Brooks said and left.

"I wonder if we should have told him Lois wants to visit some of the building owners, Mom?"

"Oh, she said she *might* go visit some people. I bet she doesn't," Rebekah speculated.

"I have my own suspicions about what's going on," Andrew said, "The guy who's doing this obviously wants property around here because he or someone else wants to build something on this block. Or he knows somebody else who wants to build something here, and if he acquires the property at a lower price, he can sell it to them for a lot more."

"Really? I never would have thought of that," Rebekah said naively.

"Stuff like this happens in business all the time, Mom," Andrew told Rebekah. "But intimidating people is not right."

"It sure isn't, son, and I'm happy I have you here with me." She smiled and placed her hand over Andrew's. "I thank God every day that you and James are in my life. Two finer men a mother couldn't ask for."

"Aww. Thanks, Mom." He hugged Rebekah and planted a kiss on her cheek. "James and I are the ones thanking God for the best mom ever."

"Now all we have to do is get James and Violet to move down here." *A mother can hope*, Rebekah thought.

"Well, let's get them married, and then we can start working on that," Andrew said with a devious chuckle. "I actually think James is jealous that I get to be here with you doing all this. He was quizzing me about how we were going to run things and made suggestions when we were in Wisconsin. Hope they come visit before the wedding. That would be great, but don't know if James has enough time off with the wedding also coming up. Have they said anything to you about coming here?"

"No, but next time I talk to your brother I'll see what he thinks. Violet needs to be able to come also. It will have to be after we've moved into the apartment. I wouldn't do that to Lois, although I don't think she would mind." Rebekah paused and then said, "Don't say anything to Rose, but Lois is seeing someone. It's for Lois to tell her."

"Yeah well, Rose and I figured that out—you know, the flowers and her odd behavior. Do you know who it is?" Andrew asked.

"I do." Rebekah smirked.

"Tell me who!" Andrew said in a voice that reminded her of a schoolgirl.

"I probably shouldn't." Rebekah hesitated for a moment, then decided, *What the heck?* "Doug Marshall. Harrison's dad."

Andrew threw his head back and laughed. "No way. Really? Why the big secret? It's actually kind of awesome, if you think about it. Harrison's a great guy, so his dad must be also."

"I don't want you to say anything to Rose now. I want Lois to tell her when she's ready."

"Geez, Mom. This is like middle school or something." They both laughed, and then Andrew became serious. "Mom, I hope you find someone like Doug Marshall to have in your life someday— I'm not saying now …." Andrew raised up the palms of both hands to stop her before she could protest. "Not now, but someday. You're too wonderful not to share your life with someone."

"Thank you. But right now, I need to stay focused on opening my teahouse and bakery. Maybe one day."

Rebekah didn't want to say it to Andrew but—yes—deep down, she did want somebody. She had a lot of love inside her wanting to break its way out. She would wait until someone appeared in her life like Doug had for Lois. What else could she do?

Chapter 13

Meanwhile that afternoon, around the same time Officer Brooks stopped by to talk to Rebekah and Andrew, Lois decided it might be helpful for her to do some detective work of her own. She figured she'd visit some of the other merchants she knew around the old shop to see if they had anything to say about the man who had wanted to buy her building. It might prove to be good information for that nice Officer Brooks.

She stopped at the bookstore, pottery shop, T-shirt and gifts shop, candle shop, and then the bagel shop, followed by the pizza place. Surprisingly, staff from each place told her their owners were not in but that they would tell them she came by.

The last place Lois decided to visit was the doughnut shop to talk to the owner, Angie, whom Lois was friends with. She knew Angie would be there, and, honestly she really wanted one of Angie's double-cinnamon swirl cheesecake doughnuts before she headed home.

Angie was indeed there and told Lois that she remembered a man who had come by wanting to buy her building last year. Unfortunately, she didn't remember his name either, because she, too, had kicked him out when he told her what he wanted. She thought she might have a business card in the back, but she would have to dig around to find it, so Lois took her doughnut to one of the booths in the front corner and sat down. This criminal investigation stuff was tough and made her hungry.

As she was enjoying her doughnut, she heard a couple of raised voices coming from the checkout counter—though not clearly enough to hear what was being said. *Sometimes customers can be so demanding*, she thought while taking another bite of doughnut. She remembered a couple of her clothing store customers who used to drive her to distraction.

Being nosy, she slowly peeked around the corner of the booth, hoping to see what was going on. A man was arguing with Angie, but she was only able to see him from the back. Then Lois's jaw dropped when the man turned his head sideways in her direction. She pulled her head back into the booth, ducking down and almost choking on her doughnut. It was the same man from the photo Harrison had shown her—the same man who had harassed Lois about her clothing store and was suspected of vandalizing Rebekah's new apartment!

What do I do? Lois thought as her heart pounded in her chest. Then she watched as the man roughly ushered Angie into a back room. Lois grabbed her purse, fumbled around to find Officer Brooks' card, dialed his number ... and got his voicemail. *Oh heck, it's going to have to be 911 then*, she thought. She dialed the number.

Before the woman who answered could say a word, Lois spoke. "My name is Lois Bender, and I need an officer or two to come ASAP to Angie's Donut Shop. The shop owner is being accosted by a bad man. I don't know the exact address—" the woman on the phone cut her off.

"No need, ma'am. I've already traced your phone and someone is on their way. Just stay hidden the best you can until help arrives, and don't do anything to endanger yourself."

Just then, Lois heard a crash at the back of the store. She could no longer see Angie or the man. *He must be beating her*, Lois thought. She had to do something. "I've got to go," she said to the dispatcher and hung up.

Lois peered around the corner but couldn't see anything, so she quickly shuffled toward the swinging door that led to the back of the store. Just as she reached to push it open, there he was. This was definitely the man from the security camera. They both stopped dead in their tracks.

"You! You're the old lady who sold your building to someone else. You're nothing but a pathetic old bag. Why didn't you sell it to me? You have no idea how much trouble you've caused me. I could wring your neck!" he shouted and lunged toward her.

Lois scrambled backward, just beyond his reach, and without thinking, turned a table over in front of the assailant. The man was moving so fast, he couldn't stop in time and tripped, throwing his hands out to break the fall.

Lois heard a *crack* as the man crash-landed on the floor. *Maybe he broke his arm*, she thought. *Good*. At the same moment, she noticed, out of the corner of her eye, a coat rack not far from her reach. She spied an umbrella—a big, golf-sized umbrella—that someone had left behind. *Bless their heart*, Lois thought as she grabbed it.

As the man fumbled to get up, she raised the umbrella and, with both hands, whacked it against the man's broken arm with all her might. The man fell to the ground, yelling in pain and grasping his arm.

"OLD BAG? OLD LADY?" Lois screamed, the adrenalin coursing through her body. "I don't think so!" She whacked him again and again, continuing to swing the umbrella like a Jedi knight.

Just then, two police officers came through the door. They immediately ran toward the man, who cried out in pain as they handcuffed him. "Get me away from her!" he screamed.

As the two officers dragged the man outside to their patrol car, another officer rushed through the door and, looking around the room, spotted Lois. "Are you okay, ma'am?" he asked Lois.

"I am, officer, but there's someone in the back who might not be," Lois responded.

The officer pointed to one of the booths. "Please sit over here, ma'am, and stay out of the way. Someone will be in to talk to you." He headed to the back room.

Soon Angie, who appeared to be unconscious, emerged on a stretcher.

Now another officer approached Lois. "Are you okay?"

"Just a little shook up," Lois responded, adding, "You might want to get a hold of Officer Brooks. All this involves a case he's working on."

"Yes, ma'am, I will." The officer pulled out a phone and moved out of earshot as he proceeded to make a call. When the officer came back, he said Officer Brooks wanted to take Lois's statement personally, so if she would kindly follow him to his car he would drive her to the station. "Officer Brooks said he would have Rebekah Hayward and Harrison Marshall come meet you there." He paused and looked around the shop as if searching for the right words. "I'm not sure what exactly happened here, but I'll be honest, I'm looking forward to hearing your statement myself." He chuckled and escorted her to the police car.

***

Just as they were locking up for the day, Rebekah and Andrew received a call from Officer Brooks asking them to come by the station. He told them he had Lois in custody and would fill them in on the details when they arrived. Rebekah was beside herself with concern.

When they arrived, Rebekah rushed into the front office where she was surprised to find Lois sitting calmly in a chair. "Lois, what happened? Why are you here?"

Just as Lois opened her mouth to speak, in came Harrison—with Doug trailing right behind him.

"My dear Lois, what in the world has happened?" Doug went straight to Lois and held her like he would never let go.

"Oh, Doug," Lois responded.

In his arms, Lois broke down for the first time, having held up like a soldier to this point. She was now safe and let the trauma of the day release, surprising even herself with her reaction.

"Okay who is going to tell us what's going on?" Harrison asked.

"It seems our friend Lois decided to do a little investigating herself by visiting some of the other merchants in the same area as Rebekah's building. At Angie's Donut Shop, her last stop, a man showed up whom Lois IDed as the man who is suspected in the vandalism of Rebekah's building. It appears that this man thought no one else was in the shop at the time." Officer Brooks tossed his head Lois's way, and she gave him a sheepish grin while batting her eyelashes. "Except 'Miss Marple,' our supersleuth here, was waiting in the corner, enjoying Angie's specialty—a double-cinnamon swirl cheesecake doughnut—and went into action when she heard distress from the back area. When the man came after Lois, she flipped a table over, causing him to fall and break his arm. She then proceeded to beat the life out of him with a golf umbrella till we arrived."

They all slowly turned to Lois who sat blank faced in her chair.

"I did what I felt I needed to," Lois proclaimed and gave a shrug.

"We have your statement, Lois, so you're released," Officer Brooks announced, waving his hand toward the door. He then turned to the others and shook his head as he broke into a smile. "She's all yours now," he said, then looked pointedly back at Lois. "Please leave the investigating to us in the future, okay?" he said sternly as he pointed a finger at her and then leaned over to say quietly, "That double-cinnamon swirl cheesecake doughnut? It's my favorite too." He patted her on the shoulder and gave a little wink.

"Yes, officer," she responded as Officer Brooks and his fellow officer left the room.

"Let's get you home," Rebekah said with concern still in her voice. "Wait till Rose hears about this."

"Listen, it's almost five o'clock. I say all of us go back to Lois's and order some pizza. Is that okay, Lois?" Andrew suggested. "We can hear all the 007 supersleuth details from the hero herself. And by then, Rose will be home too. What do you say?"

"Yes, Andrew. That's an excellent idea," Lois said, her eyes on Doug.

"Sounds good to me," Harrison said. "How about you, Dad?"

"Yes, it sounds great," Doug responded as he stared at Lois. "I don't know about you all, but I could also use a beer."

"I got you covered, Doug," Andrew said, patting Doug on the back and extending his hand. "And by the way, I'm Andrew Hayward, and this is my mom, Rebekah."

126 SUSAN AMOND TODD

"It's a pleasure to finally meet you," Doug said. He shook Andrew's hand and gave Rebekah a gentlemanly nod.

"Well, let's get out of here then. But first let me say—" Andrew turned and pointed a finger at Lois, "—you, milady, are a badass."

They all laughed as they left the precinct.

***

Since Andrew and Rebekah had gone to the precinct together in Andrew's car, he drove Rebekah back to the shop to get her vehicle. On their way, Rebekah placed an order at the pizza place around the corner from Lois's house.

"The pizza should be ready by the time I get there, so I'll run in and pick it up," Andrew told her. "You just go straight home."

"That would be great, sweetheart. It's already paid for. I can't wait to get back to Lois. What a day!"

"No kidding," Andrew responded.

Once Rebekah was safely in her car and on her way home, she took in a deep breath and let it out slowly. She was grateful Lois was okay and that the terrible man was apprehended. She imagined that over the next few weeks, they would find out what exactly was going on. Nothing like this ever happened in Wisconsin.

Rose pulled into the driveway just as Rebekah was stepping out of her car.

"Hey, Rebekah, how was your day? Mine was so boring. Can't wait till your renovation is done and the shop opens," Rose stated cheerfully.

"Well, we've had quite a day actually, but I'll let Lois tell you. Andrew should be along shortly. We're having pizza for dinner, and he's picking it up."

"Oh great. I see Harrison's truck is here. Is he having pizza with us?" Rose asked.

"As a matter of fact, he is. And so is his father, Doug."

"Okay? Cool ...." Rose said, sounding as confused as she was surprised.

Just then, Andrew pulled in with the pizza.

"Hey, Rose," he hollered. "Can you help me with the pizza? Did Mom tell you about Lois? Oh my God, she is one tough lady."

Rose looked from Andrew to Rebekah.

"Andrew, I thought we would leave it to Lois to explain. After all it *is* her story," Rebekah reminded him.

"Well, let's get inside with that pizza because you've got my curiosity for sure," Rose said, grabbing two of the pizza boxes and heading straight through the front door. "LOIS! What have you been up to?" she shouted as she opened the door.

"Come on, Mom," Andrew said, carrying two more pizza boxes. "I don't want to miss out on Lois's blow-by-blow of this." He kicked his car door shut and hurried into the house.

Neither did Rebekah, so she locked her car and quickly followed him.

Chapter 14

Over the next several weeks, the story of the man who had been harassing Asheville's store owners came to light.

The man, Albert Webster, was working for a group of investors who wanted to buy up the block to build an upscale hotel and some specialty shops. Albert had informed Officer Brooks that he was promised a commission on each building he was able to acquire. Albert—and his investor—had never dreamed he would get as much pushback as he had from the owners, and over time, he'd resorted to aggression to motivate them. According to Albert, he'd never intended to hurt anyone. Angie, the owner of the doughnut shop, had asthma and had begun to hyperventilate, causing her to grow faint after exchanging angry words with Albert. Albert helped Angie to the back room so she could sit down and was coming out to get her a glass of water when Lois encountered him. Albert never intended to harm Angie physically, nor would he have harmed Lois, or so he told Officer Brooks. He just "wanted to scare them."

Officer Brooks came over to see Rebekah at her building two days after the arrest and provided an update on the situation. He said they should just "live their lives" and "let the system handle things." They would be notified when and if their assistance was needed. Apparently, Albert had been cooperative and expounded on the tremendous pressure that had been put on him to acquire the buildings. He had no previous record and, from what they could tell, wasn't a criminal. Rebekah was still not going to let her guard down and asked Harrison if he could add a security system not only outside the building but inside, especially the shop area. He said he thought it a good idea and had actually planned on suggesting it to her.

It took Harrison several days to get his painting guys back to the apartment and paint over the black and red paint. Just as he had promised, when the guys were done, it looked like the spray paint had never been there. The final inspections all passed and, three weeks later, on the third Saturday in May, Rebekah and Andrew moved in to their new home.

***

The week before they were to move in, Rebekah received a call from Tammy. Rebekah wondered if the sale of Fred's store had gone through but wasn't going to ask. It had been a month since she was in Wisconsin, and she was aware that things like this could fall through over the simplest reasons.

"Tammy, so good to hear from you! Hope you're doing okay?" she greeted Tammy.

"I've got terrible news—well at least I think it is." There was a long pause before Tammy blurted it out. "Fred sold the store! Why would he do that?"

So he did do it, she thought to herself. She would play dumb. "What do you mean he sold the store?"

"I mean he sold the store to another company. Evidently it was an offer he couldn't refuse. He says nothing will change, but they *always* say that. He's still going to be running this one, but he's not the owner anymore."

"I hate to hear that, but you know … everything could just stay the same." Rebekah tried to sound positive, though if she were still there, she would be freaking out too.

"I just knew you would say that," Tammy huffed, sounding just as Andrew and James had when they were about ten years old.

Rebekah muffled a laugh. "Keep an open mind. You might even get a raise—have you thought of that?" Rebekah knew she hadn't.

"Well, that could be a good thing," Tammy acquiesced and then sounded a bit calmer as she added, "Where's my manners? I just jumped into my troubles. How are you doing, sweetie?"

"Don't be concerned about me. This is a big deal for you, and I'm happy you called me about it so I could help you see the possibilities." Rebekah meant it. "Just hang in there. Most of the time when things like this happen, it's a good year before they start making changes. That will give you time to show the new owners what an asset you are."

"Well, I guess you're right," Tammy acknowledged. "I am doing a good job."

"Keep that positive attitude going that you always talk about. Now, I do have good news to share. Our apartment is finished, and we're moving in this weekend."

"Well, if that isn't the best news! I can't wait till the day I come visit you and see it all. I've been to Minnesota, Upper Michigan, and Illinois—and that's it. Oh, and Canada once back in the day when you didn't need a passport. I think a trip to North Carolina is in my future."

"I would say it is. There's always a place for you in my home. Listen, Tammy. I'm sorry, but I'll have to call you back.

I'm expecting my new stove, refrigerator, and dishwasher to be delivered any minute."

"No, don't worry about it, hon. We can talk again after you move in so I can hear all about the place. You enjoy it because you deserve it. Thanks for helping me put things in perspective. We'll talk again soon. Bye."

"Bye Tammy. I'll be thinking about you."

***

In the time it took to get the inspections completed—and thanks to some wonderful help from Lois—Rebekah had purchased and ordered the furniture she wanted for the apartment. She had never had so much fun. With the exception of a few beautiful pieces Lois was giving her, everything else was brand new. Even her dishes, silverware, and pots and pans were new. And because she purchased so much at once, many of the stores were willing to hold on to her furniture until the day she wanted it delivered.

"We'll wait till after all the furniture is placed before we hang pictures and add accessories," Lois told her the morning of the furniture delivery. "I have a few things I'm ready to recycle that you can see if you would like to use."

"Lois, you've been too kind. I feel like you've given me so much already," Rebekah protested.

"My dear, don't you be concerned," Lois said with a laugh and a wave of her hand. "This means I can get something new to replace it! You'll be doing me a favor."

Both women laughed.

"Well, when you put it that way, how can I refuse?" Rebekah laughed again and gave Lois a hug.

Rebekah had decided to have her furniture delivered on the Thursday and Friday before the weekend she and Andrew intended to move in. Waiting on the deliveries was no bother since she and Andrew were downstairs both days anyway, working on the plans for the shop—which seemed never ending.

Saturday and Sunday were spent moving things around, making beds, placing clothes in the closets, and setting up the kitchen. Rose took the weekend off from work at Biltmore to help, and even Harrison and Doug showed up. By this time, Lois had told Rose all about Doug. Rose said she "couldn't be happier" to hear the news, which, in turn, made Lois happy.

Lois and Rebekah concentrated on the kitchen, leaving the men to put together any pieces of furniture that needed assembly and moving around. Rose volunteered to make the beds and arrange the bathrooms.

While Rebekah was lining some drawers in the kitchen, she wondered, *Why didn't Andrew invite Mary Sue here today?* In fact, she realized she hadn't heard Andrew mention the girl's name once in weeks. *Hmm ...* was there trouble in paradise with the two of them? She would wait and ask at an appropriate time.

By five o'clock on Sunday, the apartment had been transformed. *This is my home!* Rebekah thought as she sat in her new living room and felt her heart swell with joy.

"Can everyone meet me in the living room?" Rebekah called out.

Andrew, Rose, Lois, Harrison, and Doug all came scrambling in from where they had been working.

"I can't thank you all enough for the help you've given us, not only today but since Andrew and I arrived in this wonderful town. With that said, I can't think of anyone other than you fine folks to sit down with at this table for our first meal." She gazed toward her new kitchen table. *Her* table. "How does barbecue sound?"

"I never say no to barbecue. Where's your favorite place?" Doug asked.

"We love Bobby Perris BBQ," Andrew responded.

"No kidding, that's my favorite too! He's the 'King of Barbecue,'" Doug said with a chuckle, quoting Bobby's claim to fame.

"Well, that settles it. Andrew, go ahead and order the barbecue from Bobby Perris with all the fixings," Rebekah said, and she handed Andrew her credit card. "You can pick it up."

"Rebekah, I think I'm going to run out and pick up a couple bottles of wine so we can properly toast your first meal in this lovely home. Come on, Lois," Doug said, extending his bent arm to Lois.

Lois smiled as she took his arm, and they made their exit.

"Got it ordered, Mom," Andrew shared as he headed to the door. "They said it would be ready in twenty minutes—just about the amount of time it will take us to get there."

Their departure left Rebekah alone. It quickly became quiet. She looked around and felt a little sting in her eyes as tears pooled against her bottom lids. She went over to the sofa end table where there was a box of tissues and sat down. A minute or two later, she heard the toilet flush. Startled, she stood and turned toward the bathroom just as the door opened.

Harrison. What is it with him and the bathroom? She chuckled. In the commotion of everyone else leaving, she assumed he had gone with Andrew and Rose. She turned her head away and blinked her eyes several times to clear the tears before turning back.

"Oh, hey. Where did everyone go?" Harrison asked, looking around the apartment.

"Oh, they left to get barbecue—and wine," she responded, wondering how he'd missed it.

"Geez, I stepped into the bathroom thinking I would go to help pick up the barbecue. I guess you snooze, you lose." He chuckled awkwardly.

Rebekah looked down at her feet then back up at Harrison and chuckled as well, not knowing what to say next. After a moment, she blurted, "Harrison, this place is amazing! I never thought I would have such a beautiful home. You have utilized the space so well and made my dream come true."

"You know, I can't tell you how good it makes me feel to see the people I work for so happy. Thank you. Of course, I only have half the job done. I should be starting on the downstairs area next week though. I'm really looking forward to that."

"I am too. I feel like I have to pinch myself every day to make sure this is not make-believe. All my life I have dreamed of opening a bakery, but what I'm ultimately opening is even more than that. To think I will be a business owner by this fall .... I won't lie—it scares me a little."

"Aww, don't be worried," Harrison said with encouragement. "Look at all the help you have. Andrew is your wingman, and Lois has her retail experience to contribute, and then you have Rose to give you her support. Why, I wouldn't be surprised if your other son decides to move here. He won't be able to stand not being part of the fun!"

"I would love that, but James is getting married this year and will have a wife who may not want to move away from her family in Milwaukee." Rebekah looked straight into Harrison's brown eyes. They were so soft and caring.

He took a few steps forward until he was close to her, so close she could smell the light scent of his aftershave. She blinked a few times as she drew in a deep breath and sensed something else too.

Is he going to kiss me?

"Rebekah … I … um … well …" Harrison stammered as he ran his fingers through his hair. He inched one step closer and shifted his weight from one foot to the other. His eyes met hers and then immediately darted downward and back up again, as he hesitated, lifted his head, and opened his mouth. Another awkward chuckle escaped his lips. "I've enjoyed this project for so many reasons …. But mostly because—"

Just then Doug and Lois burst through the door, laughing, and then stopped abruptly, sensing they had walked in on something.

"Well," Lois said with a smile and a slight laugh. "Well … we're back!" She gave Doug an awkward look as they sidestepped into the room.

"Let's go put this in the kitchen, Lois." Doug smiled and looked at his son as he passed.

"Yes, I'm right behind you, dear." Lois smiled as well, keeping her eyes on Rebekah as she headed to the kitchen.

Not really knowing what to do next, Rebekah stood awkwardly next to Harrison. Within seconds, Andrew and Rose bustled in with the barbecue. The moment—whatever it was that had been materializing—evaporated into thin air, and all was as it had been just minutes before.

"Do you all mind if we use paper plates and plastic cups tonight?" Rebekah asked, turning her attention to the dining area.

There was a resounding "No."

"I can drink my wine in any vessel available," Lois said, and they all laughed.

It was wonderful to baptize their new home with friends such as these. Rebekah hadn't even been in Asheville six months and felt like she belonged. Maybe Dee had felt this way also. And to think she was living in the same space Dee had. In a strange way, that gave her comfort. Like maybe Dee would watch over her.

After everyone had left, Rebekah and Andrew sat down in the living area and marveled at their new home.

"Mom, this place is more awesome than I imagined it would be. It's so—you. Harrison nailed it."

"He sure did, son. It also helps that I was able to pick out the furniture myself! It's so much nicer to not have to live in a parsonage where someone else—with not very good taste, I might add—has picked out everything. Here I actually like everything, and I've bought each piece of furniture for the specific spot it's in—with help from Lois, of course. She is quite the decorator. I'll be using her skills for the shop also. I wish we didn't have to wait till this fall to open! Do you think there's any possibility of sooner?"

"No, probably not." Andrew shook his head and repositioned himself in the chair. "Because this is such a big job and Harrison needs quite a few of his guys, he won't start till after June first. Also, some of the guys have vacations he has to work around too. It's okay though, Mom. You have to work up your menu and test everything. I'll be happy to make myself available for taste testing—as will Rose and Lois, I have no doubt. You could probably drag Doug and Harrison in on it too." Andrew laughed.

"I figured so," Rebekah agreed and then remembered something. "I forgot to tell you about this. I found a summer class at the technical college on patisserie. Rose helped me sign up for it. I do have a little baking experience in that area, but feel I need to become more proficient, so for six weeks on Monday, Tuesday, and Wednesday mornings, starting June eighth, I'll be attending class. I figure it's a good use of my time till we get to the part of the renovation where I'll be more involved."

"Actually, that's a great idea, Mom, and you'll have fun no doubt."

"I sure will," she agreed. "I also have a question to ask you."

"Shoot," Andrew replied.

"I haven't heard you say a word about Mary Sue in some time. Anything I need to know about?"

Andrew hung his head for a moment before glancing up at his mother. "She just wasn't for me," he shared. "She's a nice girl and stuff, but after we got to know each other better, there wasn't any special magic. You know, the kind like James and Violet have. And she told me she won't be working for you after the shop opens because she's moving back home with her parents. We both decided it would be best to go our separate ways. That's okay, like I said, no special magic."

"I'm sorry to hear that. I thought she was a nice girl, but if you don't see a future, I guess it's better to move on for both of you. And don't compare your relationships to your brother's. Everyone is unique and different. The right girl will show up."

"I guess so. What about you, Mom?"

"What about me?"

"I think Harrison might kind of like you," Andrew said, snickering like a thirteen-year-old boy. "It's the way he acts when he's around you—different than when he's around me and others—don't you notice?"

Rebekah was taken aback and felt a warm wave climbing up her neck to her face. "Don't be so ridiculous, Andrew. He's doing a job for us—our relationship is purely professional. You're just confusing it with his professionalism, that's all. And besides, I'm not looking for a relationship, so put this nonsense out of your head." She waved her hand dismissively. "I'm tired and going to my new bedroom and straight to sleep! It's been a long day," she spouted and jumped up before Andrew could see the flush on her face. She could still hear him laughing at her as she closed the door of her bedroom.

Now that she was in her room, she was safe from anymore speculation on Andrew's part. She had to admit that tonight before Lois and Doug returned with the wine, she had felt a bit of an awkward—but nice—moment with Harrison, like maybe he had wanted to say something to her. She shook her head to dismiss the thought. *Nonsense.* It was probably just something he wouldn't be able to do for the shop renovation. Maybe he'd have to start a week later than planned and was afraid to tell her. She got ready for bed, climbed between the new crisp sheets, and sunk into the mattress. Her new bed felt like heaven. Her *own* bed in her *own* home. Within ten minutes, she was sound asleep.

Chapter 15

Parking at Asheville-Buncombe Technical College in the summer was nothing like what Rose had described during the normal school year. Rebekah had her pick of spaces. Now finding the right room for her class was another story. Fortunately, Rebekah had gotten directions to her classroom from Rose. Unfortunately, she took a wrong turn down a hallway that took her on a long detour though, thankfully, she eventually ended up where she needed to be. She arrived just as the instructor was getting ready to close the door.

"Hello," the instructor greeted her. "Are you here for patisserie?"

"Yes," Rebekah responded. "I took a wrong turn back there," she said with a nervous laugh as she flailed her arm toward the hall she had just come from.

"Yes, not a problem. Why don't you sit over there and we'll get started," he said and pointed to a table where a petite blonde woman close to Rebekah's age was sitting by herself.

Rebekah hadn't been sure how big the class would be and was relieved to note she was just one of eight. *A nice size*, she thought. The woman she sat next to gave her a friendly smile as Rebekah set her things down.

The instructor introduced himself as Don Lester, adding that the class should refer to him as Chef Lester or Chef. For the next six weeks, he would immerse them in all things patisserie. He proceeded to provide a summary of his work history—patisserie school in France, several baking schools in the US, participating in world-class competitions, and running several bakeries—which Rebekah found very impressive. She was ready to start baking, but Chef Lester had to go through all the rules, regulations, and basic techniques and then answer questions. It would actually be next week before they would start baking, he informed them.

Before she knew it, her first class was over.

"He's interesting," Rebekah's tablemate said in a whisper as she stood.

"Yes, he is," Rebekah responded softly. "I had it in my head we would start baking today."

The woman and Rebekah walked out the door together into the hallway, talking freely as soon as they cleared the classroom.

"I thought we'd be baking today too. Isn't that what we're here for?" she said in an annoyed voice and then stopped to face Rebekah.

"My name is Cathy Dunn." She stuck her hand out to shake Rebekah's.

"My name is Rebekah Hayward," she said as she shook Cathy's hand. "Nice to meet you."

The two continued down the hallway.

"You don't sound like you're from around here," Cathy commented.

"No, I'm from Wisconsin."

"Really? I don't think I've ever met anyone from there before. I guess I can check that one off my list now." Cathy laughed.

Wanting to take the subject off herself, Rebekah asked, "So why are you taking this class?"

"Well, I run a little bakery business out of my home, and I thought this might give me some new ideas. How about you?" Cathy asked.

"I've bought a building in downtown Asheville, and I'm starting a bakery and teahouse."

"Wow. Seriously?" Cathy stopped a moment with a surprised look on her face.

"Yes, and I say that to myself at least ten times a day." Rebekah laughed.

"It would be my dream to do that, but I don't think it will ever happen." Cathy paused for a moment and then changed the subject. "Hey, there's a little sandwich shop over in Biltmore Village. Would you like to go over there and grab a bite to eat with me? Or do you have other things to do?"

"Sure, I'd love to get a sandwich," Rebekah responded.

"Okay, why don't you follow me. That's my car over there." She pointed to the car that was parked right next to Rebekah's.

"Great! That's my car right next to you," Rebekah said and smiled.

The women got into their cars and headed to the sandwich shop.

***

As she headed home after her class and lunch with Cathy, Rebekah felt excited. She had made a new friend, and they were close in age. Her giddiness made her feel silly, kind of like a teenager. Cathy had twin daughters who had just turned twenty-one. Rebekah's first thought upon learning this was that maybe Andrew and Rose could meet them. Although Andrew seemed happy and didn't seem to miss Mary Sue at all, which she was a little surprised about, it could be nice for him to have a few friends so he could do whatever things young people like to do. All he seemed to do lately was crunch numbers, talk about the shop renovation, and hang out with Rose. He needed some more fun in his life—as did Rose for that matter. It was decided. She would invite Cathy and her girls over for dinner one night, and then she could show Cathy the shop. That would be fun.

Rebekah learned that Cathy had been born and raised in Asheville, and her husband, Hank, had been an Asheville police officer. He was killed in the line of duty five years ago, Cathy said, and Rebekah didn't press for more detail.

Always having been good at baking, Cathy had decided she could start selling cakes and cookies to her friends and acquaintances. Over time, she started getting orders for small parties and events to the point she needed help. Her daughters helped some, as did her mom and dad, but she was at a place in her baking where she had to make a decision about what to do next. That was one reason she was taking the patisserie class. If she was going big, she wanted to learn more about baking.

Rebekah had told Cathy about growing up in Wisconsin and how she learned everything she knew about baking at the hand of her grandmother. She told her about working at Fred's Market and Café but stopped at anything personal. If Cathy turned out to be the kind of friend Rebekah hoped she could be, she would share the messy stuff another time, she thought. No use in clouding a new friendship with her story. Besides, she didn't want to talk about it anyway or get sympathy from anyone.

It was so nice to meet someone with similar interests for a change. The only other person she had ever had that kind of relationship with was Tammy. The whole conversation reminded her she needed to call Tammy. Rebekah would give her a call soon.

She and Tammy had never been big phone call people since they saw each other every day at work—and Rebekah would have had to explain to Ethan whom she was talking to, *and* he would have wanted to know Tammy's background and which church she went to. Oh, that would have really gone over well if Ethan had found out Tammy worked as a bartender for Friday fish nights at a neighborhood tavern .... And that she had encouraged Rebekah to start playing the lottery. As far as Rebekah knew, Tammy didn't have a church, especially since she volunteered to work Sundays at Fred's so Rebekah could attend her church—and listen to Ethan's boring sermons. Rebekah laughed as she thought about the look he would have had on his face if he had known all of this. And then she laughed again, thinking about what might have happened if he had ever actually met Tammy. Tammy would have said she could feel that "dark energy" she was always right about. And then that dark energy would have pushed him over the top, and he would have made Rebekah quit her job for sure. She shook her head, relieved it was all in the past, and now she could just laugh about. She was so happy to have her freedom from that man so she could live her life.

When she arrived home, she popped her head into Andrew's new office downstairs. The first thing Harrison had tackled in the shop renovation was to construct an office space for Andrew to work in. It was not totally complete, but it was functional and in the footprint of where his final office would be.

"Hi, son," she said quietly.

He popped his head up from the papers he had been hunched over for hours. Yes, he was way too serious for a kid his age and needed some new friends. She would have Cathy and her girls over for certain—and Rose also.

"Oh hi, Mom. Your class was longer than I thought. How was it? Is it what you were looking for?"

"I think so, from what Chef Lester told us. He's the real deal, and I hope to learn a lot. We won't start baking till next week. He has a lot to share with us first, according to him. I guess I'll find out tomorrow," she said with a smile and sat down in the chair next to him.

"Well good," Andrew replied and looked back at the papers he had been working on.

"I made a new friend. I'm back late because she suggested we have lunch together after class. Her name is Cathy Dunn, and we're around the same age. She has a small bakery she runs out of her house and is wanting to expand her business."

Andrew looked up from his papers. "That's great, Mom. I kind of worry about you sometimes. You haven't made any friends since we got here other than Lois—which I'm not saying is bad. I just want you to make some friends close to your age to hang out with."

Who is the mother around here? Rebekah thought. "Well, it's funny you say that, Andrew, because Cathy has twin daughters who are twenty-one, and I was thinking how nice it would be for you to meet them and have some friends *your* age."

Andrew opened his mouth as if he were going to speak and then wisely closed it.

"In fact, I'm going to invite them over for dinner next weekend, and make sure you tell Rose because she can use some friends also, I think."

"Yes, ma'am." Andrew knew when not to put up any resistance.

Rebekah felt excited as she headed up the stairs to the apartment, thinking about her first real friend and the idea of entertaining in her new home. She would make something classic Wisconsin for dinner—and a fabulous dessert, of course. Oh, this was going to be fun.

Chapter 16

The laughter filled the room

"Tell us another one," begged Rose.

"Okay, okay," Andrew said holding up the palms of his hands. "What do you call a cow that just had a baby?"

Rebekah had no idea Andrew possessed this side of him. He had been telling corny farmer jokes to Rebekah, Rose, Lois, Cathy, and Cathy's two daughters, Mandy and Allie—who were blonde-haired, blue-eyed clones of their mother—keeping them in stitches.

"Do you give up?" Andrew asked.

Cathy's daughter, Allie, responded, "Yes we give up!"

Andrew hesitated before he answered to prolong their anticipation. "De-calf-inated."

They all laughed with tears in their eyes. Andrew had been telling these jokes to them nonstop, and the jokes were so cheesy, they couldn't help laughing.

"Okay, sadly cocktail time is over, ladies, as are the jokes," Andrew proclaimed. "I know you're disappointed, but it's time to go into the dining area where my mom has cooked a Wisconsin favorite for you. Cathy, if I may escort you?" Andrew offered his arm out to Cathy, who just smiled as he led her to a chair, which he proceeded to pull out for her while the younger women followed behind him, giggling.

Rebekah was glad to finally be able to invite Cathy and her daughters over for dinner. Their baking class was at its midpoint, and Rebekah and Cathy were becoming better friends with every class.

"I'm dying to find out what this Wisconsin favorite is," Cathy remarked.

The table was set beautifully, and Rebekah felt glad she had bought a table with an extra leaf. Lois had insisted she buy one with that option, and now she saw why. She first covered the table with a white cloth and yellow napkins, then set out her new white dishes with the blue floral pattern delicately scattered around the edge, some traditional stainless pattern utensils, and slightly blue-tinted glasses. The white cloth and yellow napkins were a beautiful backdrop for what she had chosen, exactly the way she had always thought a table should look.

"Dinner is coming in just a sec," Andrew said, placing a bowl of salad, a basket of his mom's homemade butter rolls, and a big bottle of ketchup on the table.

Soon, Rebekah came out and placed a large platter on the table.

"This is something my mom makes all the time," Andrew said, nodding his head toward the platter. "They're called pasties. It's like a Cornish meat pie."

"They kind of remind me of an empanada," Cathy's daughter, Mandy, said as she placed one on her plate.

"The way my brother and I—and, well, most of the people in Wisconsin—eat these is first we break them up with our fork, and then we cover them in ketchup," Andrew said, placing a pasty on his plate and grabbing the ketchup bottle. He demonstrated the process, then took a bite. "Oh my God, Mom—you did it again.

I'm in heaven," Andrew said, rolling his eyes and leaning back in his chair.

"I think Andrew is being a bit dramatic." Rebekah stared at Andrew. "Would you please pass the salad and bread to our company, Andrew?"

"Oh, yes, of course." Andrew set his fork down and did as he was told.

Everyone agreed with Andrew about how delicious the pasties were.

"So this is something y'all eat up there?" Cathy asked.

"Yes, and there are restaurants and shops that sell them also," Rebekah shared. "The way they got started was during the days when Cornish miners immigrated to Upper Michigan in the mid-1800s. They found that these were an easy meal for them to take to the mines. Inside the crust was their meat, potatoes, and vegetables made portable. A good hearty meal for hardworking men. They could also be warmed up easily. I remember my mom telling me the miners' wives would carve their husbands' initials or name in the crust when they were baked so they would know which one was theirs when they warmed them on a fire."

They dug in and were all silent for a while as they enjoyed their meal. After a couple of minutes, Lois said, "Why didn't you ever make these when you were living with me?"

"I'm wondering the same thing," Rose said.

"Are you going to have this on the menu at your new place?" Cathy asked.

"I hadn't thought of that, but maybe I should," Rebekah said, surprised by how much her friends enjoyed the pasties.

"I guess that's settled then. You said you wanted to bring some of the baked goods from Wisconsin to the South." Andrew smiled at his mom.

The rest of the evening was as enjoyable as the start. Rebekah made banana pudding for dessert, which received as many accolades as the pasties. Andrew and Rose seemed to hit it off with Allie and Mandy, and Rebekah overheard the four of them making plans to get together some night. It couldn't have gone better.

Lois and Rose insisted on staying later to help Rebekah and Andrew clean up. When they were finished, Rose and Andrew plopped themselves on the sofa and pulled a movie up on the TV while Rebekah and Lois sat in the kitchen, talking.

"Cathy and her girls are very nice," Lois said. "So happy you've found someone your age and not just some old lady like me."

"Hush, Lois, you are no old lady," Rebekah insisted, and Lois laughed. "I'm happy Andrew and Rose hit it off with Cathy's girls. I can't get over how much those girls look like each other and their mother. It's like we had triplets here tonight. Maybe Andrew will take a liking to one of the girls now that Mary Sue is out of the picture."

"Maybe—or maybe someone else." Lois paused and looked thoughtfully over at the sofa where Rose and Andrew were giggling and teasing each other. "I never did think Mary Sue was his type though," she whispered as she turned back. "Too immature. Andrew is a very mature young man. I'm guessing his brother is the same. Any word if James and his fiancée are coming to visit? Maybe even move here? We do have warmer winters you know. A nice selling point."

"No, and I don't want to put any pressure on them with the wedding coming up this fall. Violet's family is all in the Milwaukee area, so I don't think they would ever move here. I wouldn't mind though." Rebekah smiled, thinking of having them all with her—and maybe one day a baby.

"One can hope," Lois said and patted her friend's hand.

"Yes, but for now I have to focus on my shop. I think it's good I decided to take this class. There's so much going on with the construction at this point that I can't do anything about. I would just be in the way. And the class is great because it's helping me decide what I want on the menu. This pasty thing floored me tonight though. I don't think I'll add it right away, but I'll definitely keep it in mind for later—after I see how things are going."

"Good idea, Rebekah."

They were silent for a moment as they listened to Andrew and Rose laughing on the other side of the apartment.

"Oh, I wanted to tell you—I remember when Cathy's husband died. It was all over the news! A routine traffic stop for speeding that turned out to be some drug dealers. They shot him and his partner. So tragic." Lois closed her eyes briefly and shook her head.

"Really?" Rebekah gasped. "I can't imagine having to deal with something like that. She did tell me he was a police officer but no details about what caused his death. Poor thing. So sad."

"Yes," Lois agreed. "And at the time they had two young daughters left without a father."

Without a father .... Those words hit a chord with Rebekah. She thought about when her parents had thrown Dee out into the world and poor baby Rose who had grown up without a father. Now Andrew and James were dealing with something similar as adults—though in their case it was somewhat by choice. And Cathy ... she was so strong to have persevered through this. She had her home baking business and had managed to raise two lovely young women in spite of it all. Rebekah shook her head and smiled.

"I have to say, Cathy's a very good baker. She's taught me a few things over the past few weeks," Rebekah said. "There's always something new to learn."

"I have an idea. Why don't you hire Cathy to work with you? It's obvious she not only has baking talent but also seems to have business sense. And you like her."

Rebekah looked at her friend and slowly nodded as she ran Lois's suggestion through her mind. It *was* a great idea. Why hadn't she thought of it? Cathy was definitely an excellent baker and brought more than just her talent; she also had imagination, had been running a small business, and knew Asheville.

"Lois, that's a brilliant idea," Rebekah responded with a thoughtful look toward her friend.

"Well, I do still have my moments dear." Lois lifted her chin a bit and batted her eyes, and Rebekah chuckled. "Don't rush into anything," Lois continued. "Let the idea simmer, I say. You have three more weeks of your class, so see how it goes and then take your time to think about it. I have a good feeling about that girl. She's good people."

Rebekah agreed.

***

Lois and Rose left about 11:00. It had been a fun evening. Rebekah hoped she would make more friends in the future so she could do this more often. She would have to have Lois and Doug over sometime soon too, she thought.

Shortly after saying goodbye to Lois and Rose, she said good night to Andrew and checked her phone, seeing that Tammy had called. It was late and she was tired, so she resolved to call her tomorrow. Rebekah sure did miss Tammy and wondered what was going on with her as she slipped into sleep.

Chapter 17

Andrew was the first one up the next morning and decided it was time for him to make his mom breakfast for a change. It was rare for him to wake up before her, so she'd always have breakfast well underway before he rolled out of bed.

Let's see … what can I make? he thought before deciding on a simple breakfast of bacon, scrambled eggs, and toast. *Can't mess that up too much.* He grabbed the bacon and eggs out of the refrigerator.

Last night had been fun. *Cathy is a nice woman.* "Cute daughters too," he said aloud and chuckled. He was happy his mom had made a friend and was sure she would meet more people over time, but this was a good start. And as a bonus, he'd made some new friends too. Allie and Mandy seemed like a lot of fun. He did wish Cathy had some sons though—he could use some male camaraderie—but Cathy's girls had promised they would introduce him to their guy friends. Although they were identical, they had different personalities. Allie was a little more outgoing than Mandy. Allie had invited him and Rose to hang out sometime soon, which was great because Rose seemed like she could use some girlfriends herself.

Mandy had mentioned going out to a bar that had dancing next weekend, and he wasn't sure he would go. He'd immediately thought of Rose, who wouldn't be twenty-one for several more months and, therefore, wouldn't be able to go with them. He didn't want to go without her, but Rose insisted he not worry about it and go have fun anyway.

Andrew was starting to realize he had lived a somewhat sheltered life; he had never been to a bar with dancing before. His friends in college had always gone to each other's places to party because it was cheaper, but they never danced. If he did end up going, maybe he'd check out some dance moves online first so he wouldn't make a total fool of himself.

If he was being honest with himself, he'd still rather spend his time with Rose anyway. He often found himself smiling just thinking about her. Their relationship was growing into something new. Ever since that night they shared their first kiss, they'd sneak one in whenever they could. He had to admit he was falling in love with her, and he thought she might feel the same way about him.

There was the one obvious issue though. Both he and Rose weren't sure how their relationship would be accepted by his mom—and possibly others in the family—so they had decided to keep it just between them for the time being and take it slow. Mom had all the pressure of the shop opening and the upcoming wedding. She had more than enough on her plate as it was.

Andrew heard his mother stirring in her room. *She must have gotten a whiff of this bacon*, he thought and smiled, feeling quite satisfied in his decision to surprise her. He set the bread in the toaster, ready to be popped down as soon as his mom made her appearance, and he cracked the eggs into a bowl, scrambling them up with some milk, salt, and pepper.

"What do I smell?" Rebekah asked as she groggily entered the room.

"Well, I was up first for a change, and you usually make us Sunday breakfast, so I thought this time I would have a go at it."

"And I'll let you," his mom responded and laughed. "I'm going to make a cup of tea and then get out of your way."

When the tea was ready, Rebekah left Andrew to his work and went over to a chair in the living room that she had already decided would be her favorite spot to sit with a cup of tea since it offered such a nice view of Asheville in the morning.

Andrew soon had the scrambled eggs in a pan and was pressing the lever on the toaster. He set the table with a napkin, knife, fork, and glass of orange juice for each of them. Next, he set out the butter and strawberry jelly, and in just a few minutes, all was ready.

"Come and get it, Mom," he announced.

Not long after they sat down, the conversation turned to the night before and their company.

"I'm so happy you enjoyed yourself last night and made some friends," Rebekah told Andrew.

"Yes, thank you! And I might get together with Allie and Mandy on Saturday to meet some of their friends. It's at a bar, so Rose can't come along. But I hate to leave her out."

"Poor Rose. That's a shame, but she'll have her time soon. Maybe when you go out again, you can suggest a place where she can be included," Rebekah suggested.

"Good idea." Andrew hadn't thought of that.

"Now, I want to tell you about an idea Lois had last night," Rebekah said, changing the subject and taking a sip of her tea. "She suggested I think about hiring Cathy to work for me. I know I've only known her a short time, but I can tell she has work ethic and talent. I was telling Lois she's taught me a few things, and I like her personality. I've been kind of stressing over the thought of hiring capable people. This would take a big load off of me."

"Honestly it does sound like a good idea, but don't go rushing into anything. Give yourself a little more time to get to know her so you'll be sure," Andrew warned her.

Rebekah lowered her fork and smiled at Andrew. "That's exactly what I told Lois."

"Maybe she'll become your new Tammy," Andrew suggested as he put a spoonful of eggs in his mouth.

All of a sudden Rebekah said, "Oh my gosh. I'm so glad you said that." She put her fork down. "I had forgotten. Tammy called last night when our guests were here. Her message said she needed me to call back. It was too late by the time I saw it." Rebekah looked at the clock on the wall. "I know she's probably busy at Fred's with the Sunday crowd, so I'll wait till a little later. If it was urgent, she would have said so," Rebekah said and took a drink of her tea.

"I bet they miss you there," Andrew said.

"Well, I don't know about that. We're all replaceable. Everyone does things a little differently but somehow gets the same results—just in their own way. Remember, I've worked a long time with Tammy as my assistant. I couldn't have run the bakery without her. There's no doubt in my mind that Tammy is doing a superb job," Rebekah stated. "Now let me clean up here since you worked so hard making this delicious breakfast."

"And I'll let you," Andrew said, laughing. "I'm going to give James a call today. Any messages?"

"No, I need to call him also. Want to check on wedding plans and see if there's anything I can do. I would love to be able to bake their cake, but that's impossible. Not enough time before I get there, let alone a place to bake a cake that size. Maybe you'll marry someone from down here, and I can make your cake." Rebekah smiled and gave Andrew a peck on the cheek.

"You just never know," Andrew responded with a sheepish grin his mother didn't notice.

"Tell James I'll call at the end of the week," she said and took the plates over to the sink.

***

After watching some TV, Andrew announced he was going for a bike ride before it got too hot, so that left Rebekah alone. She decided to go back to her new favorite chair by the window with the view over Asheville and called Tammy.

"Hi, Rebekah. I'm so happy to be able to talk with you," Tammy responded in an anxious tone Rebekah was not familiar with.

"I'm sorry I didn't call last night, but I had some friends over, and it was late when I saw your message."

"That's okay, that's okay. I figured it must be something like that," Tammy said, and Rebekah could hear her start to cry.

"Tammy, what's wrong? Did something happen to Spencer or the kids?" Rebekah was concerned.

"No … it's …" Tammy took a breath to get herself together, then continued, "It's Fred, sweetie. He died yesterday morning. He didn't show up here at the store, so Michael went over to Fred's house and found his dad still in bed. Must have died in his sleep sometime during the night. Poor Michael. Says Fred looked so peaceful," Tammy said and started crying again.

Rebekah was speechless. Fred was about her mom's age but had always been in such good shape. Poor Tammy—and poor Michael! "How's Michael doing?" Rebekah asked.

"He seems to be keeping it together, but it probably hasn't sunken in yet. We knew something must be up because it took him some time to come back to the store. He finally came around noon and told us all the news. You know we're all like family here. Even though Fred sold the place, he was still running it. Now we wonder what will happen. Maybe Michael will take over."

"I'm so sorry, Tammy. If I'd known last night that's what you wanted to tell me, I'd have called back right away." She paused and took a deep breath. "It's going to be okay. I'm sure Michael will take over. His dad has been grooming him for running the store his whole life. It will be fine, you'll see. Will you please tell Michael, the next time you see him, that I give him my deepest sympathy? Fred was the best."

"Yes, he was. And how are things going for you?" Tammy asked, sniffling as she changed the subject.

"Actually, pretty good. The shop should be opening up in two months. Still can't believe I'm doing this," Rebekah said.

"No surprise to me," Tammy said with surety in her voice. "Always knew you would do something big."

"Well, it's just a little place, but it's mine. I'm naming it Marie Claudine's Bakery and Tea Room."

"That's your grandmother's name, right? Mère ... the one who taught you baking," Tammy remembered.

"Yes, that's right. I acquired my love of baking from her. She always wanted to open her own place, but my grandfather said no. Actually, Ethan also said no when I told him I wanted to open a bakery .... Well, that's ancient history now, isn't it?" Rebekah scoffed.

"It sure is, sweetie. The Universe has put you right where you should be, Rebekah Hayward. I can feel it."

Rebekah smiled. Tammy was such an empathic soul.

"And you are going to have a blessed and wonderful life—mark my words," Tammy added.

"Thank you, Tammy. You know I can't wait till you come visit some time—after I get the shop under control."

"I look forward to the day," Tammy said happily.

"When I visited you at Fred's, you told me Spencer wasn't well. Is he doing better?" Rebekah asked.

"No, it's his heart problems. Trying to get him to change his diet is like milking a bull. Can't make him do anything. We can only control ourselves, Rebekah," Tammy said with finality.

That's so right, Rebekah thought. "I'm taking a baking class on French patisserie at the community college while my shop is being renovated," Rebekah shared. "Something new and different for me to include in the bakery."

"I would love to do that. I bet it's fun," Tammy said.

"Yes, it is."

"Well, listen I have to go," Tammy said. "We've got a big line starting, so I need to help out. I'll keep you posted on things here. I sure miss you, Rebekah."

"I miss you too, Tammy. Can't wait till you come visit me."

"Yes, it's on my list. Love you, sweetie."

"You too, Tammy."

Poor Fred, Rebekah thought after they'd hung up. *At least it didn't sound like he suffered. If we all could be that blessed. And now poor Michael.* What would happen to the store now that Fred had sold it? She would be sure to drop Michael a card in the mail tomorrow.

Chapter 18

The patisserie class turned out even better than Rebekah could have imagined. Chef Lester had taught them so much, and Rebekah was now an expert at macarons, choux pastry, tarts of all tastes and sizes, entremets, puff pastry, and more. The class made her wish she could have gone to a French pastry school when she was younger. She would have been a natural, though she could only imagine what her parents or Ethan would have said had she told them she wanted to go to France to learn about French patisserie. Just the thought of it made her laugh.

As it happened, Rebekah's birthday was July 15, the last day of baking class. She had actually forgotten about it until that morning when Andrew wished her happy birthday and mentioned he had invited a few friends over for cake that night to celebrate.

Before Rebekah could respond, he raised a hand and said, "Cathy is making your cake, not me, so don't worry. It will be edible."

They both laughed, and she gave him a hug before she left for class.

***

After class, Chef Lester shook all their hands as they departed for the last time and wished them all success. Rebekah told him her shop, Marie Claudine's, would be opening in September and she would love for him to come by for the grand opening. He thanked her and said he would be delighted.

As they walked to their cars, Cathy said, "Since it's your birthday, let's get a sandwich to go from that restaurant in Biltmore Village and go over to the Botanical Garden. Have you ever been there before?"

"No, I haven't. Lois has mentioned she goes out there to buy plants, but otherwise I know nothing about it."

"I know it's a warm day, but it should be nice there with all the tree cover. Reed Creek and Glenn's Creek Greenway meet up there. It's my go-to place when I need alone time and solace," Cathy shared.

"I would love that." Rebekah beamed. "I don't know if I ever mentioned it, but I lived on the edge of the Nicolet National Forest in Wisconsin. My parents had several acres and a pond. I've missed walking through the woods like I used to do from my backyard. This could be a great substitute since it isn't far from where I live."

"Really? I can't imagine having a forest in your backyard," Cathy responded with a smile. "There are plenty of trails in Asheville, but I find these the most convenient, and I enjoy them."

They only had time for the Botanical Garden that day but agreed they would go walking soon on the greenway.

When Rebekah arrived home around 1:30, she met Andrew at the door.

"Great, I've been waiting for you. Having a nice birthday?" Andrew asked.

"Yes, I am. So what's up?"

"You just missed Harrison, but he'll be at your party tonight if you have any questions for him. There's three or four weeks more of construction before we can start setting up, according to him, so it's time for you and Lois to start seriously working your magic. We need to sit down and look at the calendar for an official opening date since he's given us an idea of when he'll finish up—provided all inspections pass, which I don't think will be a problem. Harrison said to go ahead and order whatever chandelier you want. It's going to be one of the last things he does, but he wants it ordered now so we can be sure it will arrive in time before the opening."

"Great!" Rebekah said.

"So have you decided on the chandelier you want? What about tables and chairs? Wall art and signs? What color are the walls going to be? We're ready to move forward and make those decisions." Andrew spoke with his clipboard in hand.

Rebekah took a deep breath before responding. "Yes. I'm trying to decide between two chandeliers I like. I want an eclectic assortment of tables and chairs, so Lois and I have been collecting some things we're storing in her garage, but we need more. I'm not sure about the wall art. I was thinking Harrison could help out with the signs, and I'm leaning toward a soft shade of robin's egg blue for the walls—and white trim." Rebekah rattled off everything and then chuckled. It made her head spin to think of the whirlwind of excitement the next couple weeks would bring.

"Awesome. Sounds like you've got it under control. Now, as I mentioned, I've invited some people over for cake and ice cream tonight around six thirty." Andrew paused. "How old are you going to be anyway?"

"What's wrong with you?" Rebekah said with an indignant tone. "You never ask a lady her age!" She laughed and then acquiesced. "I'm thirty-seven. You're not going to do something to embarrass me, are you?" She looked at him seriously. "Like putting my age on my cake?"

"Actually, James asked me, and I didn't know what to tell him 'cuz I wasn't sure." Clipboard still in hand, Andrew laughed, then enveloped his mom in a bear hug.

"Right, blame it on your brother since he's not here," she teased as she squeezed him back.

Just then, there was a knock on the front door to the shop. Andrew went to see who it was and came back with a big bouquet of white and pink sweetheart roses in a vase.

"They're for you," he said with a puzzled look and set them on a stack of plywood nearby. He handed her the envelope with her name on it.

Rebekah opened the card. "Hope you have a very Happy Birthday!" she read, then turned the card over to look at the back before looking at Andrew and shrugging her shoulders. "Huh. There's no signature. Who would have sent these?" She then cocked her head and scrunched her eyebrows.

"Maybe your brothers? Or James and Violet? Have you heard from your brothers? Or maybe Tammy? Or Lois! She would do that. We'll find out," Andrew said and then smiled a devious smile. "Maybe they're from someone coming to the party—or a secret admirer. Were there guys in that cooking class you just finished? Maybe one of them has the hots for you, Mom." He chuckled, clearly amused with himself.

Rebekah scoffed. She wasn't going there with him. "What? Secret admirer? Really? Who?"

Andrew continued laughing.

"Stop it," she said and playfully swiped at him before she let out a snicker herself.

"Okay ... okay," Andrew said and got a grip on himself. "Well, why don't you just take the rest of the day easy so you can be ready for your party tonight?"

"Ha! I can't take it easy after the long list you just gave me. I think I'll go over to see Lois and tell her it's time to start getting serious about this. I'll see you later," she said and headed back out.

As she walked to her car, she couldn't get the flowers off her mind. They were beautiful and definitely expensive. Who could have sent them?

***

On the way to Lois's, Rebekah called to make sure she was home. Now that Lois and Doug were seeing each other, Lois was out and about frequently and not always available. Fortunately, she was home this time and said she would love to talk shop.

"Happy birthday, dear," Lois greeted her as she opened the door. She gave Rebekah a peck on the cheek. "I hope it's been a pleasant day for you. I'm very much looking forward to celebrating this evening. That son of yours is so sweet to arrange a little party for you."

"Thank you, Lois. And yes, Andrew is sweet and thoughtful. I don't know what I would do without him. I really don't think I would be opening the shop if it weren't for him," she admitted.

"He is a driving force my dear. Count your blessings. Now let's get down to business and take a look at the treasures we've found," Lois said and led the way to the garage.

Over the past several months, Lois and Rebekah had been going to the occasional yard sale and flee market, looking for tables and chairs for the shop. The plan was not to worry if the tables or chairs matched but to find unique and sturdy pieces for the dining area. As a result, they had gathered tables and chairs of different sizes, colors, and dimensions.

"We should figure out how many more tables we need, but of course that will depend on the size we find. I think we need one additional larger table that can seat six, and then the rest for two-to-four people. What do you think?" Rebekah queried.

"Yes, I agree. I discovered a used furniture store recently when Doug and I were out and about. Now that your class is over, let's plan a day to go over there."

"Sounds good. Now what about art on the walls? I hadn't thought much about that, and I don't really have an opinion. Have you?" Rebekah was so fortunate to be able to rely on Lois for so much.

"I think copies of classic period paintings would be perfect, whatever we can find when we're out and about. Not too many so it looks cluttered, but tastefully hung, and some lovely mirrors. Leave that to me, dear. I may have a few things in my attic I no longer use," Lois said. "Have you decided on the chandelier?"

"I have two I'm deciding between. Andrew said Harrison will hang that last," Rebekah shared.

"Yes. Don't want any mishaps with moving things in and out, and the dust that will collect on it. Definitely should be hung at the end," Lois agreed.

"I sure do need you, Lois."

Lois smiled at Rebekah's sentiment. "Well, I guess that's enough for today. We'll do a girl's day out next week, and we could even go down to Charlotte if we aren't successful up here," Lois suggested. "How does that sound?"

"Sounds perfect to me. One more thing ..." Rebekah hesitated a moment before she continued. "Did you send me flowers for my birthday or know of anyone who did? An absolutely beautiful bouquet of about two dozen pink and white sweetheart roses showed up for me at the shop, and the giver didn't sign the card. I can't imagine who would have sent them. It's highly unlikely any of my family did. Andrew has no idea. Do you?" Rebekah asked.

"Hmm. I don't but ... hmm." Lois definitely had a thought.

"What?"

"I know you don't want to hear this, but I think Harrison has a thing for you. Maybe he sent them?" Lois speculated.

"Please, Lois." Rebekah rolled her eyes. "Harrison does *not* have a thing for me. We have a working relationship and are friends! I've had a big project for him to do, and yes, we've spent a lot of time together. He's very nice, but he's made no advancement toward me in that way. And besides, I'm not in the market for—" she paused, closed her eyes, and raised her right palm as she stated firmly, "—*that*. I have enough going on right now. The flowers must have come from my brothers. I'll ask them." She was sorry she had brought it up.

Lois threw up her hands in mock defense and Rebekah chuckled.

"Well, I need to run," Rebekah said, happily changing the subject. "Look at your calendar and let me know what day next week we can go furniture shopping, and maybe you can help me decide on the chandelier. See you tonight!" she said and headed for the door.

Lois simply nodded and gave Rebekah a sly little smile as she watched her go.

As Rebekah slid into her car, she couldn't help but fixate on the flowers. *Harrison ... ha!* She looked at herself in the rearview mirror and shook her head.

But if not Harrison, then who?

Chapter 19

A ndrew yelled up the stairs from the shop. "Hey, Mom! It's six fifteen, and people will be arriving soon. I'm sure you look beautiful as always. Cathy just brought in the cake, so c'mon down."

When Rebekah was growing up, birthdays had always been simple and low-key in her family. They would have a cake after supper and then open a present—usually something they needed at the time. She had always made sure Andrew's and James's birthdays were a bigger deal than hers had ever been. After all, she was a baker, so their cakes were always themed to whatever the boys were into at the time. She would do a special cake for Ethan too, but for her own birthday, Tammy would always make her a cake to take home. Rebekah would do the same for Tammy since they both knew that if left to decide, their husbands would just pick something up or use a boxed cake mix. Yes—they were fussy about their cakes.

After Rebekah arrived home from her visit with Lois, Andrew had forbidden her to come downstairs until he gave the word, insisting that he and Rose were busy getting the party together. *What have they been up to?* she wondered. As she opened the door to head down, the smell of food wafted up the stairs. She wasn't sure what it was, but it smelled wonderful and made her hungry.

"Ready or not, here I come," she announced as she headed through the doorway into the shop. She froze and felt her heart melt as she took everything in. In the center of the room sat a table containing a two-tiered white-frosted cake with pink cherry blossoms cascading down one side—a true testament to Cathy's talent as a baker. Next to the cake was a table with trays of sandwiches and pasta along with barbecue and fixings. Both tables were draped with pink tablecloths, and all around were streamers of pink, blue, green, and yellow with a big "Happy Birthday" banner suspended above the food table. The entire scene was beautiful and brought tears to Rebekah's eyes. She had never in her life been celebrated like this before.

Behind the table stood Andrew, Rose, Cathy, and Harrison with big smiles on their faces. The tears Rebekah had been fighting back escaped down her face.

"Why are you crying, Mom?" Andrew quickly came to his mother and wrapped his arms around her.

"They're tears of happiness, son," Rebekah managed to get out.

"Happy birthday, Rebekah!" said Rose, who was next to give her a big hug.

Cathy followed suit, but Harrison stayed right where he was, said, "Happy birthday," and gave Rebekah a big smile and a nod.

"Well, our other guests should be arriving any—" Andrew started, but before he could finish his sentence, Lois and Doug came through the door yelling, "Happy birthday!" in unison.

Next was Sam Brooks, Harrison's friend and the officer who had helped them during the vandalism, Cathy's girls Allie and Mandy, and then a big surprise: Don Lester, her patisserie instructor.

"Chef Lester! How nice of you to come!" Rebekah welcomed him, her tone expressing her surprise and delight. "I'm so happy for you to see my shop—or its 'before' look, anyway."

"Cathy invited me before class today. I'm thrilled to see one of my students branching out like this. Such an inspiration. And please, call me Don." He was so gracious and showed not a shadow of the serious, no-nonsense man who had taught their class.

"Okay … Don," Rebekah said and happily shook his hand.

They all fixed a plate and headed upstairs to eat and visit in the apartment. Officer Brooks asked them to please call him Sam, so now everyone present was on a first-name basis. As it turned out, Sam had known Cathy's husband, so he spent some time talking to her and Cathy's girls. Don hit it off with Lois and Doug, and Rose and Andrew were downstairs, which left Rebekah and Harrison together once again.

"Beautiful flowers," he said as he bent over to smell one of the roses, twirling its stem between his fingers. "From someone special?"

"I—don't know," Rebekah stammered. "The sender didn't put their name on the card. They are beautiful, though, and in the colors I love."

"Did you know you can call the florist that delivered them and ask who they were sent by?" Harrison suggested.

"Oh, I hadn't thought of that, but I guess you're right. At first, I thought maybe my brothers had sent them or my son James, but I spoke with James earlier, and he said it wasn't him. I can't imagine who else would have sent them. That's a good idea though. I'll call tomorrow. I certainly want to thank the person who sent them."

After a pause, Harrison started, "I hope you've had a good day. I mean your birthday *is* only once a year." He glanced down at the flowers thoughtfully and then back up at Rebekah. "I was an only child, so my parents made a big deal out of my birthday when I was a kid."

"Really? I can't imagine that. I had five siblings, so birthdays were not that big of a deal at our house. This is pretty over the top for me." She looked around the room and laughed slightly. "I mean, in a good way though! I have had a wonderful day, and this has been a great grand finale. I can't tell you how special this all makes me feel."

"Well, you're a special woman, Rebekah."

Harrison cocked his head to the side and their eyes met. This time, she couldn't look away.

"You've only been in town a short while, and look at the friends you've made." Harrison lifted his hand and looked around the room briefly before locking eyes with her again. "But you have that kind of personality. People want to know you." He paused and smiled. "I'm happy *I've* gotten to know you—and that you've had a good birthday."

"Yes, I have. Today was my last day of baking class, so Cathy and I picked up lunch at a little sandwich shop we like and headed over to the botanical garden. I had heard of the garden from Lois but hadn't gone by there yet. I'm looking forward to going back. A lovely place."

"There are some greenway trails connected to the garden that are great for a run or a walk. I'd love to show them to you one day if you'd like, and then maybe we can have lunch?" Harrison responded, not realizing Cathy had walked up behind him.

"Yes, I found out about that today also and—"

"That's a great idea, Harrison!" Cathy interjected. "Maybe we could get a group to go and then have lunch after?"

Harrison opened his mouth, closed it, and then hesitated a moment before he finally responded. "Uh, yeah, sure. That would be fun." Before he could say another word, Andrew walked in with the birthday cake, prompting everyone to sing "Happy Birthday."

Rebekah blew out the candles, and Cathy cut the cake for everyone. The cake was fabulous: chocolate with a salted caramel filling and vanilla buttercream frosting, garnished with white chocolate cherry blossom flowers, and served with vanilla ice cream. Beautiful *and* delicious.

A while later, when everyone had finished eating their cake, Rebekah looked around to see where Harrison was and saw he was speaking with Andrew and Sam. She hadn't visited with Chef Lester—Don—so she sat down next to him.

"I'm so happy Cathy was able to invite you here today, Don," she started. "I've learned a lot in your class that will give me confidence once my shop opens. I hope you'll become a regular visitor."

"I definitely will. I ran my own small bakery at one time and worked in several bakeshops over the years. In fact, if you have any questions or ideas you want to bounce off me, give me a call." He pulled out a card and wrote a number on the back of it. "Here's my personal number. You see, when I was early in my career, someone did that for me, and I just want to pass it on."

"Thank you, Don. I'm very touched by your offer," Rebekah said and meant it. A resource like Don could be very helpful. "I'll probably be taking you up on it!" she added, and they both laughed.

Before he left, Rebekah spoke briefly with Sam. He told her he'd been keeping a close eye on their area and to feel free to let him know if she saw anything she thought might be suspicious.

She told him she or Andrew would definitely let him know.

The party wound down, and people began to head home as the next day was a workday.

As always, Lois, Doug, and Rose stayed after to help clean up.

"Did you find out if Harrison sent you those lovely flowers?" Lois pulled Rebekah aside to ask. "Those were not sent by your brothers but a man in love—if you want my opinion."

"Lois, I'm not going to ask him, but I really don't think it was him. He noticed and mentioned them but not in a way that would make me suspect anything. When I told him I didn't know who they were from, he suggested I call the florist to find out. If it were him, I don't think he would have suggested that—would he?"

Lois thought for a moment. "No, I suppose not. Make sure you let me know who it was after you call, dear. I'm so curious." She raised her eyebrows and gave Rebekah a funny little smile. "Good night, and happy birthday!" She hugged Rebekah and gave her a peck on the cheek before she and Doug left.

What a wonderful night, Rebekah thought as she locked the door behind Lois and Doug. In just a short amount of time in Asheville, she had made friends she was sure would be there the rest of her life. She headed upstairs and found Andrew and Rose waiting for her.

"I didn't realize you were still here, Rose. Andrew, make sure you walk her to her car when she leaves."

"Don't worry, I will, Mom."

"Andrew, you went above and beyond for this little party. Thank you so much. And you too, Rose! I feel very special."

"You *are* special, Mom." He gave her a big hug. "You are an amazing woman."

"Everything he said." Rose giggled and gave her aunt a hug.

Rebekah gave them each a kiss on the cheek and was headed to her bedroom door when Andrew spoke.

"Oh, by the way. I asked Harrison if he sent you those flowers, and he said no. Just thought you might want to know," Andrew volunteered, smiling like he had done her a favor.

Rebekah stopped dead in her tracks and turned to face Andrew. "I can't believe you asked him that, Andrew! I'm a little embarrassed now," she responded.

"Why?" Andrew asked, truly puzzled.

Rose laughed and shook her head.

"*Really?* Never mind. If you don't understand why, I'm not explaining. Maybe you can explain to him, Rose." *What is wrong with him?* She stood silent for a few moments then took a deep breath and got herself together. "I just want you to know how thoughtful it was for you to do this for me tonight. I appreciate it more than you can imagine. And now I'm going to bed. Good night."

"Good night, Rebekah," Rose said.

"Good night, Mom. Sweet dreams."

Rebekah got ready for bed and crawled under the covers, still thinking about the evening. *What a wonderful birthday.* She had been surprised to see Don Lester there and was so happy he had extended his expertise to help when he could. She would definitely take him up on that. Very nice of Sam Brooks to be there too. Lois, Doug, Rose, and Cathy were so supportive of her.

And then there was Harrison.

Their conversation ran over and over in her mind—the garden and the hiking trails. And then Cathy's interruption had really seemed to catch him off guard. Was he … getting ready to ask her out? Or was it just a friendly invitation? Either way, she would like to check out the trails, and if Harrison did ask her to go, she would happily agree. *Why not?*

She smiled, took a deep breath in and out, and slipped into sleep.

Chapter 20

During the party, Harrison and Andrew had spoken and decided that since Rebekah's baking class was over, the three of them needed to get down to business. They planned a meeting to go over Harrison's finishing timeline so he could make sure they were all on the same page. The early September shop opening was just six and a half weeks away. To Harrison, it sounded like a long time, but he knew from experience that it would go fast. He and Andrew had decided to meet the next morning.

But as he got ready to leave that morning, the first thought on Harrison's mind was how Andrew had asked whether he had sent Rebekah that bouquet of flowers for her birthday. It wasn't him, though honestly, he wished he *had* sent them, and he couldn't stop thinking about who did. Much to his dismay, it seemed she had another secret admirer. Although he really wanted to ask her out, he knew he shouldn't until the job was done.

Admittedly, he had pushed it a bit when Rebekah told him about her trip to the botanical garden and he suggested they walk the trails together sometime. In his mind, he was just setting things up for the future. Paving the way so to speak. And she was about to answer too—until her friend Cathy had to pipe in, so he never got his answer. He wondered what she might have said had they not been interrupted.

Harrison arrived at the shop around 9:45 to find Andrew and Rebekah waiting for him in the large open space that would soon be the shop.

"Good morning, Harrison," Andrew greeted him. The young man had his ledger books spread out on a makeshift table made from a board laid over two sawhorses.

Harrison smiled. Andrew was always well prepared. Rebekah was lucky to have his help, and it had crossed Harrison's mind a few times that maybe he should hire him to help with his books. That kid would go far someday.

"Good morning, and thanks again for the invite to the party last night. I enjoyed helping you celebrate," Harrison said with a smile and nod toward Rebekah.

"I should be thanking you and everyone else who came out!" Rebekah said. "It made me realize how many friends I've made in such a short time here." She smiled and swept a strand of hair behind her ear.

"No surprise there, Rebekah." Harrison glanced at his feet, smiled, and scuffed one foot a little before changing the subject and getting down to business. "I wanted to meet with both of you to go over my plans for completing everything so we're on the same page."

"Sounds good," Andrew said. "I know we've been talking a lot, but it's still good to set all our expectations."

"Definitely. Now, Rebekah, I know you need your kitchen available as soon as I can get it finished. You'll want some time for set up and recipe testing, so my plan is to complete that area first and have it sealed off from the rest of the building so you can do your thing."

"That sounds great. I've worked with commercial ovens my whole baking career, but I think these new ones will take a little adapting. I want everything perfect by the time we open. I can't believe we're almost there," she said with excitement.

"Do you have your staff yet?" Harrison asked.

"Well, I've got my core team, but I need to hire more people. I've been keeping this to myself but was thinking of asking Cathy to be my assistant. I've been waiting for our baking class to finish—you know, to make sure she's as good as I thought she was." Rebekah gave a sheepish grin. "I feel like she is. And of course, both Rose and Lois are going to work for me." She tossed her head Andrew's way. "And I'll drag in this one from time to time."

"Me? Ah, I don't know about that." Andrew scowled and shook his head as they all laughed. "I wonder if Don could help you out with hiring? He probably knows some capable people looking for a job."

"Great idea, son," Rebekah said. "I'll give him a call when we're done here to find out when I can go see him."

"Well, it all sounds good," Harrison said and turned to Rebekah, looking her straight in the eyes. "I'd also like to spend some time with you, Rebekah—um, you know, ah—going over your signage and the bakery cases. I can head you in the right direction and help you order those things."

"That would be great," Rebekah said, holding back a laugh.

They spent the rest of the meeting walking through the space that would soon be the teahouse and bakery, clarifying the schedule for the next few weeks to avoid any confusion between now and the grand opening.

Then Harrison sat down with Rebekah to order the bakery cases and put her in touch with a friend of his who could create a painted sign for the shop front just like she wanted.

The dream was all coming together.

***

"How do you feel after the meeting with Harrison? I feel pretty good about it—but how about you?" Andrew and Rebekah sat in Andrew's office later that morning, working on staffing.

"Yes, I'm excited," Rebekah responded, although that was putting it mildly. She was ecstatic. Her dream was coming to fruition. *How many people get to do this?* she wondered. She paused and took a deep breath then looked back to Andrew. "And you have helped me put this all together. I love you, Andrew," she said as unexpected tears began to well up along her eyelids.

"Aww geez, Mom. I love you too. Now let's not get off our focus here," Andrew said with a big sniff. He grabbed a tissue and blew his nose. "I hate it when you do this to me. You know I'm your chief financial officer, and I have an image to uphold. This is business," he said and sniffed again.

They both laughed.

"By the way, I called Don, and he said I could come by and see him around two o'clock today, so I'm going to head over to the school after I grab something to eat. I think I'll go upstairs to the apartment and make a sandwich. Can I make one for you?"

Andrew, who had been glued to his computer screen, looked sideways at her. "Ah, yeah that would be great. Not too heavy on the mustard."

"Got it," she said and headed upstairs.

Rebekah put together a couple of ham and turkey sandwiches with sharp white cheddar, baby lettuce, homemade sourdough bread, and mustard—not too heavy—and brought them downstairs. Andrew was still glued to his computer screen—until he saw the sandwich she had made for him.

"This looks great, Mom." He took a bite and grinned with his mouth full of food. "Why is it that a sandwich always tastes better when you make it?"

"I don't know. Maybe it's the love I release when I spread the mustard—extra lightly?" She laughed and Andrew rolled his eyes.

"So what did you tell Don you wanted?" Andrew queried with a mouth full of sandwich.

"I asked if he had time to give me some advice on staffing. He said he would be delighted to. After that, I'm going to swing by Cathy's house and offer her the position. You agree that's the right move, don't you?"

"Yeah, I do. Let's hope she accepts. That'd be a big load off our shoulders."

***

The meeting with Don was helpful. At this point she needed to hire at least four to six additional people, they decided, and more if she got busy. Don also helped her decide on business hours—seven to five to start, closed on Sundays. She would take appointments after-hours for people wanting cakes and catering who couldn't get in during shop hours since she would be closed in the evenings.

Next was her stop at Cathy's house. She had called ahead to tell Cathy she was stopping by for a short visit.

"Well, hey, c'mon in. To what do I owe the surprise?" Cathy greeted her as they walked in and sat down in the living room.

"Well, I'm not going to beat around the bush. I came here for a specific reason. I want to offer you the position of being my assistant at Marie Claudine's. I think we would work well together. I love your talent and vision, I've seen and tasted your incredible baking, and I know I need someone with creativity like yours. So … what do you think?" Rebekah exhaled, having laid it all out.

"Wow, I wasn't expecting this." Cathy hesitated for a short moment, looking down and then back up at Rebekah with a smile. "I'm so surprised." She paused and sat straight up in her chair. "Well, I've been wanting to expand my home business, which can be very irregular and a lot of stress at times."

"I have an idea." Rebekah leaned forward in her chair and looked Cathy in the eyes. "I know I sprung this on you, so think about it tonight and, if you'd like, come over to the shop tomorrow and we can talk with Andrew about the particulars. We can give you an idea of the pay and responsibility—you know—and answer any questions."

Cathy nodded her head slowly as she contemplated. "That sounds good. I'll do that. How about I come by at eleven? I'm so excited," Cathy said.

"Great. I would want you to begin as soon as the kitchen is set up so we can start testing and developing our menu. I have an idea of some specific things I would like to do, but having you to bounce those ideas off would be priceless. All I know is that I need someone like you." Rebekah stood up and gave Cathy a big smile and hug. "I have to run now, but I'll see you tomorrow!"

As Rebekah backed out of Cathy's driveway, she had a very good feeling her friend would say yes.

***

Where had the day gone? It was already four o'clock when Rebekah arrived back at the shop to find Andrew sweeping the floor.

"What are you doing?" Rebekah asked.

"Oh!" Andrew jumped, startled by the unexpected voice. "I've been looking at my computer all day and needed some physical activity. I heard Harrison tell one of the guys the floor needed sweeping earlier and thought I would give him a hand. It actually helps me focus my mind. I've helped Harrison with a few little things before. I kind of like it."

"Your grandpa would be so proud after all those projects you and James did with him." She smiled and swallowed a little lump that had formed in her throat. She remembered how much her dad had loved doing projects with the boys when they were young. He always said, "Every young fella needs to know the basics of building no matter what they do in life."

"Yeah, that was fun. I miss Grandpa. He knew how to do a lot. I never did well with the car stuff he taught me, but James sure did. I think Grandpa hoped James would take over the family auto shop one day, but it's really not his thing. Do you know if anyone will?" Andrew wondered.

"Not sure who, but between my brothers, I'm sure one or more of your cousins will step up and take the helm. I've never been involved in the running of the place, so I haven't bothered to keep track of it. I'll ask next time I talk to your uncles."

Just then, Rebekah's phone rang.

"It's Tammy. I'll be back in a bit," she told Andrew and headed upstairs.

"Hi, Tammy," she said as she stepped into her living room.

"I didn't have a free minute all day yesterday to call and wish you a happy birthday, so I thought I'd give you a call today. Happy birthday!" Tammy's voice bubbled through the phone.

"Thank you. Actually, I've been wondering about you and how things are at Fred's. How's Michael doing?"

"Well," Tammy started, "the week after Fred passed away, the people who bought the store came in and told Michael they didn't need him anymore! So he's gone, and we haven't seen hide nor hair of him since."

"You're kidding! That seems so cruel."

"It sure is. Someone from the deli went over to Michael's house to check on him, and there's a For Sale sign in the front yard. They knocked on the door, but there was no answer, so they peeked in the window, and it's empty. Not a stick of furniture—nothing. And no one knows where he's gone."

"Well, that sure sounds odd to move out so fast. Why would he do that? Poor Michael. Where would he have gone? I know he doesn't have any family in the area—his older brothers moved away, and it was just him and his dad in Rhinelander as far as I knew. Not sure where his brothers live since they were never involved with the store." Rebekah scratched her head and thought for a moment. "Did he have a girlfriend?"

"A few of us wondered that also, but if he did have a girlfriend, he never spoke of it. He's got loads of money from the sale to do whatever he wants now, so maybe he decided to move to a new place where he's unknown. You know what? I bet he's probably on an exotic island where the sun shines every day and it never snows, living with his beautiful islander girlfriend," Tammy fantasized, ending with her infectious laugh.

"I wouldn't start that rumor just yet, Tammy, until you have the facts," Rebekah said, then also laughed.

"Oh, no. Me? I would never do that." Tammy paused and then cackled.

"What about your family? What's going on?" Rebekah asked, wanting to change the subject.

"Not much. Same old stuff. I'm keeping as low a profile as I can at the store because I don't want them to find any reason to send me down the same path as Michael. I like what I do and want to keep doing it."

Rebekah understood just how Tammy felt. Had it not been for all that had happened with Ethan, she would still be there in

Rhinelander, happily running the bakery at Fred's. But now that she was where she was, she was even happier.

"If it happens, Tammy, don't worry. Life may take you somewhere you never thought you might be. I'm proof of that," Rebekah attested.

"You're right, sweetheart. You're right." Tammy paused and cleared her throat. "Rebekah, I'm worried about Spencer. Even though I'm cooking good healthy meals for him, I know he's out there eating and drinking things that might not be good for him—the son of a buck."

"Keep doing your cooking, but if he doesn't take his heart problems seriously, there's only so much you can do."

"I know," Tammy said. "Enough of that. Tell me about your new place. Is it all coming together still?"

"The speculation is Marie Claudine's Bakery & Tea House will open the beginning of September. Not sure of the exact date yet. I can hardly believe it. Pinch me so I know it's real!" Rebekah exclaimed. "We've had a few ups and downs, but everything's coming together. These last six weeks are going to be a whirlwind, I expect."

"I want to visit you next year for sure. How's that?"

"I can't wait," Rebekah agreed. "Oh, and I found out a few weeks ago that James is getting married the first weekend of November in Milwaukee. As if I didn't have enough to deal with! Don't know if I'll get a chance to see you though."

"I understand. You'll be busy with the wedding. That's exciting though! Listen, I'll keep you updated on Michael if I hear anything. I've got to get back to work here. Glad your birthday was nice. Have a good rest of your day."

"You too, Tammy. I sure do miss you. Take care."

Chapter 21

I t was the first week in August. *How could that be?* Rebekah thought as she peered into one of her brand new ovens where she had just placed a batch of cinnamon chocolate chip scones, replacing the pound cake loaves that were now cooling.

Much to Rebekah's delight, Cathy had decided to come work as her assistant. So as soon as the kitchen area was set up, the two women had begun their test baking to determine what would be on the menu.

Rebekah had never experienced a year in her life quite like this one, and it didn't look like this new path she was on would slow down anytime soon. Then she thought about the previous year and all the changes that had brought her to where she was now. She was sure her success and happiness would continue to manifest from all she had muddled through.

"Come look at these macarons," Cathy called out excitedly. "I love these ovens! You really picked some good ones. I think these are the most perfect macarons I've ever made. Ideally, I like to wait till the next day to fill mine, but once these cool, I'm doing a taste test because I can't wait to put one in my mouth," Cathy proclaimed.

"Wow, they do look good, Cathy," Rebekah said as she lightly touched the tops of a few of the pink, blue, green, and yellow circles cooling on the counter. "They have a nice shell on top and perfect feet on the bottom." She looked at Cathy with a smile. "No doubt these will be a favorite of our customers. What are you going to fill them with?"

"They were a big seller in my home baking business. I'm going to use an assortment of fruit flavors to fill these, but I can do any flavor. You know, I'm sure I've made thousands of these in my lifetime. How's the pound cake coming? People do love them some pound cake down here, you know. Are you having success in converting it to a large batch?"

"I feel I am," Rebekah replied. "Just took some out of the oven a few minutes ago. I'm making a smaller loaf size to start out with, and if there's interest in a larger size, I might do them by special order. Lois is stopping by around eleven to taste test them, since it *is* her recipe. If I get the thumbs up from her, I'm on to the next thing."

"And what might that be?"

"Since we took a class in patisserie, I figured I should be making my own puff pastry," Rebekah said matter-of-factly. "We can make it up ahead of time, then you and I can decide what items we want to make with it later. We'll have it all rolled out in sheets ready to go in the freezers."

"Good idea," Cathy agreed.

"Cathy, I was thinking ... when you finish with your macarons, how about doing some pâte à choux? I would like to carry the standard eclairs and crème puffs all the time, but I think we should do some specialty things, especially around the different seasons of the year."

"Oh, I would love that," Cathy proclaimed. "You know you can even do savory crème puffs? I've done them for parties. Also, we can offer croquembouches at Christmastime. I've done them. They're a nice dramatic centerpiece that people love."

"I've done them also, but I've never done the little swans or a Paris-Brest. Have you?" Rebekah inquired.

"No, but we can now!" Cathy laughed.

"My head is spinning." Rebekah laughed nervously. "Oh, and I'm looking forward to wedding cakes. They are my favorite thing to bake. Andrew and I talked about getting the bakery and tea part established before I start doing special occasion cakes. I think it's a good idea unless someone specifically asks if we can do a cake for a wedding or party—then I'll do it. I'm not going to miss a sale. I'm sure I'll have to hire more people when I go big into cakes. The business side is all new to me, and I don't want to make any mistakes by overextending myself."

"I thought that's why you had Andrew!" Cathy laughed and gave Rebekah a sideway glance and smile before she continued. "Well, you're going to make some mistakes for sure, but you'll learn from them."

Rebekah smiled and nodded. "Amen to that."

"Well, hello ladies. Looks like y'all are having lots of fun. It sure does smell delicious in here." Lois had popped in right on time to test the pound cake.

Lois came straight over to Rebekah and hugged her. Rebekah let out a sigh. Lois had been such a big support, and Rebekah was especially glad she'd be helping with the tea side of the business.

As Lois pulled away from Rebekah, she spied Cathy and her rainbow of macarons.

"Hi, Cathy. Did you make these? *My Lawd*, my mouth is watering."

"Yes, ma'am, I did!" Cathy responded, beaming. "When they're done, would you like to taste test a few of them?"

"That's a definite yes," Lois confirmed with a grin.

Lois had been so animated, Rebekah almost didn't notice Rose standing quietly behind her.

"Rose! I didn't see you hiding there. I'm so happy you tagged along. I miss seeing you every day. How have you been?" Rebekah inquired as she engulfed the girl in a hug.

"Hey, I miss you too, but between the class I've been taking this summer and working at Biltmore, I've been busy."

"I bet you have, but it's all worth it." Rebekah smiled at her niece.

"I don't know if Andrew told you, dear," Lois interrupted, "but we've decided on the company we're going to use to provide tea for the shop. I've tried everything they offer, and all are superb." She chuckled and added, "I have even gotten Doug drinking tea now." She raised her eyebrows and gave a smile. "The company only deals with independent retailers like you, and they are also providing us with all the proper appliances to make the best tea in Asheville. They even come in and train you and your employees on how to use the machines. We will also have coffee to offer our customers, but our main focus is tea."

"That sounds great, Lois. Thank you so much for your hard work." Rebekah was more than grateful.

"Also, we're allowed to sell the tea in bulk to people. We can package it in bags or tins—we can even come up with a signature blend we can sell with the store name on it. How do you like that idea?"

"I like that a lot, Lois. So, Marie Claudine's Special Blend? Yes! I like that. Can I put you on it?" Rebekah bubbled with excitement.

"Already started," Lois responded and they laughed.

"Lois, how do you know so much about tea?" Cathy inquired.

"Oh, my mother and father were English, and that's what we English do—drink tea. It was an integral part of my life, actually. When I was a child, we had friends over for tea all the time. If done properly, tea is truly a lovely experience. I hope to carry the tradition on here," Lois declared.

"I love that, Lois," Rebekah said with warmth. "It's what will make us different from other bakeries. I've been looking over the list you gave me of tea sandwiches and cookies—or biscuits as the English would call them. I had some other ideas I would like you to look over too."

"I will be happy to. I can't tell you how much I'm enjoying this." Rebekah could tell Lois was in her element.

"Now, I need you and Rose to taste this pound cake," Rebekah started. "I'm not even going to tell you how many times I've multiplied the recipe, but I think I've got it. Try it out." Rebekah handed Lois, Rose, and Cathy each a piece of the pound cake as well as fixing herself a piece on one of her new white plates dusted with delicate pastel flowers.

Before tasting hers, Rose asked, "What about Andrew, Rebekah? Shouldn't he try the pound cake too?"

"Oh, Andrew's in his office. I guess you could go surprise him with some pound cake. I'm sure he would love to see you."

Lois watched as Rose eagerly grabbed a second plate and then scurried off, lickety-split, to Andrew's office. She had noticed a difference in the girl lately, and come to think of it, she seemed especially different around Andrew. A little giddy. *Hmm. Could something be going on between those two?* she wondered. She would have to keep an eye on them.

"C'mon, ladies," Rebekah said and led the way to a table. Then she turned back to Lois, who seemed distracted. "Lois?"

"What?" Lois asked as if startled, then shook her head. "Oh, yes. My pleasure, dear," she said and followed Rebekah to the table where they sat down with Cathy.

Rebekah's eyes were fixed on Lois as she tasted the cake—one, two, and then three bites before she said a word.

"Rebekah …" Lois was stone-faced as she looked her in the eyes. "I think Mabel, the woman who gave me the original recipe, would be so pleased to know this wonderful cake is on your menu. Don't change a thing."

Rebekah looked at Cathy, let out a giant sigh, and laughed. "Thank you, Lois. I'm so relieved you think so. If you think it would be a good idea, I might try adding things like fruit and chocolate to make some different versions?"

"It's my opinion you can never go wrong with chocolate. Yes, let your creative juices flow," Lois responded with a wave of her hand.

Rebekah gave Lois a hug. "I love you, Lois."

"I love you too, Rebekah."

The three women sat and talked a little longer before Lois announced she had to run along. They all went back to the kitchen, and Rebekah gave Lois a bag with two of the fresh pound cakes to take home with her.

Lois gazed up at the ceiling as she and Rebekah walked out of the kitchen. "When will that chandelier be going up?"

"In two weeks. They're holding it for safekeeping at the lighting store till Harrison finishes up."

"Smart idea. Can't wait to see its sparkle." Lois smiled.

Lois started toward the door and called for Rose.

Then turning back to Rebekah, she asked, "So how is dear Harrison?"

"He's fine. Working very hard to get everything done. I'm so happy you insisted he do this work. I'm pretty sure he's ready to finish and move on to his next project."

"Hmm, I wonder what that next project might be," Lois inquired. "I'm sure he'll come by to check up on things here though. Maybe will even be a regular customer."

"I'm not sure about a regular customer, but I would imagine he'll follow up," Rebekah answered, wondering why Lois would think Harrison would frequent a bakery and teahouse. *He doesn't seem like the tea type at all*, she thought, *more like a sports bar kind of guy.*

"We shall see, we shall see. Rose, I'm leaving!" Lois called again. "What's taking that girl so long?"

Rose came out of Andrew's office with the empty plates. "Here's the plates, Rebekah. It's the best pound cake I think I've ever had."

Lois turned and gave Rebekah a peck on the cheek before heading out the door. "Let's go, Rose."

"Actually ... I'm going to stay and hang out with Andrew. He'll bring me home," Rose said and smiled. She had a little glow about her that Lois didn't miss.

"Okay. I'll see you later then." Her gaze stayed on Rose for an extra few seconds before she exited.

Rebekah chuckled to herself as she walked back to the kitchen, thinking about Harrison with his pinky extended, drinking tea from a teacup and eating dainty little tea sandwiches. *Okay, maybe he'll stop by for something from the bakery—like a pastry or a sandwich and an iced tea.*

"Glad Lois gave her approval on the pound cake," Cathy said to Rebekah as they both settled back into their baking. "Hey, I was thinking about this while you were with Lois. How about seeing if Chef Lester would come by sometime and do a little taste test for us?"

"Good idea. And he said to call him Don, Cathy."

"He told *you* to call him that, not me. I'm still a little afraid of him," Cathy confessed and laughed.

Rebekah smiled. "I am a little also, honestly, but he's been a great help, and I think he likes us. He sure is a wealth of information for me. He did offer to give me advice if I needed it." She shrugged as she pulled out her phone and gave him a call.

***

It just so happened that Chef Lester—Don—was going to be in the area around two o'clock and said he would love to come by and do some taste testing for them. He showed up at 2:15.

"Hello, anyone home?" Don called from the back door. Rebekah had told him to park in the back of the building and let himself in.

"We're in here," Rebekah called from the kitchen door and went to greet him.

Don looked up and down and all around the space before speaking. "This place is looking amazing, Rebekah. You're putting together a very unique environment."

"Thank you! Oh, and up here I'm hanging a fancy chandelier, but we're waiting till the very end to keep it safe and clean." She looked around and then said softly as if she were talking to herself, "It's been my lifelong dream since I was a girl, really, to do this." She turned and smiled at Don. "My grandmother, Marie Claudine, not only taught me everything she knew about baking but also ignited my love for it. She had wanted to open a bakery herself, but my grandfather wouldn't hear of it. He said, 'Women don't do that.' So I decided I would open one for her—hence the name."

Don pursed his lips and nodded, appearing very moved by what Rebekah had just told him. She knew he understood and shared the same love of baking.

"Thank you for sharing that. Your love shows within these walls." He placed his hand on her shoulder. "Now where are these goodies you want me to try?"

Rebekah laughed and led the way.

Don spent the next hour and a half visiting, touring the premises, and tasting what the women had made. He shared stories with them of his successes and failures, leaving them in stitches with some of his anecdotes.

"I started out baking very young like you, Rebekah. My grandfather had a bakery where he did mostly doughnuts, Danishes, and small cakes. No special orders or imagination for anything else. The whole family helped to make it run. When he retired, one of my uncles took it over and didn't change anything with the times, so the bakery eventually closed. That's something you want to make sure you do, Rebekah, is change with the times. Today there's always the new flavor and twist ready to make its way in the culinary world. Keep up with it."

"When did you start teaching—Don?" Cathy asked with a sideways glance toward Rebekah.

"It was after my wife died ten years ago. We never had children, and I needed something different in my life, you know, to help me cope. A friend told me about the community college wanting a teacher in their food service area, so I applied and got the job. I've enjoyed it. I haven't shared this, but I'm retiring after this last class I'm teaching. Looking for the next challenge." He smiled.

Just then, Rebekah had an idea.

Don stood up and said, "I need to let you ladies get back to your fun. I sure enjoyed this. Kind of jealous of you, Rebekah. I've started up many bakeries but never one that was my own. I wish you great success."

"Well thank you, Don. Let me walk you to the door." Rebekah led him to the back of the shop and then stopped and held up an index finger. "Don, I have a question for you. Would you like to work part-time for me? Even though you're retiring, I bet you would like a little something to do, and I could use your expertise." Rebekah was excited at the prospect. His expertise and experience were exactly what she needed.

"Wow, Rebekah. You've taken me by surprise." Don scratched his head as he looked at her. "It could be fun. Can you let me think about it?"

"By all means. Take your time. We can talk about what kind of hours work best. I'm only open during the day, so your evenings would be free. Maybe you could supervise the kitchen so Cathy and I can work on other things. Please consider it."

"I certainly will," he said and gave Rebekah a hug before he departed.

Rebekah saw him off and then went to check on Andrew.

"Hey, Mom, how has the baking gone today? It sure smelled good, and that pound cake Rose brought me was *so* good." Andrew relaxed back in his chair and smiled.

"So you already took Rose home? I didn't see you leave. Did you have a nice visit?" Rebekah asked.

"Umm, yeah, we did."

"I miss seeing her, but she'll be working with us here soon, and we'll be seeing her regularly again."

"Nice," Andrew said with a smile and drummed his fingers on his desk awkwardly.

"The baking went well today. Those ovens are amazing. I think I could bake anything in them."

Andrew laughed. "Mom. You've always been able to bake anything. You're my hero," he leaned back in his chair once more, his hands locked behind his head, and smiled.

"Aww, thank you, Andrew. I did something kind of spur of the moment today, but I think it was a smart decision. I asked Don Lester to come work for us."

Andrew sat up straight in his chair and placed both hands palm down on his desk. "But he already has a job, Mom. Would he even have time to work here?"

"He told me today he's retiring, and I thought having him on board, in a part-time position, could be helpful. He's run bakeries and restaurants before. I thought it was a good move," Rebekah defended herself.

"How much are you going to pay him?" Andrew questioned.

"Well ... I didn't think of that. It just seemed like a good idea," Rebekah mumbled.

"Okay." Andrew, clearly agitated, paused as he chose his next words carefully. "Mom ... I think from now on, we need to have a new rule that no one gets offered a job until you and I discuss it."

Rebekah raised her eyebrows. Andrew sounded like *her* parent. But she knew he was right. She had been impulsive. "I can agree with that, Andrew. But I still think I would like Don working with us in some capacity. He knows the business, and we're learning as we go."

"True, and I can agree that Don would be an asset. Did he say yes?"

"No, he wanted to think about it. He may say no," Rebekah admitted.

"So let's wait and see, then go from there .... But no more hiring beyond what we've already decided. Agreed?" Andrew laid down the law.

"Agreed," Rebekah said sheepishly.

"I'm ready to call it quits. So do I get to taste test any more of the goodies you made today? I had to sit here and smell it while I toiled away in my office in front of this computer all day." Andrew was pathetic.

Rebekah laughed. "Of course. I saved a little of everything for you, but first I'm going to cook our supper."

"I'll help," Andrew offered. He turned the lights off, and they headed up to their apartment.

Chapter 22

Everything was coming together, and today was a big day for Rebekah. There were just two and a half more weeks until Marie Claudine's grand opening on September 3—and today, they were finally hanging her chandelier. It was the final finishing touch and an image she'd held in her mind for so long. There was one person she wanted to share this moment with more than anyone.

"Hi Tammy, it's Rebekah," she said as Tammy's always-exuberant voice came across the line.

"Hey, I have been thinking about you! How is it all going? I hope good. You haven't opened your new place yet, have you?"

"No, not yet. You have no idea the hoops you have to jump through when opening a business," Rebekah proclaimed. "It's beyond ridiculous."

"Oh, yeah, yeah, I bet it is. Dealing with the bureaucracy," Tammy stated and laughed.

"You got it. Everybody has to give their okay and get their money, but I guess we don't want people taking short cuts. That would cause problems down the road," Rebekah rationalized.

"So tell me everything about the place." Tammy was eager.

"Well, of course I think it's fabulous. I had Marie Claudine's Bakery and Tea House painted on a traditional wooden sign hanging across the front of the building. It's very simple in white, black, and what I call 'French blue.' Inside are twelve-foot ceilings, eight-foot glass windows across the front, and two heavy dark-oak antique doors with lead glass windows. They're beautiful and, according to Lois, the building's original doors. She estimates they could be about a hundred years old. The glass is that old thick kind with ripples in it. When you come in, you're greeted by seating on the left and the bakery on the right. The wood floors are original too. We had them refinished, and they have that beautiful patina you can only get with age. By any chance, did you ever go to that department store in Wausau with the wood floors?" Rebekah asked.

"The one with the floors that creaked? It was called Landry's." Tammy was quick to answer.

"Well, that's what my floors sound like," Rebekah said, laughing.

"You know, somebody has renovated that building and divided it into some restaurants and shops. It's as cute as can be, but I'll be darned if those floors don't still creak just like they always did." Tammy laughed.

"Well, that's just what my place sounds like—except not quite as loud, fortunately. But I doubt you'll be paying any attention to the creaking floors when you walk in because your eyes will be drawn to the *fabulous* crystal chandelier hanging at the entrance. In fact, we're hanging it today in a few hours. The last thing to be done—like the icing on a cake. We're still not ready to open by any means just yet. A lot of prep work and training needs to be done. I've hired five young women, in addition to my niece Rose, my friend and bakery assistant Cathy, and Cathy's two daughters.

That gives me nine people to start with. I met Cathy in the baking class I took. Then, of course, I have myself, Lois, and Andrew on board. I'm sure I'll have to hire more after people start discovering us, but this should work for now—I think," Rebekah shared.

"Sounds like you have your ducks in a row. I'm proud of you."

"Thank you, Tammy. The only thing that would make it more perfect is to have you here by my side. We're a good team."

"Yes, we are, we are. I miss you at the store." Tammy paused for a moment before adding, "Oh! I have to tell you the latest. The new owner just renamed the store. It's now Northern Market and Café, and *man* are they making changes. I'm still trying to keep as low a profile as I can so I keep my job, but you know I'm not good at that," Tammy admitted with a tone of worry.

"Just stick to the bakery. What about Michael? Last time you said he had disappeared. Any word on his whereabouts?" Rebekah was curious to hear what had happened to him.

"Well, it turns out he's up in Phillips. Spencer went up there fishing one weekend and stopped at a tavern with his buddies where he bumped into Michael. Michael told Spencer he was selling his house in Rhinelander and was buying something up there in Phillips. He's got enough money now so he doesn't have to worry about work, and evidently, he met a woman there he's head over heels about, so I'm guessing they'll get married and live happily ever after. The woman is a German teacher at the high school."

"Well, I think that's good. Michael is really a nice guy, and he deserves to find someone. If by chance you see him, let him know I wish him the best." Rebekah meant it. She thought about when she was home this past spring and how Michael had asked her to dinner or lunch. If circumstances had been different, maybe she would have gone out with him, and who knows what may have developed. But she was learning, life seems to head us in the right direction. She was happy Michael had found someone not too far away to help him through this new direction his life had taken.

"What's the news on the wedding for James in Milwaukee?" Tammy asked.

"Still set for the first weekend in November. I wish it weren't so close to my first holiday season with the shop." She took in a deep breath and let it out. "Just a lot going on. I haven't even started looking for a dress for the wedding."

"You'll do fine with the holiday season. It's not going to be much different than when you worked here around that time of the year I would guess. You know your baking like it's a part of you, and that Cathy sounds like she could be your clone. You're a natural, and you have such great support. You can't go wrong the way I see it. As far as finding a dress, take that niece with you, and I bet you'll find a dress no problem."

"Thank you, Tammy. I need *you* to keep me grounded. I just wanted to share this moment with you."

"Hon, I think about you all the time."

"And I think of you. Well, I have to run. I just needed to hear your voice." Rebekah felt a knot in her throat. "They'll be here before I know it with my chandelier, and I don't want to miss that." Rebekah laughed, easing the emotion.

"I need a picture of that thing," Tammy demanded and laughed.

"Will do. It has been so good catching up with you. I'll give you a call after my grand opening and send a few more pictures," Rebekah told her.

"Oh, that would be great. Send more than a few. You know you'll be a great success. You can do it, Rebekah. You can do anything," Tammy assured her.

"Thank you, my friend."

***

Harrison pulled up just as the guys from the lighting company were opening the back of their truck.

He stopped next to the truck and rolled down his window. "Hey, guys. I'm going to go park in the back, then I'll come open the front doors for you to bring the chandelier in."

"Sounds good," said the foreman, and his assistant gave a thumbs up.

After parking his truck, Harrison walked through the back door and paused a moment, looking at how great the place had turned out. From the refinished original floors to the custom work he'd done on the walls, trim, and ceiling—the place didn't look new; it looked better, as if it had always been there. This was definitely the finest work he'd ever done, and he was proud. The chandelier would be the perfect finishing touch. He hated that the job was finished, but then again, maybe now he could get up the nerve to ask Rebekah out. Harrison closed his eyes, lost in his thoughts for a moment, until he heard one of the lighting guys knock on the front door. He chuckled to himself and quickly scooted over to open it.

"Sorry, c'mon in." He smiled at the two men, letting them in and gesturing to the spot on the ceiling he had marked for where the chandelier would go. He pulled out his phone and quickly texted Rebekah, *They're here*. She responded with a happy face, and in a moment, he heard her light footsteps gliding down the stairs, soon followed by Andrew's much heavier, look-out-here-I-come gait. Harrison smiled and laughed to himself.

"Pretty exciting day today," he greeted them.

"It sure is, Harrison, and I wouldn't be here if it weren't for you," Rebekah declared and gave him a hug. "You brought my vision to life. I will always be grateful to you."

Harrison could feel the flush coming up his face. *How embarrassing*, he thought, but fortunately Rebekah was distracted, speaking with the guys who had just brought in the box containing the chandelier. Unfortunately for Harrison though, Andrew *had* been watching him.

Andrew approached Harrison, leaned over, and quietly spoke. "Your secret is safe with me, man." He put his hand on Harrison's shoulder before he softly chuckled.

Harrison looked down at his feet, hoping the brim of his ball cap would shade his face.

"Don't worry, buddy. Your time will come. Be patient. And besides—" he gave Harrison a pat on the back and extended his hand, "—I'm on your side. We all are."

Harrison laughed and shook his hand.

Andrew gave Harrison a wink and another chuckle before proceeding to his mom's side.

Just then Cathy, Lois, and Rose arrived.

"You made it. Thank you for coming." Rebekah greeted each of them with a hug.

"My dear, we wouldn't miss it," Lois declared.

The men opened the double oak doors to bring in the equipment that would hoist the heavy chandelier up to the ceiling for installation. Rebekah was beside herself with excitement watching her vision come to fruition.

In a little over an hour, the chandelier was in place. Rebekah had the honor of flipping the switch.

It's lovely, Harrison thought as his eyes moved from the massive light fixture to Rebekah. He smiled.

"This is even more beautiful than I thought it would be." Rebekah was in awe. The majestic chandelier was about thirty inches wide by thirty-six inches tall, though still delicate in appearance. Its dainty crystal prisms didn't overtake it like some gaudier pieces Rebekah had seen but were instead lightly interspersed, looking like little fairies who had decided to settle there for a while.

"It sure is beautiful. I thought the picture you showed me was amazing, but the real thing is even more so," Cathy exclaimed. "Simply beautiful."

"It reminds me of you, Rebekah—graceful and gentle," Rose shared, not taking her gaze from the chandelier.

"It looks—magical. And perfect," Harrison said as Rebekah turned to him. He set his gaze on her face, which glowed under the warm light.

For a moment, Rebekah drank in the silence before she smiled and said softly to Harrison as she looked into his eyes, "Yes, magical. That's exactly what I thought the first time I saw it too."

Harrison smiled back, catching Andrew out of the corner of his eye who gave him a wink and nod of his head. Harrison quickly turned away lest he start blushing again.

"Harrison, since it's so close to lunchtime, our Marie Claudine crew here was planning on picking up some barbecue to continue our celebration. Why don't you join us?" Rebekah suggested and then added, "Unless you have another job to go to."

"Yes, Harrison," Andrew chimed in. "You need to be part of our celebration, since you've worked so hard on our renovation."

"Well, I don't have to be anywhere, but I also don't want to intrude," Harrison stammered.

"Intrude?" Rebekah scoffed. "Nonsense." She looked around at everyone. "You're a part of this team. I'll never forget everything you did to make my dream come true. Just because this job is done doesn't mean our friendship has to be."

"Yes, I couldn't agree more, Mom," Andrew said and gave Harrison a toothy Cheshire cat grin.

"Well then—sure." Harrison gave in. "I'd love to join you."

"Andrew, you order the food, and then maybe Harrison can ride with you to pick it up," Rebekah dictated.

"Yes, ma'am."

"Cathy and I have been baking up a storm, so we have plenty of dessert, don't we?" Rebekah looked to Cathy.

"That's an understatement. In fact, maybe we can send you all home with a little care package," Cathy suggested.

"I would never refuse that," Lois responded. "How about you, Harrison?"

"I was afraid they would never ask." Harrison gave a chuckle and a big smile.

A moment later, Andrew hung up his phone and gestured to Harrison. "Barbecue ordered, let's go."

"Can I come too?" Rose asked.

"Sure," Andrew said, and they were out the door.

"That Harrison is such a nice guy—and cute," Cathy commented after the guys had left. "I wonder if he has a girlfriend?"

"You know I'm actually dating his father, Cathy. Are you interested in him?" Lois inquired.

"I mean … I wouldn't mind finding a nice fella now that my girls are older and on their way. I don't want to spend the rest of my life alone, and he seems more than eligible," she added, then turned to Rebekah. "How about you, Rebekah? Ever think of finding a fella?"

"I've got this project," Rebekah said and looked around the shop. "I think it's about all I can handle right now."

"I suppose so," Cathy responded. "Hey, I'm going to go use the restroom before the guys get back."

After Cathy was out of earshot, Lois spoke. "I wonder if Cathy is serious about Harrison?"

"I don't know," Rebekah responded. "First I've heard of it."

"Rebekah …" Lois took a deep breath in and let it out. "You're a beautiful woman and very special. You should be sharing this time of your life with someone."

"I appreciate your concern, Lois, but I've been through a lot, and I'm still trying to put the pieces back together. I feel I've done pretty well so far. My whole marital situation, hoping to find Dee, moving to Asheville, opening this place—I'm not sure a relationship is right for me or fair to someone else, at least not now."

Lois took Rebekah's hand. "I understand. I'm just saying, stay open to possibilities for a special person in your life, and if someone comes along, don't let them pass you by, dear. Just look at Doug and me." Lois laughed a bit and then became serious. "Anyway, I feel like I'm your surrogate mother just like I was for Dee." She touched Rebekah's cheek. "You've done amazing, darling, and I believe there are more amazing events in your life yet to come."

A tear rolled down Rebekah's face. "Lois, you are the kind of mother I never had growing up, and I'll bet Dee felt the same way. I mean, she did make you guardian of her child. That says it all. My friend Tammy is a very spiritual woman, not in a church kind of way but a universal way. She told me, 'Everything and everyone is here to help you along your path. Not just the good stuff, but even the not so pleasant events, as well as the people you meet.' Actually, she says the unpleasant things will move you further along to where you *need* to be, and I agree with that."

The two women were silent, smiling softly at each other for a moment.

"I have to say I agree with your friend Tammy," Lois commented. "She sounds like my kind of girl. I sure hope I can meet her one day."

"Yes, she's amazing, and there's no one like her." Rebekah felt a little pang in her chest, thinking about how she wished Tammy were by her side right now. "I believe when I discovered that Ethan—my so-called husband—was still married, it was the most unpleasant thing that has ever happened to me …. But it led me here to do this." She paused and looked around the room before looking Lois in the eyes.

"I'm living a wonderful life, and I'm happier than I have ever been. All of those unpleasant events have led me here to where I should be, and I'm doing what I should be doing. I have every hope that someday, someone will enter my life at the right time who wants to share this with me—even if I can't imagine it right now. I still have some wounds to heal, and that wouldn't be fair to someone else."

After a long, thoughtful pause, Lois responded. "I understand, my dear, I understand." She took Rebekah's hand in hers once more. "I love you, Rebekah." A tear rolled down Lois's cheek as she wrapped her arms around her friend.

"I love you too, Lois," Rebekah said, hugging her back.

"Did I miss something while I was in the restroom?" Cathy asked with a concerned look on her face when she came back.

Before they could respond, Andrew, Rose, and Harrison burst through the front doors, laughing and toting Barbecue.

"Lunch is here!" Andrew announced as he charged in, then stopped dead in his tracks when he noticed the three solemn-faced women. "Everything okay here?"

"Couldn't be better," Lois said with a chuckle. "Now let's eat!"

Chapter 23

The past week had gone by in a whirlwind, and Marie Claudine's Bakery & Tea House had passed all the final inspections with flying colors. It was one week before the grand opening, and Rebekah thought a practice run—or as Andrew called it a "soft opening"—with some invited guests sounded like a good idea. She had invited not only her usual group of friends but also other store owners in the area and the students from the patisserie baking class she had taken. The guests were invited to drop in from 5:30 until 8 p.m. It was now 4 p.m., and Rebekah was getting a little nervous thinking about this dry run.

She stood by herself in the dining area, listening to the hustle and bustle coming from the kitchen. It felt so familiar, and she thought of when she was manager of the bakery at Fred's Market; the memory made her smile. For a moment, she closed her eyes and thought, *Thank you, God. I'm in my element, and I'm grateful.*

Rose stuck her head out of the kitchen and called to her, "You okay, Rebekah?"

Rebekah came back to reality and smiled with a little shake of her head. "I'm fine. Never been better." She chuckled and took a few steps toward the front door where she turned around so she could take a moment to assess the space for the hundredth time. The first thing you saw when you entered was the beautiful chandelier welcoming you in. To her right was the shining glass bakery case, and behind that was the kitchen. The wall between the bakery and kitchen was a half wall with a full glass window on the upper part so customers could watch the baking magic unfold.

At the end of the bakery case was the register and a suggestion box that read "Dear Marie Claudine" where people could tell Marie Claudine—or Rebekah—about a favorite bakery item they would love to see in the bakery case. Rebekah's hope was that customers sharing their favorite baked goods could help her broaden the horizons of the shop. There also was a large open antique cabinet that held, for purchase, tins of all the different teas they served as well as other items like tea infusers, cloths, cups, cozies, engraved spoons, teapots, and other products pertaining to "the art of tea," as Lois put it.

Left of the door was the dining area filled with the eclectic tables and chairs Lois and Rebekah had collected over the past several months. In the middle of the pale-blue shiplap wall was an 11x14 portrait of Marie Claudine. Lois had a local artist she knew create the painting from a picture Rebekah provided of Mère. The rest of the wall was filled with Lois's flea market finds: framed pictures of long-ago English and French countryside and the people who had lived there. Lois had done a wonderful job of setting the mood; to Rebekah it felt both elegant and fun.

Across the back wall was the beverage station that provided hot tea, coffee, soda, iced tea, flavored water, and juices. They eventually intended to offer some specialty iced teas, using some of the unique teas they offered for sale in the shop and adding a little uniqueness to their menu.

People would order and pay at the end of the bakery counter, then choose a table to sit at while they waited for their food and beverage to be delivered to them. The whole space had a nice flow to it.

In addition to the bakery items, they would offer tea sandwiches as well as basic deli sandwiches. The tea sandwiches came on a plate alone or with a pot of tea, and for two or more people the shop offered a traditional high tea stand—three-tiered—with sandwiches on the bottom; scones with jam, lemon curd, and cream in the middle; and sweet treats on the top. It was an eventual goal of Rebekah's to find a few local farmers from whom she could buy seasonal produce to integrate into the menu.

When they were working on the shop layout, Andrew had suggested that they might benefit from including a party room so they could offer a space for tea parties and other meetings. It could be not only for adults who wanted to meet there but also for children's birthday parties. Rebekah loved the idea, so Harrison had created the room in the back of the shop opposite Andrew's office and next to the space Rebekah would eventually use as her cake room in the future. The back also featured several storage areas. Harrison had helped them utilized the space well—just as he had done with the apartment upstairs.

"Hey, Rebekah, everyone is here in the kitchen. Did you want to talk to the staff before we start?" It was Cathy. Rebekah was so grateful for her.

"Yes. I'll be right there."

Along with Rose and Cathy's girls, Mandy and Allie, who would work part-time, Rebekah had hired five young women named Katy, Sara, Karen, Pam, and Stacy to work full-time behind the bakery counter, checkout, beverage station, and dining area. They were all dressed in crisp white pants and shirts finished off with light-pink aprons embroidered with Marie Claudine's name. Rebekah and Cathy wore white chef coats. Lois, who was also present, would serve as more of a hostess, so she wore whatever she chose.

As of yet Rebekah hadn't heard back from Don about the part-time position she had offered him. If he turned her down, her hope was that a couple of the full-time workers she had hired would want to learn more about baking, since she realized the kitchen was going to be quite a challenge for she and Cathy alone. Granted business would likely be slow starting out, but she anticipated they would get busier as word got around about Marie Claudine's and she began to build up a clientele.

"Hello, ladies," Rebekah began as she joined her staff in the kitchen. "I hope you're as excited as I am today. The people here this evening are all friends, but I want you to treat it just like things will be when we open for real next week. What I also want you to do tonight is make mental notes of anything you think we can do better or any ideas you may have to change something. One thing you should know about me is I have an open-door policy for any suggestions. I ran a bakery for many years in Wisconsin, where I'm from, and found my employees had the best ideas to make things better. So with that said, let's relax and have fun tonight."

The young women smiled and nodded their heads, a couple saying "Yes, ma'am."

Lois came over to give Rebekah a quick hug and a smile before she said, "Good job, dear. It's going to be great."

Next, Rebekah went to find Andrew—where else but in his office, looking at a computer screen. He didn't notice her standing in the door, so she spoke. "I knew I would find you here. I hope you're not going to hide here all night?"

Andrew reluctantly looked up, "Ah, no Mom. I'll be out there right by your side. Have you heard if Don is going to take you up on that position you offered?" That boy was always business.

"No, but he'll be here tonight. I'll find out from him. I either need someone with experience like his or to start training a couple of our new employees in baking. By any chance, do you want to learn baking, Andrew?" she joked.

He looked up at her as if she had sprouted a horn in her forehead. "What? Are you serious?" Andrew leaned back and spread his arms out, hands up, finding no humor in what she had said. "I have my hands full with this."

"I'm just kidding, son. Calm down." Sometimes Andrew could be a little too serious for someone his age. Maybe after everything got going, he could start to have more fun.

"I'm going back out there," Rebekah told Andrew and headed to the front of the shop where she found Doug and Harrison in the dining area talking to Lois. "Hey, when did you sneak in?" she asked and proceeded to hug both of them.

"Rebekah, this place looks amazing," Doug said.

"I have your son to thank for that, Doug. I told him what I needed, and he had the vision." Rebekah turned and smiled at Harrison.

"Just followed what you asked for," Harrison humbly answered with a smile.

"I think you need to give yourself more credit, Harrison dear," Lois said. "Remember this used to be my clothing store. You worked magic not only here but upstairs in that apartment. Pure talent."

"I agree, Lois." Doug was beaming and patted Harrison on the back. "My son is good at what he does. Always has been."

"Well, after all that, I think I deserve to go check the treats." Harrison grinned and walked toward the bakery cases.

"I'll join you." Rebekah laughed and followed him.

"Everything looks so good here," Harrison said, looking from one confection to the next. "Not sure what I would pick."

All of a sudden Cathy popped in out of nowhere. "Hey, Harrison," she drawled. "So happy you're here. Looking for something sweet?" she asked with a flirtatious smile on her face like Rebekah had never seen before.

"Oh, ah, just looking, Cathy. Maybe later," Harrison fumbled.

Before Cathy could say anything else, Lois and Doug stepped in. "Harrison, you probably want to go say hi to Andrew," Lois suggested. "Rebekah, I'm going to camp out by the tea tonight, but you know Doug and Harrison can help out if things start getting crazy. I mean, what are friends for?"

"Yes, Rebekah. Whatever you need. Right, son?" Doug said and raised his eyebrows at Harrison.

"Yes, of course."

"That's very kind of you, but you are to be guests tonight. This is practice for my staff so they'll know what to expect for the grand opening," Rebekah assured them.

"I guess you're right," Doug said, and he and Harrison headed to Andrew's office.

"Rebekah, I don't want to make you nervous, but it's five o'clock. I'm so excited for you." Lois grabbed Rebekah's arm with a giddy look on her face.

"I guess you and I better get back to the kitchen for one last check, Cathy." Rebekah turned to Cathy and laughed. She felt surprisingly relaxed and was looking forward to the evening.

At 5:30, Rebekah was at the front door, greeting her guests as they entered and thanking them for coming. By six o'clock, the dining area was more than half filled with people. The staff was flowing along here and there, and everything was running smoothly. Cathy had things under control in the kitchen, so she decided this was her chance to find Don Lester and ask about the job she had offered him.

"Don." She found him sitting with some of the people from the patisserie class. "Can I talk to you for a minute?" He nodded, and she led him to Andrew's office.

Before she could even ask, Don started, "You want to know about the offer you gave me, yes? I've done a lot of thinking about how much fun it would be to help start a new business—but I'll have to turn you down. I have decided I want to take some time off and not jump into anything. I may change my mind down the road, but not for now. You can still count on me for advice though. I definitely will be coming by to check up on you regularly, and you can always give me a call. I want you to succeed."

"Well—" she paused, "—I am disappointed, but I understand and appreciate your support, Don. I'm going to see if a couple of the people I've hired would like to learn the baking business. On-the-job training might take a while, but it's my best option right now."

"I feel honored you asked me, Rebekah. It's just—I'm ready to take some time for myself. Isn't that what retirement's for?"

"It sure is. Thank you for considering though."

Don gave her a big hug, and they walked back out into the shop. "I have to say, Rebekah, this place is beautiful and unique." Don looked around from floor to ceiling. "You'll have half the people in Asheville coming in here for tea and pastries before you know it. I wish you great success."

"Thank you, Don. I appreciate it. Now, I better go check on how things are going."

Don went back to his table and Rebekah to the kitchen.

Rebekah spent most of the rest of the evening in the kitchen, helping to prepare food for her guests. It felt good to be back in a bakery kitchen again. She would stick her head out now and again to greet her guests and receive accolades and wishes for success as folks came through the line. All in all, it had turned out to be a good night. The front door was now locked, and Rebekah would talk to the staff before they left tonight to tell them how much she appreciated their hard work and ask them to think overnight about how things went. Tomorrow they would all meet at 9 a.m. to go over the evening.

It was 8:30 p.m. now, and the only people still left were Cathy, Rose, Lois, Doug, Harrison, Don, Andrew and, of course, Rebekah. The kitchen was pristine and ready for the next day, so they all sat down at one of the large tables with something to drink and something from the bakery case, talking about the evening.

"I want to make a toast," Doug said.

Everyone raised their glasses.

"To great success and smooth sailing for Rebekah, and may Marie Claudine look down on you tonight with great pride on her granddaughter's accomplishment."

They all clinked glasses and a few chimed in with "Hear! Hear!" or "Congratulations."

"Thank you, everyone. You all have been great support for me. What would I do without my friends?" She raised her glass and a few tears of happiness trickled down her cheeks.

Rebekah was soon getting hugs from everyone, and they were all talking at once when Cathy looked to the front door.

"Looks like someone's out there knocking on the door. They must think we're open," she said.

Rebekah scrunched her face. The front lights were off, and the sign on the door listed an opening date, but still some people just never paid attention to signs.

"They'll eventually figure it out. Let's just ignore it," Cathy suggested.

But whoever it was wouldn't give up and cupped their hands around their face to look in through the door window. As far as Rebekah could tell, it wasn't someone she recognized, but between the distance and the rippled antique glass in the door, she couldn't be sure.

"I wonder if it's someone who was invited tonight and couldn't stop by till now," Rebekah queried.

"Ah, geez. Let me go find out," Cathy said with a sigh and got up to head that way.

"I'll go with you," Andrew said with slight concern.

Everyone continued their conversation for a few minutes until Cathy came back alone.

"This guy says he knows you, Rebekah. His name is Michael Wagner?" Cathy reported, sounding confused.

Rebekah turned to Cathy for a moment and just stared as she thought. She only knew one Michael Wagner—Fred's son—but according to Tammy, he was with his new girlfriend in Phillips, Wisconsin.

"Are you sure he said Michael Wagner? I know a Michael Wagner from *Wisconsin*." Rebekah got up, and she and Cathy headed to the door where Andrew stood waiting.

"He says he knows you, Mom."

Rebekah peered through the rippled window, her scrunched face expressing her bewilderment as she saw that it was indeed Michael Wagner, Fred's son. "Open the door, Andrew," she said.

Andrew raised an eyebrow and then did as instructed.

"Oh, for cripes' sake, Rebekah, it's so good to see you," Michael said and gave her a big hug.

"Michael, what are you doing here?"

"It's a long story. But, hey, I'm starving. Ya got anything I can eat?" Michael proclaimed.

Before Rebekah could respond, Cathy jumped in. "I'll go make you a sandwich, but don't start your story till I get back," she said, and off she went to the kitchen, not taking her eyes off Michael.

"Michael, I'm in shock," Rebekah said bewildered.

"Well, it's me for sure," Michael responded with a chuckle and smile.

"Why don't you come back here and sit down?" Rebekah led the way to her friends at the table. "Everyone this is Michael, a friend of mine from Wisconsin who I've known most of my life," she said.

Everyone said hi, and then Doug, ever the voice of reason, stood up and said, "Rebekah, I think it's time we all said good evening anyway and part ways so you can visit with your friend. Thank you for inviting us all to partake in this celebration of your new endeavor. It was a very pleasant evening."

"Yes, Doug, I think you're correct," Lois chimed in. "It was a lovely evening, everyone. We all wish you the greatest success, Rebekah."

Everyone agreed as Lois showed them to the door, but she and Doug came back to wait for Cathy who was finishing up Michael's sandwich.

"Come, come, Cathy." Lois pointed her finger at the table they had been sitting at. "Give the man his sandwich, and let's go. We need to leave Rebekah to her friend. We'll be back in the morning, Rebekah!"

Cathy looked distraught as she set the sandwich on the table. She was quickly ushered out by Lois who handed Cathy her purse, then shooed her toward the door.

Lois and Doug trailed right behind her. "Would you be kind enough to lock the door, Andrew?" she asked, and they were all gone in a flash.

"Let's sit over here at the table, Michael, so you can enjoy your sandwich." Rebekah escorted Michael to a table and raised her eyebrows as she looked toward Andrew. "I'll be right back, Michael," she added, and she walked Andrew to his office.

"What's going on, Mom? This is a little weird—even for a guy from Wisconsin. I mean it's a pretty long road trip."

"I'm not sure, son, but I'm fine with him. Don't worry. You go on upstairs while I talk to Michael and find out what he's doing here. I'm as puzzled as you are. His dad was Fred—remember, the man I worked for in Rhinelander? Fred passed away at the end of June. There's more to the story, but I'll fill you in later. It's fine. I'm safe."

"Okay, if you say so, but I'm keeping the door open, so just holler."

"It's going to be fine," she assured him as she closed her eyes and softly chuckled. She gently pushed Andrew toward the stairs to the apartment. "Now go on."

With a raise of his eyebrows, Andrew reluctantly obeyed.

Rebekah paused a moment before heading back to the table where Michael was eating his sandwich. She took a deep breath, trying to get her thoughts together before she heard his story.

What was going on?

Chapter 24

As she sat down next to Michael at the table, he looked up and smiled.

"Hey, that woman makes a good sandwich," he said and took another bite.

Rebekah smiled and nodded, deciding to let him finish eating before she asked any questions. For a moment, she watched her old friend—the scene feeling so familiar. He still had the same tall, thin stature and blond hair, and he really didn't look that much different than he had when they were teenagers, just a little more tired around the eyes.

"So what's going on, Michael, and what brought you here?" she finally began as he finished his last bite.

"Oh, it's a long story." Michael leaned back in his chair and took a deep in-and-out breath. "Can't tell you how good it is to see you though, Rebekah. I know I told you about Dad selling the store when you were visiting this past spring, so I don't have to explain all that," Michael started.

"Yes, I didn't breathe a word about it. Tammy eventually told me and then shared the sad news about your dad passing away. I was so sorry to hear that. Your dad gave me a chance years ago when I was just a kid. His faith in me helped me to get to where I am now."

"Yeah …. Oh, and I did get your card. Thanks." He paused and took a big breath to control his emotions before he continued. "Dad was a good guy." Michael then gazed at the floor for a bit before he went on. "He would be madder than hell right now if he knew they booted me out of the store after he died. That was not the way we understood the agreement, but they said it was only Dad who they had agreed to keep on and that allowing me to stay there was a 'kindness.' Now that he was gone, I would have to find something else. Jerks. I worked just as hard as Dad did to make Fred's what it was."

"That's true. You had your dad's flair for business."

"Yep, I sure did. Fortunately, Dad made a lot of money off the deal and even had it set up so he would receive a profit percentage the first five years. Dad was one shrewd business guy," Michael scoffed. "I wish I were half the man he was." Michael's voice was a little strained, prompting him to take a long gulp from his water glass before he went on.

"Tammy told me no one knew where you had gone after your dad passed away," Rebekah said. "She said several people from the store went over to your house but there was no answer when they knocked on the door. Everyone was concerned and worried." Rebekah decided not to say anything about the woman in Phillips whom Tammy had told her about. She wanted to hear the whole story from Michael.

"Oh, that Tammy is one sweet lady. Let me tell you, she really stepped up to fill your shoes after you left. I've missed her. I didn't mean to make anyone worry. I just didn't feel I belonged in Rhinelander anymore after Dad died and the store was gone."

"So tell me what happened once you left the store," Rebekah said, trying to keep him on track and wanting desperately to get to the part about why he was there in Asheville.

"Well, after I cleaned out my office, I decided I needed to get away for a while, so I threw some stuff in a suitcase and headed up 47 North to some places where Dad and I used to enjoy going together." Michael looked down at his folded hands resting on the table and breathed in and out before he looked back up and spoke. "Stopped on the way and saw a hunting buddy of mine who has a place around Lac Du Flambeau for a couple days, then visited a college friend and his wife in Ironwood before arriving at my destination: Copper Falls. Dad, myself, my brothers, and Mom, when she was alive, used to go up there every summer." He looked at Rebekah. "Have you ever been there?"

"No, but I heard about it. We always headed over to Upper Michigan to see our family if we had some time off, and Ethan never wanted to go anywhere. I've heard that it's beautiful though."

"It is. On my way down here, I stopped at a few places in the mountains, and I have to say, it could rival some of the spots I visited. Nobody thinks there's stuff like that in Wisconsin, but there is. It's not all flat plains or farmland." Michael paused and looked at his watch. "Am I keeping you from anything?"

"No, no. I really want to hear how you got here," Rebekah replied, not wanting him to get sidetracked.

"Oh yeah, sure." Michael shook his head up and down and gave a weak, forced smile as he continued. "Had a great time in the Falls area, so decided to go home down through Chequamegon-Nicolet National Forest and ended up stopping in Phillips—nice little town—and decided to stay awhile, so I got a hotel room. To make a long story short, I went to a tavern, a little place close by where I was staying, for fish on Friday night. It was so crowded, I ended up sitting at a table with some other folks and made a few new friends. One happened to be a woman who was the German teacher at the high school, and well, we kind of hit it off, so I hung around town for a while and rented a short-term, furnished place. Things seemed to be going very well with the German teacher—until her old boyfriend came back to town. Some fancy lawyer. He had gone down to Milwaukee a while ago to find fame and fortune and decided he liked things better in Phillips—along with missing my new girlfriend, the German teacher. Apparently, she had missed him too."

"I'm so sorry to hear that, Michael. So … all that's what brought you here?"

"Yep. I got to thinking about my life. I needed a new start— kinda like what you did—and the more I thought about it, I realized I could go anywhere I wanted to. Maybe I should head to Asheville where Rebekah is. See how she's doing. Start over. You seemed to like it. I decided, what the heck, I would start there."

Rebekah wasn't sure how to respond, so she kept silent.

"I've been down here a week and love it. I'm in a short-term rental for now. Wasn't hard to find you. I knew you were opening a business, and I knew it was a bakery and teahouse, so I drove the streets in downtown Asheville and found you tonight. I could see people were inside here, and I took a chance." Michael spread his arms as if to say "ta-da."

Rebekah was still dazed that Michael was sitting there. "Wow, that's quite a story. So what do you plan to do now you're here?"

"To be honest, I don't really know. Kind of making it up as I go along. I don't need to work, but I'd like to do *something*. Going to do a little more exploring of Asheville and the South. Never been down this way before, so I'll take my time. I like it so far. You do like it here, right? Glad you came?"

Rebekah was still processing all he had said and felt taken off guard by his question. "What? Ah—why, yes. I wouldn't be opening a new business if I weren't. So … you said you have a place to stay then?"

"Oh yes, I have the place I'm renting on a month-by-month lease."

Feeling somewhat relieved, Rebekah smiled and nodded. She didn't want to have to invite him to stay with her and Andrew—her plate was certainly full enough at the moment—though she would have if he'd really needed a place.

"I was actually going to drive down to Charlotte tomorrow and check it out. Heard that it was pretty nice for a big city. Like I said, I'm going to explore the area and see if I want to permanently stay here or try somewhere else." He smiled at Rebekah and looked down at his watch. "I think I've kept you long enough though. How about I come by again during the day. Let's say—Monday? And you can give me the grand tour then. How does that sound?"

"I think it sounds fine. My son and I actually live upstairs here. We have a nice apartment." There was an awkward silence as Rebekah felt unsure how to continue. "I'm sorry, but I'm still in shock with your appearance here, Michael."

"I understand, Rebekah. Let me give you my phone number if you want to get in touch with me before Monday."

Rebekah grabbed a pen from the nearby counter, and he wrote it down on a napkin.

"It's really good to see you and how well you've done for yourself. I'll come by this Monday, say around one o'clock? I'm sure you'll be working on getting things ready for your grand opening. When is it?"

"Next Thursday. I'll probably be a basket case by that day, I'm sure."

"No doubt." Michael gave a soft chuckle as he stood up from his chair and started to the door. "I won't keep you any longer. Good night, Rebekah. See you soon."

"Good night, Michael." She followed him to the door, then locked it as she watched him climb into his truck and drive away.

As she turned off the lights and finished closing up the shop, Rebekah pieced together what had just happened. *How strange.* Why had Michael chosen Asheville of all places? After a few minutes, she realized Andrew was probably upstairs pacing the floor, so she went up. True to his words, he had left the door open and was there to greet her.

"I listened to the whole thing—hope you don't mind?"

"Of course not, son. Glad you did because now I don't have to repeat it. What did you think?"

"Well, I feel bad for the guy. His whole life was the store, and now he has nothing. I mean, there's room in Asheville for another person." Andrew paused and hesitated before he continued. "Does he have a thing for you, Mom?"

She had been waiting for that question and stared down at her feet for a second before she spoke. "Not sure. He seemed to like me back when I was a teenager. When we were up there this past spring, he told me his dad was going to sell the store and asked me to not tell anyone. He also asked me if I wanted to grab lunch or dinner, but I think it was just that he felt comfortable talking to me about the sale of the store since I didn't work there anymore. Honestly, I don't think he had anyone else he could talk to about it. He's never been married and is only a couple years older than me. I don't know. I really don't have time for that kind of stuff now." She looked up at her son.

"I had to ask. Maybe he thinks you're going to be his new girl."

"I really don't think so, but I couldn't say it's impossible." Rebekah was past the point of tired.

"I say let's go to bed. It's been a long day, and we're both tired. We can talk about this tomorrow."

"Yes. I told our staff to be here at nine tomorrow to talk over how things went tonight. I need to be my best. Love you, son," she said, and she wrapped her arms around Andrew.

"Love you too, Mom. Go get to bed. I'll make sure all is locked up."

Rebekah headed to her room. *What an evening.*

She thought about what Andrew had asked her about Michael. He was a nice guy but not the one for her. She had never been interested in him in that way; they were just longtime friends, and she felt it should stay that way. Still … all this talk had her thinking about how she would like to share her life with *someone*—someday. After all, she was now thirty-seven and not getting any younger. She wouldn't admit it to anyone, but she had actually begun to wonder if Harrison could be that someone. There was something Rebekah liked about Harrison. He was such a gentleman, kind and talented. He had real focus in his life, and … she loved how warm his eyes were when he looked at her.

Although she was happy her business was finally opening, she had to admit she was also a little sad that the project was finished. She wondered if she might never see him again—other than the occasional drop-in to make sure all was running smoothly or to grab a doughnut. It had been really fun to do this remodel with him. Plus, he was a great role model and friend for Andrew. But shoot. Wasn't Cathy quite smitten with him too?

Oh well.

It was time to put all this in the back of her mind anyway; she needed her sleep. It would soon be showtime for Marie Claudine's, and that needed to be her main focus now.

After getting ready for bed, she crawled under the covers and opened a book she had been reading. She liked to read a little every night before bed to relax her mind, but tonight her mind would not stay with the words on the pages. It was no use, so she put her bookmark in, set the book on the nightstand, and turned off the bedside lamp, willing herself to sleep.

Chapter 25

The next morning, around 8:15, Rebekah thought she would go down to the shop early and get a few things done before everyone else showed up—only to find Cathy already busy in the kitchen.

"When did you get here?" Rebekah asked, startling Cathy.

"My *Lawd*, you just scared the bejeebers out of me." Cathy put her hand over her heart and sat on a chair.

"I'm sorry." Rebekah chuckled a little bit. "Just surprised you're here so early. I didn't expect anyone to arrive before nine. What time did you get here?" Rebekah asked.

"About eight. I'm putting away a few things we let air-dry from last night and just checking the kitchen." She hesitated with a guilty look on her face before she continued. "Oh all right." She paused for a moment, pursing her lips as she decided how to begin. "I want to know who that guy was last night and figured I'd ask you before everyone else got here. He's obviously one of your people from the North by the sound of his accent."

"What accent?" Rebekah said, feigning offense. "We don't *have* an accent in Wisconsin. You people down here have an accent." She turned to cover a smirk, knowing she would get a rise out of Cathy.

"Whaddya mean?" Cathy started, but Lois appeared, putting a halt to their conversation.

"Good mornin', ladies," Lois greeted them.

Rose, who had ridden with her, gave a smile and a wave.

"I didn't expect you here so early, Cathy," Lois said.

"Didn't expect you here either," Cathy countered with the hint of attitude.

Rebekah started laughing. "Okay, ladies. Put some water on to boil so we can have a cup of tea, and let's grab a couple scones from the bakery case. I'll tell you all about Michael."

Rose shook her head and chuckled, turning to her aunt. "You all go right ahead. Is Andrew awake?"

"Yep. Why don't you go on up and hang out with him? We'll still start right at nine," Rebekah informed her, and Rose hightailed it upstairs.

The three sat down and Rebekah, as promised, told them all about Michael, beginning with when she was sixteen and had just started working at Fred's, all the way up to what she had learned last night. She gave his explanation for why he was in Asheville and mentioned how he was going to come by again Monday afternoon so they could talk some more.

"I have to say, he's kind of cute, Rebekah," Cathy declared. "How old is he?'"

"I'm not exactly sure, but probably a couple years older than me. I got married when I was eighteen, and I know he was already gone to college by then. I never paid much attention to that. I led a very sheltered life. I do remember he always worked during the holidays and summer at the store while in college. When he was done with college, he came back to work as his dad's assistant at the store."

"So he's closer to my age then?" Cathy asked with a note of curiosity.

"Yes, around there I guess," Rebekah replied.

Cathy looked at her watch. "Oh, I left my chef's jacket in the car! Let me run out and get it."

Lois watched her leave and frowned. "I swear that girl is on a man hunt," she proclaimed once Cathy was outside and out of earshot. She then turned back to Rebekah and looked her in the eye. "I want to know. Are you interested in this Michael, dear?"

"No, not really. He's always been a friend. Why do you ask?"

"Just curious dear, just curious."

In a moment, Cathy was back, with the rest of the staff trailing behind her.

"Look what I found wandering around outside!" Cathy laughed.

They had a productive meeting as they reviewed the details of the night before. Everyone had suggestions and ideas, which made Rebekah happy.

"I know our official grand opening is next Thursday, but Andrew and I decided we will start work on Monday in preparation for a soft opening of the shop on Tuesday, unofficially, to get comfortable before Thursday's big grand opening. Lots of places do that. I've made a schedule for all of next week. Andrew's going to print it out and make sure you each have one before you leave today. I'm only going to keep you here till one. We'll work on the suggestions and ideas you all had about last night till noon, and then we'll have lunch. We're going to practice by making one of our coworkers a sandwich—the way they request it. Don't make it easy for each other."

***

Rebekah, Cathy, and Lois ended up staying until 4 p.m. that afternoon, making signs and going over the menu and pricing with Andrew one final time.

Cathy and Lois had been gone no more than a few minutes when Harrison showed up.

"Hey, y'all. How's it going? I think things went well last night." Harrison looked the place up and down. "I have to say I'm proud of the way it looks. Do you mind if I take some pictures to use as an example of my work?" he asked.

"Well, of course not," Rebekah said.

"Be our guest," Andrew added. "Happy to have you show off our place. Make sure you tell them where it is and how much they'll enjoy it also."

Rebekah and Harrison looked at each other, then laughed. Andrew always had the business aspect in mind.

Andrew continued, "Hey, you aren't going to be a stranger now that the job is done, I hope? You better come by and see us, friend. I think Mom will agree."

Rebekah nodded and smiled at Harrison.

"Well, I feel the same way. I've enjoyed getting to know you two—more than just clients."

"Absolutely," said Andrew. "And lunch is always on us when you come by. Right, Mom?"

"That's right. Your money's no good here, Harrison."

"Thank you. I appreciate it," Harrison said, catching Rebekah's eyes for a moment.

Andrew clapped his hands together and walked toward the bakery case. "Tell you what, let's go grab something to drink and something sinful to eat so we can all sit down for a visit."

Harrison let out a quiet snicker and shook his head as he turned to Rebekah who threw a hand over her mouth to suppress a laugh.

"Sounds good, Andrew," Harrison said with a cheesy grin as he and Rebekah followed the young man. The three sat at one of the tables for a chat while Harrison filled them in on his next project.

"My next big job is out of town in Lake Lure for the next several months. I'm renovating a house for a family. I'll be back and forth to Asheville but probably staying in Lake Lure for long periods of time. I'll still have some smaller jobs going on here also, you know, like what I did while working on your project. Most contractors work that way," Harrison explained. "Got to always have a couple irons in the fire."

"Makes good sense from a business point of view," Andrew concurred.

Harrison looked at his watch. "Oh, got to run. Told Dad I'd come by and fix a loose board at his house. He told Lois he was going to climb up a ladder and fix it, so she called me, and I put a stop to that." Harrison chuckled. "Crazy old man."

They all laughed.

"Don't leave just yet." Rebekah stopped him and ran to the bakery case to retrieve a couple of boxes. "I fixed you and your dad each a little box of baked goods. We need to use this all up since we'll be baking all new things for the soft open on Tuesday."

"I'm not going to say no to that, and Dad will be thrilled. Thank you, Rebekah." Harrison's eyes twinkled and lingered for a moment as he gave Rebekah a smile and a look that made something stir inside her—in a very good way—before he was out the door.

After the door closed, Andrew turned to his mom and just stared at her for a moment, not saying anything.

"What?" Rebekah asked with a hint of impatience.

"Mom."

Rebekah could see Andrew was struggling to get the right words together and tried not to laugh.

With an exasperated look on his face, Andrew finally gestured to the door Harrison had just left through. "*He* is an awesome guy!

And *I* think *you* two were meant for each other." Before Rebekah could say a word, he quickly put his hand up as if he were stopping traffic. "Just—listen to me. I understand your hesitancy after going through what you did with Dad. Dad ... is a self-centered jerk. Harrison is not. And it's so obvious to me that he likes you. There's a chemistry between you two. I could see it before my eyes, right now, before he left. Could you maybe do more to encourage him? I know you like him too."

Rebekah stared at the ground for a moment and got her mom face on. "First: I have a full plate right now, son. Second: I think Cathy has a thing for him, and I don't want to have any trouble in that area. And third: I plan on being a success, and that means I have to concentrate and prioritize. I would have loved it if Don had come on board to help take a little pressure off me, but he decided not to. I understand why. I know I can do this because I know this business, and I have lots of support. I just need to focus. This is my dream." She paused and took a deep breath. "If it's meant to be with Harrison, it will be. Please try to understand."

"Okay." He sighed heavily. "I get it, Mom. I just want you to find someone to share your life with."

"Let me make a suggestion before you start on me," Rebekah said with a touch of irritation in her voice. "Why don't you concentrate on yourself in that area? I also want *you* to find someone to share *your* life with. How's that?"

Andrew looked at his mother sheepishly. "Don't worry about me," he responded, blinking his eyes several times.

"I'm sorry to throw that back at you," Rebekah said, "but next time, look at yourself before telling others what to do with their life, especially when they didn't ask for advice."

"Yes, ma'am, I'm sorry," Andrew responded flatly and knew it was time to change the subject. "I'm kind of tired and need a break from the shop. I think I'll go find a mindless movie to watch so I don't have to think."

"Sounds good. After we open, we may not have this luxury, so let's take it now. Better yet—let's go out to the barbecue place you love so much first. That sounds good, doesn't it?"

"Actually, it does. I was afraid you were going to say, 'Let's make a sandwich in the shop kitchen.' I figure we will be having a lot of those in the future."

Rebekah went upstairs to change out of her work clothes and get her purse. In spite of everything she had gone through with Ethan, she sure was a blessed woman. Had she not been married— although falsely—to Ethan, she knew she wouldn't be here now. She wouldn't have two awesome sons, wouldn't have found out what happened to Dee, and wouldn't have Rose in her life. She wouldn't have met Lois or made friends with Cathy. And she wouldn't have won the lottery so she could do all this. And—she sighed—yes, she wouldn't have met Harrison.

Time would only tell with that last one.

***

After pulling out of the parking space at Marie Claudine's that he had used every day for the past several months, Harrison had to admit he felt somewhat sad. He really enjoyed working with Rebekah and Andrew. Their project was the biggest job he had ever done, making it a feather in his cap as an accomplishment. His success there was what got him this next job in Lake Lure. But more than that, he felt forlorn that he wouldn't be seeing Rebekah every day. And now that friend of hers from Wisconsin had showed up. Michael, was it? Harrison wanted so badly to ask Rebekah about him, but how pathetic would that be? After all, the guy had come here all the way from Wisconsin for Pete's sake. His intentions were kind of obvious, even if Rebekah didn't see it.

Harrison pulled into his dad's driveway and saw Lois's car was already there.

He knocked twice on the front door and then walked in. "Hey, Dad. I'm here to fix that piece of wood falling off your house."

Doug and Lois both came walking into the foyer to greet him.

"You are the best," Doug said and patted him on the back.

Lois just smiled.

Harrison was glad his dad was seeing Lois. It was as if the happier, more youthful Dad was back.

"Got a little present from Rebekah for you," he said. "I just left there. Wanted to check and see if there was anything that had popped up that needed attention, but it seems all is well. She sent me out with a box of goodies—and one for you when she heard I was coming over here."

"Bless that dear girl," Doug said, thrilled to try some more treats. "I'm going to take this to the kitchen, and then I'll meet you out back to show you what needs to be fixed." He puttered off to the kitchen.

Before Harrison could turn to head outside, Lois said, "Hey, did Rebekah tell you about that man who showed up last night? Turns out he's *just a friend*. Nothing going on romantically there. His dad owned the store where Rebekah worked in Wisconsin. Yes, just friends. Thought you might be curious. I'm keeping an eye on the situation though." She winked at Harrison.

Harrison felt himself turning twenty shades of red before he responded, "Oh, okay," and turned abruptly to leave.

"One more thing, Harrison," Lois said, tapping his shoulder to stop him. "I'm curious about something." Lois hesitated several seconds and took a breath in and out before she continued. "This may be a silly question, but ... do you know if there's anything going on between Andrew and Rose?"

Uncertain he'd heard Lois correctly, Harrison just stared at her blankly.

"What I mean is, well, I might as well just say it ... do you think they are more than just ... *cousins*?"

Harrison blinked his eyes several times and felt his jaw drop as he pondered Lois's question. Andrew and Rose were very close and seemed to enjoy each other's company .... But something more? He couldn't say. "Lois, I can't say I've noticed anything. They are very close, I know that. Did you think of asking Rose that question?"

"Oh, just forget I asked this, Harrison, please. Can we keep it between us?" Lois appealed to him, feeling her cheeks flush. "I'm just being silly."

"Sure, Lois," Harrison replied. "I won't say a word. I better get out back before Dad starts wondering where I am," he said, and he took off. *Wow*, he thought as he walked out to find his dad.

Doug stayed outside and chatted with Harrison while he nailed the board, but as soon as he was done, Harrison said he needed to run. He was afraid to go back in the house for fear of what Lois might say or ask him next—though he wouldn't admit that to his dad. He also had the new project starting up on Monday and, truthfully, had some organizing to do. He told his dad to say goodbye to Lois for him and was out of there faster than lightning.

Driving home, he considered what Lois had told him about Rebekah's friend Michael, and he was glad, if a little embarrassed. He felt better about leaving Asheville now, knowing the guy wasn't much of a threat. Better yet, Michael was under Lois's "watchful eye"—although, it appeared, so was he.

... And Andrew and Rose?

They were *cousins* … though not by blood. So it wouldn't really be a problem for them to be "something more" …. Right? Neither was seeing anyone else to his knowledge, and they were particularly close, always together. Now that he thought of it, it did seem plausible. *Poor kids, having Lois's eye on them.* Harrison laughed. Better them than himself though.

Chapter 26

Monday afternoon, a little before 1 p.m., there was a knock on the door of Marie Claudine's Bakery and Tea House. As expected, it was Michael. Rebekah unlocked the door and let him in.

"Welcome, Michael. Please come in." She closed and locked the door behind him, and the two hugged. After they stepped back, she got a better look at Michael in the daylight, noticing he had aged a little, with gray hair shining at the temples of his mostly blond head and wrinkles around his blue eyes. He was still in good shape though—not a trace of the pot belly a lot of men his age had seemed to develop.

Michael looked the shop over from top to bottom thoroughly before he spoke.

"Seeing this place in daylight has just reinforced what I saw the other night—this is an amazing place. Has it always been a restaurant?" he asked.

"No, it was a clothing store before, believe it or not. We remodeled the upstairs and downstairs down to the studs."

"Seriously? Wow, so you gutted the whole place? How cool. I hope you'll give me a tour of your apartment also?" Michael asked.

"Of course. But let's sit down and chat first. How about a cup of tea or coffee and a custard-filled doughnut with chocolate frosting?" she asked.

"Are the doughnuts like the ones you made at the store?" Michael asked with a hopeful look.

"They sure are," Rebekah responded with a soft laugh. "When you've got a winner, you don't mess with it."

"Then yes please, and coffee with cream." Michael sounded like a little boy.

Rebekah handed Michael the coffee and doughnut before leading him to the table that was farthest from the kitchen where her employees were busy at work. She made sure she sat facing the kitchen and that he sat with his back to it. Both Lois and Cathy would surely be on a reconnaissance mission, observing anything they could. She wasn't going to make it easy for those two spies.

"How was your trip to Charlotte?" she asked him. "I've driven down there once but was spared from driving too far in. I've heard horror stories about the traffic."

"Sure isn't like what I was used to in Rhinelander and the surrounding area." Michael took a big bite of doughnut, closed his eyes, and threw his head back, "Oh my gosh." He held up the pastry with reverence. "Just as amazing as I remember." He set the pastry down and took a sip of coffee before he continued. "I don't mind the traffic though. I went down to Milwaukee and Chicago many times to see a couple of my buddies there. You know I went to college in Madison, so I used to head down there for Badger games and over to Green Bay for Packers games. Dad had season tickets. They all have traffic, so Charlotte wasn't too bad. I kind of liked it. And there are some nice smaller towns around its outskirts that give it that small-town flare."

"I guess I'll have to venture in further the next time I go down there," Rebekah considered.

"You should go there occasionally and check out places similar to yours. Keep up with the trends and competition—even if it's not in your town. That's what Dad and I would do. Any time I went out of town, he gave me a list of places he wanted me to check out. If we found a new idea, we would tweak it and make it ours." Michael took a breath in and out. "I miss that."

"I bet you do. I can't imagine losing your dad *and* a place in the company you helped him build all at the same time. You lost your identity." As the words left Rebekah's mouth, it occurred to her that she and Michael were not dissimilar in that regard. She, too, had lost her identity after all was revealed about Ethan. No wonder Michael had come down to Asheville to find her.

"Yes," Michael said simply. "I did. Now I'm searching to find my next chapter. Just knew it wasn't up there." He tossed his head. "Enough of me. I've told you all there is to tell. I want to hear about how you got to this place."

She told him her story about moving to Milwaukee to live by the boys and how her search for her sister had brought her to Asheville only to find that Dee had passed away. She talked about finding Rose and meeting Lois, and she explained how she and Lois had "worked out a deal" so Rebekah could open Marie Claudine's and stay in Asheville to be a part of Rose's life—the next best thing to being with Dee.

"Wow, kinda like it was meant to be," Michael said, his face beaming.

"Yes, exactly. That's why I went for it. I didn't think I could go wrong. I might add that Dee and Rose actually lived in the apartment upstairs. Even though I had it gutted and everything reconfigured, I find contentment in knowing she lived here." One little spontaneous tear formed in the corner of Rebekah's eye that she discreetly wiped away with her finger.

"Man, Rebekah, this could be a great book—or a movie," Michael said, not noticing the tear.

They continued to chitchat for another thirty minutes about home in Wisconsin.

"Would you like me to give you the tour?" Rebekah asked as Michael took his last sip of coffee.

"I thought you'd never ask," he responded, and they both laughed.

Rebekah started by sharing how she and Lois had spent months collecting the tables and chairs to give the space that "eclectic but traditional" look. "I don't know how she did it, but Lois came up with all these great pictures," she said, gesturing to the wide shiplap wall in front of them. "She also asked me for a snapshot of my grandmother and then found an artist to paint this lovely portrait of her."

Michael walked over to the painting and scrutinized it for a moment before he commented, not taking his eyes off of it, "I don't imagine you know this, but I enjoy painting. This is an exquisite job. Haven't picked up a brush in a while myself though."

"No, I didn't know you painted. That's amazing. I'd be afraid to see what I might come up with if I tried to paint. Definitely abstract art." Rebekah laughed.

"You might surprise yourself. Makes me think maybe I should start again." He turned away from the painting and faced Rebekah before he continued. "Lots of beautiful scenery here. Now show me the rest of this place."

She took him to the kitchen next so he could meet her staff. Rebekah knew some of them—Cathy and Lois in particular—were dying to talk to Michael. He shared a couple of funny stories about working with Rebekah at Fred's in Rhinelander and ended by telling them how great she was.

"Thank you, Michael, you're too kind, but I do remember some run-ins we've had also," Rebekah admitted.

"I don't remember that, Rebekah," Michael said with a very serious and concerned look on his face, then crossed his fingers on both hands and placed them behind his back. He stared at Rebekah for a moment until he broke into a big smile that made everyone laugh.

"Michael, let me take you over to the tea area. I'm in charge of that. Would love to get your expert opinion if you don't mind." Lois took Michael by the arm and led him that way.

"It would be my pleasure, Lois," Michael said and followed her lead.

"He seems like such a nice guy, Rebekah," Cathy said with a rather excited tone, gazing at Michael as he left the kitchen.

"He is. I've known him a long time. I was sixteen when I started working as a cashier for his dad's store. So much has happened since then." Rebekah let out a deep sigh, shook her head, and was back to business. "How's everything going here?" she asked Katy.

"It's great, Miss Rebekah," said Katy. "Miss Cathy here runs a tight ship."

"That's how we become successful," Cathy added, "right, Rebekah?"

"I couldn't agree more," Rebekah concurred. "So show me what you all have been working on."

After a few minutes, Rebekah could see that Lois was having way too much fun with Michael in the tea area and that maybe she should rescue him.

"I better save Michael from Lois. I'm going to show him the rest of the shop and the apartment, and then I'll be back." Rebekah headed out to the store where Lois was laughing and talking a mile a minute.

"Rebekah, you'll never believe it. This nice young man is living in a house in my neighborhood. You'll just have to come to dinner sometime." She turned to Michael. "I insist," Lois added, with her usual charm.

"Well, okay. Umm, sounds good. You folks are going to be busy the next couple of weeks so, you know, don't feel you have to invite me over. I'll probably be by here for some of my meals for sure," Michael said, blushing.

"Leave the poor guy alone, Lois," Rebekah laughed as she spoke. "He's not used to Southern hospitality yet."

"Oh hush, Rebekah. We'll talk again soon, Michael." Lois gave him a little pat on the arm before departing.

Rebekah couldn't stop smiling. "Glad we got that out of the way. Lois is a dear soul, and I don't know what I would do without her, but—" She turned and looked as Lois went into the kitchen. "—she is a *presence*. Now let me show you the back of the shop and the apartment before I take you to meet my son Andrew. He handles all the business end and has a degree in accounting from UW Milwaukee."

Andrew was in his usual position, looking at the computer screen with papers organized in neat stacks all around him. Rebekah gave a little knock on the open door, and he looked up.

"I want you to officially meet Michael, son."

Andrew stood up and gestured for them to come in. "Michael—" Andrew extended his hand. "—pleased to meet you. Mom has nothing but good things to say about you. Welcome to Asheville."

"Thank you, Andrew. So far, I'm enjoying it," Michael responded and shook his hand. "How's it going? Your mom says you're the business brains of this operation."

Andrew laughed. "I guess I am. I do enjoy it though."

"I've seen the whole place, and I have to say you've done a great job. I did a lot of the business end for my dad also at the store. Everything good with your computer programs? I did purchasing also. Any challenges there? I'd be happy to give you any advice if you need some help."

"Well, now that you mention it, I have a couple of things I'm working through that are new to me that you may be able to clear up. Mom, do you mind if I monopolize Michael for a bit?" Andrew turned to his mother.

"No, son. You two take your time. I'm heading back up front to see how things are going since we open tomorrow at seven." Rebekah opened her eyes wide and took a deep breath. "Michael, you and Andrew enjoy yourselves, but make sure you say bye before you leave." She gave a wave and headed to the kitchen.

All was under control, and at 4 p.m., Rebekah sent everyone home, telling them to get a good night's sleep. They opened at 7 a.m. but would arrive to work at 5 to start baking. The time might even be moved earlier as business picked up.

Rebekah stuck her head in Andrew's office where he and Michael still had their noses glued to the computer screen.

"Hey, guys. Need to come up for air?" Rebekah teased.

"Ah, hi, Mom. We're good. Michael helped me figure out something," Andrew responded.

"We're doing good here. This boy of yours is a smart son of a gun." Michael chuckled and looked to Andrew. "I guess I better be heading out, but I am coming by for lunch tomorrow, so I'll see you then." He turned to Andrew. "Hey, if you have any more questions, you can ask me tomorrow. How's that?"

"Great," Andrew replied and got up to let Michael out the locked front door.

"Michael—" Rebekah stopped him. "Would you do one thing for me tonight? Please call Tammy and tell her where you are. I'm assuming no one knew you headed down here? Everyone at Fred's has been very concerned about you," Rebekah pleaded before he left.

"Why sure, Rebekah. It's nice of them to be concerned about me. I'll let Tammy know and tell her what a great place you have." Michael gave Rebekah a warm smile, and he walked to the front with Andrew.

Rebekah went upstairs to the apartment to cook supper. When she finished, she hollered downstairs for Andrew to come up.

They sat down to eat, and Andrew started the conversation.

"Mom, you know how bummed you were when Don didn't want to come to work here?" Andrew asked.

"Well, yes, but it will all work out. Why do you ask?"

"I want to hire Michael. He knows everything about running a place like this. I mean, there is no way we can't succeed with him on board. He taught me more this afternoon than I've learned since we started this place. He suggested a few things I never even thought of for promoting us. I don't know that we could afford to pay him enough with all the stuff he knows, but I would like to at least ask him. How do you feel about it?" Andrew looked hopeful.

This took Rebekah by surprise. Michael working for them? It would take a lot of pressure off her and Andrew. Maybe he would work part-time? He did know the food part as well as the store part—and staffing.

"You've taken me off guard. How about I think about it?"

"Sounds fair. We'll see how things go and then decide. We may do better than we think. Just have to build up our confidence," Andrew asserted.

"True. We don't know until we get started, right?"

"Right. We've got this."

As they ate silently, both were thinking the same thing. Michael could be a win for them. But how could they make it work? That was the question.

Chapter 27

The next ten days were a test of endurance for Rebekah and her team. She and Cathy baked their hearts out. Word was out about the new teahouse, and people were curious. Needless to say, the grand opening was a huge success. Rebekah was grateful for all the traffic—and also that they were closed on Sundays.

Monday morning, Stacy, one of the young women she had hired, gave notice because she had found another job. Then Sara called in sick because she had a headache. Rebekah called Katy to see if she could come in, but she was out of town and wouldn't be back until that evening. Cathy's girls and Rose were in classes that morning but would be in around noon. That left Andrew to don an apron and fill in until more help arrived.

When Rebekah locked the door at five that afternoon, Andrew said, "We need to talk."

"We'll talk after all my work is done," she told him.

At 7:15, Rebekah was finally able to sit down in his office. She collapsed into the chair across from his desk and held her head in her hands, exhausted.

"Have you given my idea about hiring Michael any more thought?"

Rebekah had figured that was what he was going to ask. "I have, but what I really think I need is another baker to free me up," Rebekah answered.

"Honestly, Mom, I don't think that is the total answer. Yes, you need another person who can bake, but we're talking about a guy here who has *so* much knowledge and sense about the business we've entered into. You know baking, and I know accounting—but Michael knows *business*. Having him on board would increase our success rate, *and* he would be teaching me things for the future. I looked up some statistics. The first year, sixty percent of new businesses like ours fail. I don't want us to be in that statistic." Andrew's voice was strained, and he cleared his throat. "And what about when we have to leave for James's wedding in November? Have you thought about that? You, me, and Rose are going. I don't want to even think about how stressed out you and I are going to be while we're there."

She had thought about the wedding and knew it was going to be tough, but now that Marie Claudine's was open, reality was sinking in. Rebekah felt sick to her stomach, and a wave of panic came over her. Maybe she shouldn't have opened the business. She took a breath and shook her head. *No.* This was her dream. And then she thought of the promise she had made to Mère about opening a bakery someday. This wasn't just Rebekah's dream but Mère's also. Rebekah was the one blessed with the task of making it come true. She closed her eyes and said a silent, heartfelt prayer. *Oh God, what should I do?* After a moment, she felt the heavy feeling lift and the sick churn in her stomach dissipate as it was replaced by a wave of calmness. A voice spoke in her mind. *Don't let your energy flow that way. You choose where it should go. Focus on the positive. You have the power within you.*

"Mom. Mom! Are you okay?" Andrew was at his mother's side.

"What? Yes, son. Why?" Rebekah responded.

"For a moment I thought you were going to pass out. Here's some water. Take a drink."

"I'm fine." Rebekah put her hand up and assured him. "Yes, give Michael a call and ask if we can meet with him tomorrow, right after closing. How does that sound?"

"Sounds good. I've been doing research on situations like ours where you take someone on who helps with company organization. I propose we offer him a low base pay and then a percentage of yearly profit with a cap for his services. This is pretty common in the business world. What do you think?" Andrew waited while Rebekah thought for a few moments.

"I'm impressed with your research. You're quite the businessman, Andrew. This definitely is your calling. Yes, I think let's do it. After my conversation with him the other day, I think Michael is looking for something to do, and this might be just what he needs to help him find his way. Good job." She got up and gave Andrew a hug and kiss on the cheek.

"Thanks, Mom," Andrew said, hugging her back. "I'll have to get some legal papers drawn up if Michael agrees. Oh, and tonight you also need to give Don a call to see if he can suggest someone to hire as a baker."

"I will. Now let's call it a day."

"Sure, Mom. Let me give Michael a call first."

***

The next day, right before closing, Michael stopped by. Andrew met him at the door and ushered him to his office.

"He's back, Rebekah," Cathy said, checking Michael out as the men walked across the store. "Are you dating him yet?"

Rebekah laughed. "No, Cathy. I told you. We're just good friends."

"Then what's he doing here again?" Cathy asked.

She certainly is nosy, Rebekah thought. "Not sure" was all she answered as she shook her head.

Soon Lois, equally as nosy, was interrogating Rebekah.

"I see your friend is back. Anything special going on tonight?" Lois asked, raising an eyebrow.

Rebekah pulled Lois aside. She didn't mind telling her what was going on, since Lois had been in business herself for years. She might even give Rebekah some good advice. "Andrew suggested we might want to hire Michael to help out around here. I'm not going to lie, Lois. I'm overwhelmed. You have been a huge help, but I need more. Michael has tons of experience, and he is a hard worker. We're going to ask him if he would consider coming to work with us."

"Dear, I think that's an excellent idea. I'm happy to work all that I can, but this place has taken off like a *rocket*. If we can't service the customers, we will lose them."

Rebekah opened her eyes wide and nodded. Lois spoke the truth.

"Exactly. And I also called Don to send us some people we could interview as bakers. That will help free me up some and give Cathy a day off during the week. Also, having Michael here will be great help when we go to James's wedding. I can't believe I was concerned about not having enough business." Rebekah rolled her eyes and scoffed.

"The problem you have is one that most new businesses would love to have, Rebekah," Lois assured her. "But business can go up and down. It did many times with our clothing store. It was feast or famine for us."

"I expect after the first of the year we'll have a better handle on this and know what to expect," she said. "If you think you have everything under control, I'm going back to Andrew's office."

"Why yes, dear. I'll take care of things. Good night in case I leave before you're finished with your meeting. Hope all goes well." Lois gave her a smile and hug.

"Oh, great. Here's Mom, so let's begin," Andrew said as Rebekah entered his office. He and his mom had decided he would to be in charge of working out logistics with Michael.

"Hi, Michael. We appreciate you coming by," Rebekah said.

"You've got my curiosity going." Michael had a big smile on his face, looking from Rebekah to Andrew. "What's up?"

"After being open for just over a week," Andrew started, "we've realized we need some help. Our uniqueness has already attracted a lot of customers, and we can't keep up. I'm not going to beat around the bush, Michael. We were wondering if you would be interested in coming on board with us. You would be a manager like my mom and me. Only thing is, we don't have a lot of capital right now to pay you a big salary. So here's what we propose: a nominal salary, but at the end of the year, we'll give you ten percent of our profit—up to a certain amount. I talked with our lawyer, and he'll draw up some papers with all the details if you think you might be interested."

Michael sat for a good long while before he spoke. "I wasn't expecting this. I honestly didn't want to work for a while but ..." He trailed off and sat, his face puzzled as he thought.

It was Rebekah's turn. "Michael, we want you to think about it—be sure you would want to work with us. You don't have to decide right now."

"You have the experience and knowledge we need to run this business. I knew that immediately the other day when we talked. I would consider you a mentor," Andrew shared.

Again, Michael sat for a long while before responding. "I can't deny, your little place here gives me a bit of excitement. I miss Fred's Market—but mostly being there with Dad." Michael thought a moment. "Send me your offer, and I will look it over and think about it. Give me the weekend. Would that be okay?"

"Sure," Andrew answered.

"How about you stay and have supper with us?" Rebekah suggested. "Andrew and I are just going to make a couple of sandwiches in the kitchen and take them upstairs. We would love it if you joined us, wouldn't we Andrew?"

"Yes, we would," Andrew agreed.

"Sure," Michael answered. "I was just going to eat some leftovers I had from yesterday that I didn't really want." He chuckled.

Rebekah led the way. She was hoping if Michael spent some time with them, he would see how nice it could be and feel more receptive to Andrew's offer.

Fingers crossed.

Chapter 28

On Monday, Michael gave Andrew a call and said he would like to come by. Andrew told him closing time would be best, and Michael was there five minutes before they locked the door, with Andrew making sure he was available to greet him.

"Michael, glad to see you." Andrew shook his hand. "Let's go back to my office."

As soon as Rebekah could get away, she joined them. Fortunately, Cathy had left an hour early that day, so Rebekah was able to avoid any further interrogation from her. But Lois still gave her a wink and a smile as Rebekah headed back to the office to find out what Michael's decision would be.

"Michael," Rebekah greeted him, "I hope this visit is because you've made your decision." She felt a fluttering in her stomach and was hopeful.

"I have." Michael paused, causing Rebekah's stomach to flip-flop, and then gave them a big smile. "I'm gonna do it.

"Oh, Michael. I can't tell you how happy that makes us." Rebekah looked to Andrew who was smiling and calm.

"Wait a minute .... I do have some stipulations," Michael added.

"I'm ready to hear them." Andrew grinned.

"I only want to work Monday through Thursday, but I can help out in a pinch on a Friday or Saturday if really needed. Otherwise, I like your terms. When can I start?" Michael asked with a big smile on his face.

"Wonderful! How about tomorrow at seven? I'm serious." Andrew chuckled and extended his hand to Michael who shook it.

"Tomorrow it is," Michael said and smiled.

"Wow! Michael, I can't tell you how much this means to me. I feel a load lifted off my shoulders," Rebekah said and leaned back in her chair.

"It means a lot to me also," Michael admitted. "I've been trying to figure out what I should do next and where I fit in. I thought I knew where my life would go—running the store that Dad and I built together. I have to admit, I've been kinda lost since he passed. This has given me the direction I really need in my life right now, and I'm grateful."

"Well, so are we," Andrew said. "I'll get the final paperwork together with our lawyer. He said he could get it ready in a day or so. Let me give him a call in the morning, okay?"

They said their goodbyes, and Andrew walked Michael to the door to let him out.

"I better call the lawyer," Andrew said when he came back to the office, and he dialed the number. "Hey, man," he said when the attorney answered. "Listen, that deal I was working on came through, so let's go ahead with the paperwork. When can I get it? … Okay. Sure, just email them to me. Everything good where you are? … When might we see you? … Well, make sure you come by. Remember lunch is on us. Thanks so much, man. Don't know what we'd do without you. Bye."

He hung up and let out a sigh, then glanced at Rebekah who was staring at him with a puzzled expression. She hadn't even known they *had* a lawyer, let alone one who Andrew was so friendly with.

"Sweetheart, who were you talking to?" she asked. "I have to confess, I don't even know our lawyer's name. Shouldn't I?"

Andrew stared at her for a moment then laughed. "Seriously? You know him very well, Mom. It's Harrison. Remember, he has a law degree?"

Rebekah's jaw dropped, and she nodded in slow motion. Andrew laughed again when he saw her expression.

"Ah, right. So he can do that kind of business stuff?"

"Sure can. I've been using him for *all* our legal stuff." Andrew smiled from ear to ear. "And if it's something Harrison can't do for us, Doug takes care of it. Don't know what I would've done without that. Harrison's the one who suggested we pay Michael a lower salary and then a yearly profit share. Gives Michael a vested interest in our success."

"Seems Harrison is a very multitalented individual," Rebekah concluded and raised her eyebrows.

Andrew looked at her with a serious, unwavering glance. "I'm glad you're finally figuring that out, Mom. You should tell him that next time you see him," Andrew teased, just barely containing his laughter.

Rebekah gave him that special look only your mother can give you, said, "Oh you," and left the office.

Chapter 29

"I can't tell you how much I appreciate you doing this with me, Rose. The wedding is the first weekend in November, only a month away, and I have to get my dress. I've never shopped for something so formal before," Rebekah confessed to Rose as they headed out to visit a couple of bridal shops in the Asheville area. Rebekah was happy to be able to spend some time with Rose that didn't involve work for a change. It also gave her a chance to see how things would run in the shop if she weren't there.

"Well, you're lucky you have me here then, because I never have either! I ordered my senior prom dress online. We can figure it out together," Rose rationalized. "Did you have a certain color in mind?"

"Not really. I've been told Violet's mom is wearing a long sage-green satin dress with a chiffon overlay and silver beading. No surprise, but Violet's bridesmaids are all wearing tea-length taffeta dresses in a *violet* shade." Rebekah chuckled. "I thought we could just find something to help me blend in that won't fight with those colors. And we need a dress for you too of course."

"Don't worry about me. I don't need a dress. I'm excited to have a chance to wear my prom dress again. It's a soft shade of periwinkle blue. I really like it—and know I look good in it." Rose giggled and tossed her hair playfully.

"I'm sure you look beautiful in it, but if you see something you absolutely love, I'll buy it for you. That's what aunts are for," Rebekah said and patted Rose on the arm.

The first bridal shop had several lovely options, but all of them needed to be ordered at least six weeks ahead of time. The second shop had a stock of discontinued dresses that could be purchased off the rack.

Rose came running over to Rebekah holding a blue dress and said, "This is the one. I know it."

The dress was lovely. It was a deep royal-blue color in a long, flattering A-line silhouette and was made of lightweight taffeta with a chiffon overlay. The top featured a scoop neck with a delicate floral lace accent woven into the chiffon around the upper bodice area, with the same floral lace used to make up the full-length sleeves. In the lower bodice, the chiffon was gathered up with accent ruching on the left side.

"Oh my" was all Rebekah said as she took in the stunning gown.

"It looks like you, Rebekah. This is your color *and* your size. Let's try it on," Rose said and took her by the hand to head to the dressing room.

The dress fit as if it had been made for Rebekah. The only alteration needed was taking up the hem a bit, and according to the woman at the shop, that could be done by the next week. While there, Rebekah found low-healed silver shoes and a clutch to match, as well as a simple silver rhinestone drop necklace and earrings. She was all set. Since it took less time than they had expected to accomplish their mission, and Rose hadn't found anything she liked more than her prom dress, Rebekah took Rose to lunch at her choice of restaurant before they headed back to work at Marie Claudine's.

***

It was soon approaching the end of October, and the business was running much more smoothly with Michael on board. Marie Claudine's now had the focus they had been searching for. Michael knew his stuff, and just as importantly, Michael and Andrew got along well and were a solid team. The whole experience—running his mother's new business and working under Michael's mentorship—was wonderful for Andrew. Even though Andrew had done well in college, he had been thrown into this venture only months after graduating and lacked practical experience. Michael had excellent hands-on experience and was a true mentor. He quickly showed the young man that just because Andrew had learned something in college did not mean it was necessarily the hard-and-fast rule for how to do things. Those textbook techniques and models were more of a guide, and you always had to adapt the rules to your individual business.

Just like life, Rebekah thought as she watched the two men work their magic during Michael's first few weeks at the shop.

Changes had already been made in the kitchen as well. Don Lester had given Rebekah the names of several people who might be interested in the bakery job. Rebekah interviewed all of them, but none seemed like the right fit, and they all wanted a supervisor position, which she couldn't offer.

Then one day, Katy came to her, said she would love to know more about baking, and asked if she could be trained on the job. Rebekah was thrilled at the idea because she knew she could train Katy for what she needed. So instead of hiring a new baker, she hired a front-of-house replacement for Katy, which saved the shop both money and time.

Fortunately, Katy followed instructions well, so Rebekah could leave her with Cathy. This allowed Rebekah to stay on top of all the little surprises that seemed to pop up here and there on a daily—sometimes hourly—basis.

Rose, as it turned out, was a bit of a tea expert herself since she had lived with Lois for so many years. It therefore seemed logical that Rebekah make her Lois's assistant in that area. Lois worked part-time, mostly mornings, so it was helpful to have Rose—who went to school in the morning and would work afternoons and Saturdays—to pick up the slack.

All employees were required to go through a Tea 101 education with Lois, including Rebekah, Andrew, and Michael. Tea was a big part of their business, so they all needed to be knowledgeable. Fortunately, Michael had come up with a computer program Lois could use to monitor tea inventory whether she was in the shop or at home. This made things very easy.

Rebekah was so pleased with the party room they had decided to include in the remodel. She and Lois had decorated the room in the same eclectic style as the front—with some variations. The walls were painted white with a hint of pink. As they had for the main dining area, they selected tables and chairs in different sizes and styles, but to make things extra festive, they covered the tables with different-colored pastel cloths and the chairs with white slip-covers sprinkled with little flowers in coordinating pastels. The room was so popular, they already had party bookings through November and people asking about December.

Lois happened to be in that day, even though it was a Saturday, setting up for an afternoon bridal shower. Rebekah walked in to see if she needed any help.

"How's it going?" she asked.

"Going well. I just love setting up these parties," Lois bubbled as she began setting cloth napkins at each place setting.

"Well, you're very good at it. It's the little touches you think up, Lois. You have exquisite taste."

"Oh, you make me blush," Lois sputtered. "I've always enjoyed doing this kind of stuff. I loved it back in the good old days when I would host dinner parties with my husband and our friends—using our china, crystal, and silver. It was so much fun."

"I've never had any of those things, so I wouldn't know," Rebekah confessed. "I lived in a parsonage, and my mother never had anything but stainless steel, plastic glasses, and everyday dishes. Most of what I had in the way of dishes and utensils up until now in my life was just functional. That's why I love my place upstairs so much; it's filled with all new stuff, picked out by me and not someone else."

"You're my kind of woman," Lois chortled as she started to place little vases of flowers on each table in the room. "Here, grab some of these vases and help me, dear."

Rebekah smiled at her. "Sure, Lois."

"Since I have you alone—" Lois stopped, looking from side to side even though no one else was there and the door was closed. "did you know Cathy has her sight set on *Michael*? I think he likes her also."

"No, I didn't. I guess I'm so busy, I missed it. Anyway, how do you know this? You're part-time and always out here—not in the kitchen," Rebekah noted.

"Rose keeps me abreast of the goings on here. Just call me if you're ever wondering anything."

Rebekah shook her head and laughed, then thought of something she *was* wondering about. "I *was* curious about how that job is going that Harrison is working on at Lake Lure? He came by here last week one day, but I was involved with a delivery from our food supplier, and I didn't get a chance to say hi. Hope all is okay. I asked Andrew how he was, and well you know how it is with boys, all he said was 'fine,'" Rebekah said, rolling her eyes as she imitated Andrew's baritone.

"Doug mentioned Harrison hasn't been home much, but it sounds like the job is going well. I believe in a few more weeks, it will be done and he'll be back here." Lois was very nonchalant. "Would you mind placing plates around each table?" she asked, and after a long pause, she added without looking at Rebekah, "You miss him, don't you?"

Rebekah, taken off guard, stopped in her tracks. "Ah, well, I—"

Lois laughed. "You don't have to pretend with me dear. And besides, I'll drag it out of you anyway."

It was true. Lois could extract information better than anyone Rebekah knew.

"Yes, I have missed seeing him," Rebekah admitted with a sigh, "which has surprised me. When I didn't get to talk to him the other day, I just wondered if all was good with him and when he would be finished, that's all. You've provided that information for me. Thank you."

"Okay, okay. Here, could you put these on each table." Lois gave her a sideways glance, smiled, and handed her a tray holding some small bowls of dinner mints. "So let's change the subject to something *I* want to know. When do you leave for your son's wedding, and when will you be back?"

"We're going to fly into Green Bay the Sunday before the wedding so we can visit my mom. Sadly, according to my brothers, she's not in any shape to travel and attend the wedding. My oldest brother, Tom, said she seems so frail, he's afraid all the travel and festivities would be too much for her. We'll stay at her house while we're there. On Tuesday, we drive down to Milwaukee. Thursday is a bridesmaid luncheon. This will give me a chance to meet some of Violet's family before the wedding. I've met her parents before, but I don't really know them. Friday night is the rehearsal dinner, which I'm paying for. I told James he and Violet should just pick a place they like and set everything up. Then wedding is Saturday, and we'll fly back on Monday." Rebekah took a deep breath and let it out slowly. "Phew!"

"So you'll rent a car?" Lois asked.

"Yes, and return it in Milwaukee before we fly back to Asheville."

"Is the wedding large?"

"It sounds like it's not too terribly big. It's mostly her family and friends and I imagine some of James's friends. I really don't have many friends up there, you know. My brothers and some of their family members are coming also, I think. The wedding and reception are all in the same place, at a hotel, so I've made reservations for Andrew, Rose, and me to stay on Friday, Saturday, and Sunday night. I got a suite. Just makes it easier."

"You have everything all set it sounds like. Maybe Andrew will marry a girl from down here and we can plan a wedding …. Did you notice I included myself in that?" Lois chuckled.

"I did and wouldn't have it any other way." Rebekah smiled.

"I was wondering if there was any special girl in his life now?" Lois queried, making sure she didn't make eye contact with Rebekah.

"None that I'm aware of," Rebekah responded. "It would be nice if he and Rose could both find someone."

Yes it would, Lois thought, continuing to set the tables.

"Lois, I hope you know how much I appreciate you offering to work every day while we're gone."

"It's my pleasure, dear. I'll just defer to Michael." Lois smiled.

"As I do all the time," Rebekah agreed.

"The wedding is two weeks from today, and you leave a week from this Sunday, yes? I sure hope Harrison comes to see us before you leave," Lois said as she pointed to some sugar bowls filled with sugar cubes. "Could you place those next, dear?"

"Stop it," Rebekah warned with a half smile on her face before she went to retrieve the sugar bowls.

"Okay, okay, but there's one last thing I have to ask about the wedding. Will the boys' birth mother and father be there?" Lois had asked the one main thing Rebekah was wondering herself.

"I don't know, and I haven't asked James. I'm preparing myself for a yes—they probably will be—and if they aren't, great. I really don't think James cares either way if his dad comes." Rebekah paused and rubbed the back of her neck for a moment. "I'm not going to lie, Lois; I feel sick to my stomach just *thinking* about them being there. I know my four brothers will be bodyguards to protect me. They never did really like Ethan that much, and now they despise him. One of my brothers offered to go beat him up after I told them about Ethan's deceit—and he meant it."

"Be aloof but polite. That has always served me well in awkward situations." Lois put her hand on Rebekah's shoulder. "You are a tough one, a survivor, and you will survive this. I can't wait till it's over and I can hear all the juicy details from you and Rose. I would love to be a fly on the wall," she said, rubbing her hands together.

"Oh, I'm sure we'll have lots of 'juicy details' for you—even if Ethan and Emily don't show up. Between my family and Violet's, there are some characters, and it *is* a Wisconsin wedding. They are never boring." She chuckled and shook her head. "I've got to go check the kitchen," she said and left Lois to finish setting up the party room.

Chapter 30

"What kind of scone of the day have you decided on for next week while I'm gone, Cathy?" Rebekah asked.

Rebekah, Andrew, and Rose were leaving the next day to head to Wisconsin for the wedding.

"Let me see here," Cathy said and then read from a typed-up list: "Monday and Tuesday, Pumpkin Caramel; Wednesday and Thursday, Lemon Dream; and Friday and Saturday, Triple Chocolate Obsession—everybody's favorite."

Rebekah contemplated. "Okay, but I wonder if we should swap out the Friday and Saturday flavor since it's such a big favorite and we usually have to make double if we don't want to run out—just to make it a little easier on you?"

"You're right, everybody seems to buy two or more of those. Good call. Hey, how about cinnamon raisin? It's a nice fall flavor."

Rebekah thought a moment. "I think that's a great idea. Let's do that one. See how it goes, and we can maybe add it to the rotation."

"There's something else I want to experiment and try." Cathy paused for dramatic effect and raised her hands a bit. "How does a maple, brown sugar, bacon scone sound?"

"Oh my gosh, yes!" Rebekah gasped. "I'll be happy to taste test that one. Let's try it when I get back. People are crazy over anything bacon. I was thinking we need to come up with some good savory scones, say in a mini size. People will want to order them for parties, don't you think?"

"Oh, I have a bunch of recipes for those. I used to make them all the time for my home baking business. I think we've got a lot to do when you get back." Cathy gave a lighthearted laugh.

Rebekah patted her on the back. "Yes, we'll be gearing up for our first holiday season. I'll be back a week from Monday, so Tuesday morning after the rush is past, let's you and I have a meeting to talk things over so we're on the same page. I have several ideas in mind, but I want your thoughts also. I need to go talk to Michael and then the sandwich staff unless there's anything else we need to go over?"

Cathy shook her head no, and with a quick wave, Rebekah headed out to look for Michael who she found in the storage room. He had graciously told her he would work every day while she was gone.

"You sure got us well stocked, Rebekah. Don't worry about a thing—this place will still be standing when you get back," he assured her with a chuckle.

"Honestly, Michael, I don't know how I would even be able to leave tomorrow if you weren't here. I'm so grateful. I just want to give you a big hug," she said. She playfully threw her arms around him and gave him a peck on the cheek as Michael warmly returned her hug. At that precise moment, Cathy walked in and stopped dead in her tracks. Rebekah and Michael both looked toward her, mortified as they stood there wrapped in each other's arms.

"Oh, I—" Her chin quivered as she stumbled over her words. "I'm so sorry—I didn't know." Her face quickly reddened as she turned and rushed out.

Rebekah frowned, remembering what Lois had told her about Cathy having her sights set on Michael. "Oh, my goodness. I better go check on her," she said, gave Michael a quick pat on the shoulder, and left him standing there, dazed.

Rebekah found Cathy alone in the kitchen, crying. "Hey, you. What was that about?"

"I didn't realize you and Michael were seeing each other," Cathy said, now beyond distraught.

"We're just longtime friends, Cathy. I've told you that several times. We're not seeing each other. Why? Do you like him?"

Cathy turned her back to Rebekah as she wiped away a tear and blew her nose. After a moment, she slowly nodded.

"Then go for it! He's a wonderful guy. We've known each other since we were kids, and there's nothing more than friendship between us—I promise. If you like him, let him know. I think he's lonely and would like some companionship."

"Do you really think so?" Cathy asked red-faced but finally having gotten control.

"Yes." Rebekah opened her arms for a hug, and Cathy sheepishly accepted. "And you know he could use someone to help him adapt to the South."

"You're right, Rebekah. I bet he could." Cathy chuckled as she wiped a few lingering tears from her cheeks. "Hey, I think I'll invite him to my church this Sunday." Cathy's whole demeanor changed as she realized she still had a chance.

As Rebekah turned and walked away, she let out a sigh, hoping beyond hope that Michael would be fond of Cathy too—otherwise who knows what she would have to deal with when she returned.

***

Michael was kind enough to offer Rebekah, Andrew, and Rose a ride to the airport Sunday morning to catch their flight. They had decided to fly out of the Asheville/Hendersonville airport, which meant a slightly longer flight but made the trip there easier so they wouldn't have to drive all the way to Charlotte Douglas Airport now that Marie Claudine's was in the picture.

On the plane, Rose and Andrew sat together in one row, and Rebekah sat behind them by herself. She was relieved to have no seatmate—no awkward stranger wanting to talk and make friends—because she had something to think about.

The night before, Harrison had showed up just as they were closing the shop. He went to talk with Andrew in his office for a while, but after everyone else had left, he sought her out when she was alone in the kitchen.

"Hey, Rebekah. I was just talking to Andrew, and he was telling me how well you all are doing. I can't tell you how happy that makes me. I'm so excited for you."

"We're not setting the world on fire yet, but I've got my fingers crossed," she said, and they both let out a little chuckle.

There was an awkward silence as they both looked down at the floor then back up at each other.

Harrison removed the well-worn navy ball cap he always wore and ran his fingers through his disheveled sandy-brown hair. "Um, Andrew said you get back a week from Monday?"

"Yep. I hate that we can't fly back Sunday, but the only flight we could get that day has several stops and gets in at ten at night. Instead, we got a flight with just one stop early Monday morning that gets us in here at one o'clock. At least then I can get back to the shop before we close for the day and be ready to go on Tuesday."

"Great. So …" He looked down again and fumbled his cap in his hands for a moment before he spoke. "I was wondering if you would let me take you out to dinner sometime after you get back?" He looked her in the eyes warmly and smiled.

Rebekah's heart did an immediate flip-flop. She hadn't been expecting this. Having been married at age eighteen, she had never had a man ask her to dinner before—not like this. What should she say? She hesitated.

As Harrison studied her face, his eyebrows drooped, crestfallen with the long silence.

She took a breath. "Yes, Harrison." Another breath. "I would love to go to dinner with you." She smiled and exhaled.

The color came back to Harrison's face. "Well, great. Great. That's just great!"

"Great!" Rebekah repeated with a little laugh.

"How about I call you on Monday? Or maybe even better—I can stop by here, and we can see how things are after you being gone, and then we can pick an evening for dinner."

"I think that sounds—lovely." Her eyes met his, and she beamed.

"I better let you go. I'm sure you have things to do yet tonight."

"I do," she responded.

"Do y'all need a ride to the airport?"

"No, Michael has already offered to take us and pick us up, but thank you. I appreciate your offer."

"Okay then. Have a safe trip." He quietly looked her in the eyes and took a slow breath, hesitating only for a moment before he stepped forward and engulfed her in his arms.

Rebekah felt the gentle rise and fall of his chest against her cheek and lingered there a while until he slowly pulled back and softly kissed her lips.

With a wide grin, Harrison replaced his ball cap, gave her a quick wink, and headed out the door.

She noted a slight lift in his step as she watched him depart, and it was only then that she exhaled.

Just then, the airplane captain announced he had turned off the Fasten Seat Belt sign, allowing passengers to move about the cabin, and Rebekah was pulled back to the present.

Andrew stood up and looked over the back of his seat at his mom. "You doing okay, Mom? Why are you smiling like that?"

Rebekah shook her head and chuckled. She hadn't even realized she was smiling. "Just happy to be going to the wedding, son." *Good answer*, she thought.

They had a layover in Chicago before arriving in Green Bay where they picked up the rental car they would be using and embarked on the two-hour drive to visit Rebekah's mother Ruth.

Ben greeted them at Ruth's house when they arrived. Since he now lived in Green Bay, he would always stay with his mom when he visited the family. He informed them that Ruth was taking her afternoon rest. This gave Rebekah a chance to freely ask Ben about her.

"How is she doing?" Rebekah asked.

"Better, I think, than the last time you saw her. I don't see her as often as our brothers do, but she doesn't seem any worse. Even though she looks frail—like a strong wind could pick her up and blow her away—she's got a strength about her. Mom was never a big woman, but she's always been tough as nails and held her own. For the most part, she still cooks for herself, but we still keep her freezer stocked with meals to make it easier if she has a rough day. She has a woman close to her age who comes in two times a week to help clean, take her shopping, and be a companion. Mom seems to like her, which helps. I always stay with her whenever I come home to visit."

Rebekah felt sad, a little guilty, to hear all this. Being so far away in Asheville, she hated that she couldn't help, and she had said as much to Andrew several times before. His response was always the same: "Mom, you have been drawn to where you are. Your brothers are where they are and more than capable to take care of things. You have no reason to feel guilty." She sighed. Maybe he was right.

"We figured tonight you would be tired from your flights and the drive here, so we're going to order pizza," Ben continued. "Tom, Steve, and Jake are coming over, and tomorrow we're going to have an early Thanksgiving as a family at Steve's house. Turkey with all the trimmings. You're leaving on Tuesday to drive down to Milwaukee, right?"

"Yes," Rebekah confirmed. "Got to take part in all the wedding festivities, you know. You're all coming to the wedding, aren't you?"

"All of us except Mom. We didn't think the trip would be good for her—too much excitement."

"You know what's best," Rebekah said.

"Hey Mom, Rose and I will get the luggage out of the car," Andrew said, and they headed out, leaving the siblings alone.

"Rebekah, before they come back, we were all wondering if Ethan was going to be at the wedding? We're just worried about you."

"I have no idea, Ben. I'll admit, I've been afraid to ask, and I think the boys are afraid to tell me. Honestly, I never bring up his name, so neither do they. I hope he's not, but he is James's dad. I'll find out later this week and will just have to deal with it if he's there. No need to worry about it right now and spoil everything," she said assuredly.

"Well, you won't be alone at the wedding if he is there. We've discussed it amongst ourselves, and we will protect you from him.

That son of a—you know what—won't get near you," Ben said with determination.

"I was kind of hoping that." She smiled and gave her brother a hug. "Emily also. Don't forget about her. I don't think the woman is stable."

"Oh, don't worry, we'll have all the bases covered." Ben chuckled and nodded his head.

"Hey, Ben," Andrew called, interrupting them as he came in with their suitcases, "same rooms as last time?"

"Yeah, sounds good," Ben responded.

Rebekah went upstairs to settle in. Soon her mom would be up from her nap.

***

Later, when her mom was up and Rebekah's other brothers came over to visit, they all gathered in the living room to reminisce. It was nice that it was a Sunday and they could all relax together.

"Do you remember the time we were driving to Upper Michigan to visit relatives and left Steve in the gas station restroom?" Tom said. "Rebekah you were probably too small to remember, but if it weren't for you, I don't think we would have missed him till we got there. You were about three and kept saying 'Seeve!' which is how you said his name. Your voice was so soft, and we were all so loud no one heard you. Dee finally said, 'Mama, I think little sister is trying to tell us something. She keeps saying Seeve.' Mom turned around, did a quick head count, and immediately said 'Darrell, turn around! We lost Steve!'"

Everyone was laughing hysterically.

Ruth let out a few more chuckles and wiped tears from her eyes before she spoke. "It's true! When we got there, Steve was sitting on a bench waiting. I jumped out and hugged him, but your dad came over and asked him why he wasn't in the car. I shot your dad a dirty look. As we walked to the car, Steve looked up at me with big eyes and said, 'I told the lady inside the gas station not to worry, because you would be back for me.'"

"Well, I guess it's time to tell you the truth, Steve," Jake said with a solemn look as he scanned his other siblings. "You may not know this, but the family did take a vote before coming back for you and well … it was only by one vote we ended up coming to retrieve you," Jake said flatly and shrugged his shoulders.

Everyone roared even more with laughter.

"I don't remember everything from when I was young, but I do remember that," Steve said with a fixed gaze. "Made a permanent, etched memory. From that time on if we ever made a bathroom stop, I made sure I was the first one in the restroom and first one out of it—and back in the car."

"And I always did a head count from then on," Ruth added.

It had been a fun night.

"Look at the clock," Jake said. "It's ten o'clock. I bet you guys are tired. You had a long day."

"We did," Rebekah concurred. "How about you, Rose? Are you tired?" The girl had been quieter than usual.

"I am tired, but I'm really enjoying all these stories. Mostly I'm looking forward to tomorrow," Rose replied. "My first Thanksgiving with my family."

"That's right! We have many reasons to celebrate tomorrow," Tom replied, "and we sure want to know you better, Rose. In fact, we closed the auto shop tomorrow because we're having our Thanksgiving early with you all. I'm going fishing in the morning and would love it if you and Andrew tagged along. How does that sound?"

Poor Rose was taken by surprise. "I don't know much about fishing."

"Nothing to it," Andrew said and patted her on the shoulder, sensing her discomfort. "Count us both in, Uncle Tom."

Rose just smiled.

Tom, Jake, and Steve left. Andrew and Rose went up to bed as did Ben, leaving Rebekah and her mother alone.

"It's so good to have you here, Rebekah, and to see Rose again. Such a beautiful young woman," Ruth remarked.

"Yes, I love being in her life. She's a great addition to our family for sure." Rebekah loved the girl as if she were her own.

There was a pause as the two women sat in comfortable silence. Then Rebekah took her mother's hand before she spoke again. "Mom, I can't tell you how happy I am to see you. You seem to have settled into your life as it is now, and I think that's good."

"Yes, it is but I think it's coming close to my time, and I'm ready," Ruth responded.

This took Rebekah by surprise. She remembered Mère stating something similar not long before she passed away.

"I try to keep going, but I don't know. I don't feel I belong in this world anymore."

Ruth looked at her daughter, and Rebekah could see the love in her mother's eyes, something unfamiliar to Rebekah. Rebekah had always felt she never measured up to what her mother expected of her. Even after she married Ethan at her parents' insistence, her mother had always found fault with what Rebekah chose to do, ranging from her job at Fred's to the way she did things at home and how she raised the boys. Never a kind word. But now her mother had transformed into someone kind—and thoughtful. Rebekah wasn't going to question the transformation but rather accept it, and gladly.

"Just keep trying, Mom. I'll come back again for a visit next year. I have to get through this first holiday season in my new shop. I wish you could see it. My wish is for you to feel better so you can come visit me and see it. Maybe one day you could?"

"Oh my, no, I'm not sure Rebekah. You just come here and see me." She patted Rebekah's hand.

"Well, let's keep it in mind, Mom." Rebekah smiled.

"I think it's bedtime," Ruth announced.

They went upstairs and Rebekah gave her mom a long hug before they went to their separate rooms and closed the doors. Rebekah sat on her bed and immediately began to cry. Why couldn't her mother have been more like she was tonight when Rebekah was a girl? All her life Rebekah had wanted to feel the love her mom seemed to give so freely now. Why did she have to wait so long? What had made her mother change? Maybe it was knowing what had happened to Dee and having Rose as a part of their family now. They were finally complete.

Rebekah dried her tears, feeling somewhat better with the release. As she got ready for bed, she sighed, resigned to the fact that at least she had a warm relationship with her mom *now*. She would be grateful and move forward with that.

Chapter 31

"I know I say this every year, but that was the best turkey and meal I think we have ever had," Jake said, turning to his mom.

"Thank you, Jake, but I had help from Rose this year, and the rest of you brought all the side dishes, so I can't claim all the glory."

"I just did what Grandma said." Rose raised her hands in the air. "She was the brains behind this bird. If she said jump, I asked how high, if you know what I mean."

"Oh, we sure do," Jake responded. "Do you still have that large wooden spoon in the second drawer in the kitchen, Mom?"

"I guess the next time you act up, you'll find out, son," Ruth said and gave her son the stink eye.

Everyone laughed. It was so nice for Rebekah to hear Rose call her mother "Grandma." Surely Dee was looking down on them at that moment with a smile.

"Jake may say that every year, but I do *this* every year," Tom said as he leaned back, loosened his belt a notch, and undid the top button on his jeans while letting out a sigh, causing hysterics at the table.

"I was just thinking the same thing, Tom," Jake said and followed suit, causing more laughs. He gave his brother a high five and said, "When in Rome …."

"Does that mean you guys have no room for pumpkin pie?" Deb, Tom's wife asked.

"No, sweetheart, I did this just to make sure I had room for it," Tom said.

With that, Steve and Ben exchanged a look, then also loosened their belts and unbuttoned their jeans.

"What about you, Andrew?" Ben gave the boy a look.

"Guys, I already planned ahead and wore my gym pants," Andrew sat back in his chair and pulled at his stretchy waistband, giving them a thumbs up.

"Now that it's unanimous, bring on the pie, please—and don't skimp on the whipped cream!" Tom said, patting his belly.

Rebekah laughed until her sides hurt. She wiped the tears from her eyes and looked around the room, smiling. Oh, how she had missed this. For a moment, she thought about a day in the future when her boys and Rose would be married with their own families who would come to her house for Thanksgiving so she could cook this special dinner for them. *One can dream*, she thought.

As was usual in her family, she and her sisters-in-law—Deb, Lori, and Jane—cleaned up, with Rose tagging along. Rebekah enjoyed this time, getting caught up on her nieces and nephews, since she wasn't around anymore to pick up the bits of information here and there when she saw her family. This time the women were mostly interested in Rose and bombarded the poor girl with questions about her life and what she was going to do in the future. To be honest, Rebekah was interested too, because Rose had been very closedmouth on the matter.

"Well," she started, "Andrew and I talk about this a lot. He and Rebekah have encouraged me to continue my education. I'm just taking basic classes right now, but I'm thinking about a major in business."

This was new information to Rebekah, and she paid attention.

"I haven't told anyone but Andrew that I'm going to take a couple of business classes next semester to see how I like it. I've really enjoyed working in Rebekah's new shop and would like to stay on after I graduate. Andrew likes the idea too and said that would make it a true family business."

"That sounds great," Rebekah said. "There is nothing I would love more."

Rose smiled.

Tom's wife, Deb, spoke. "All of us knew and loved your mom and know how proud she would be of you if she could see you now." Deb and Jake's wife, Lori, each put an arm around Rose.

Rose looked back and forth between them, and just when it seemed like she would smile, she broke down into a sob.

Rebekah's eyes immediately teared up, which then got Jane started as well. "All of you stop it now," Rebekah proclaimed as she and Jane joined the group hug.

Just then, Jake walked into the kitchen and abruptly stopped.

"What's wrong? I was just wondering if there was any pumpkin pie left. What happened?" Jake asked, his eyes wide with equal parts concern and confusion.

Rebekah looked to him, tears running down her cheeks. "It's a girl thing. Go away."

He paused and scratched his head, then proceeded with caution. "Oh … okay. Mom also wanted to know when you were coming back out to visit some more."

Rebekah lifted her head from the group. "Tell her five minutes," she said and then rejoined the group hug.

The women started laughing as soon as Jake left the room.

"Let's go on out before any more of them come looking for us," Rose suggested.

They all visited in the family room for a couple more hours until Rebekah could see her mom's eyelids drooping. She suggested they head home since they had a long drive to Milwaukee the next day and a full rest of the week. She was glad she would see more of her brothers at the wedding on Saturday.

The next morning, they packed up their rental car and headed out. Rebekah hated saying goodbye to her mom, but she felt better doing so than she had the last time she was there. Although Ruth looked frail, she seemed as if she were participating in life again, which was a big improvement. Rebekah told her mother that she hoped to come visit again in the spring. "I can come help you plant some flowers and a little garden like we used to do," she suggested, which seemed to make Ruth happy, and Rebekah was glad to give her mother something to look forward to.

***

They left Ruth's house Tuesday morning at around 10:30 and, after stopping for lunch on the way, arrived at James and Violet's place close to 3 p.m. Both James and Violet had taken the full week off for the wedding as well as the following week for their honeymoon to the Florida Keys.

The couple looked so happy. Rebekah couldn't wait for Violet to be her new daughter-in-law.

"Mom, I was thinking some hamburgers and brats on the grill tonight would be good, even though I know it's November. Figured you guys would like some local food."

Rebekah nodded her head enthusiastically. James had that right.

"Have you got all the stuff to put on it? Like sauerkraut?" Andrew questioned hopefully.

"As a matter of fact, brother, I do—in addition to Violet's homemade dill pickles and her secret-recipe potato salad. I'm shocked you would even ask about the sauerkraut since it's a given." James smiled at Violet who rolled her eyes and laughed.

"I'm in heaven." Andrew made prayer hands and closed his eyes dramatically.

"We'll go get checked in at the hotel, unload, and come back around 5:30. Does that sound okay?" Rebekah suggested.

"Sounds good, Mom. We're happy we don't have snow yet, and the weather isn't going to get really cold till the end of next week," James remarked.

"You know, we do get cold weather in Asheville, just not as long and severe as yours here." Rebekah laughed. "It's just enough to satisfy me."

The hotel was nice and looked like a place that could cater to both small and large events. Down a hall to the left was a fancy-looking restaurant, where Rebekah figured they would be having the rehearsal dinner, and a little sandwich place was tucked away just off the lobby. On the right was a hallway lined with doors where she figured the rooms for the wedding ceremony and reception must be. In the suite, they each had their own bedroom, but they did have to share a bathroom. A small kitchenet and living area finished the space off.

The first thing Rebekah and Rose did was get their dresses out of their suitcases to hang and let the wrinkles start to smooth out before they all headed back to James and Violet's place for supper.

As Rose, Andrew, and James visited, Violet filled Rebekah in on what was going on leading up to the wedding.

"Andrew, as you know, is James's best man, so he'll need to get measured tomorrow for his rental tux now that he's in town. Nothing else is going on during the day, but my parents want to have you over tomorrow night for supper—just our two families. Thursday we're having a bridesmaid luncheon that you and Rose are invited to, and Friday is the rehearsal and dinner. I know you said to choose wherever we wanted for the dinner, so James decided to make reservations at the hotel restaurant. It's really nice."

"Yes, I saw it when we checked in. It does look nice. That all sounds good to me. You have everything well planned out, Violet. I would expect no less from two accountants."

"Oh, and I'm sure James didn't tell you this, but we've been taking ballroom dancing lessons, so we'll look good for our first dance. And you know there's a mother-son dance, don't you?" she asked.

Rebekah hadn't been to many weddings as fancy as this one, so she was ignorant on what was proper, but she nodded and said, "Yes, of course," as if she'd known all along.

"Oh, good. You don't have to worry about him not knowing how to lead you around the dance floor. He's rather good," she gushed with a giggle.

"I can't wait. James always had good rhythm," Rebekah added.

The hamburgers and brats were good. Not only had Violet made the homemade pickles and potato salad, but she had also prepared pickled beets. That girl had talent.

After they got back to the hotel, Rose suggested it might be fun if she and Rebekah checked out a shopping mall the next day. She figured Andrew and James might want to hang out together after they went to get Andrew measured for his tux.

It will be nice for the boys to have some alone time together, Rebekah thought.

***

Violet's parents, Betty and Jerry Wolfman, were very nice people. They lived in Wauwatosa, which was just outside of Milwaukee. Betty had made pork tenderloin with roasted vegetables, mashed potatoes, and gravy. It was delicious. For dessert she made cheesecake with strawberries on top.

"I was very nervous cooking for you," Betty admitted. "Violet has told me how well you cook and bake. I mean, after all, you own a bakery!"

"I would hire you in a minute, Betty. That cheesecake was amazing, and I'm wanting to ask for the recipe. You have a talent yourself, and so does Violet. I've tasted her jam before, and yesterday we had her pickles and pickled beets as well as one of the best potato salads I've ever had. Did you teach her?" Rebekah inquired.

"Well, thank you. And I did, but she's a natural. She has two younger brothers, so she and I stuck together, and cooking was our thing. Now, I would really love to hear more about your bakery."

Rebekah told her all about how exciting it was to renovate both the shop and the upstairs apartment where she and Andrew now lived. "I've wanted to open a bakery since I was a girl, and making that dream come true feels a little surreal at times. My grandmother inspired me."

"I can tell it's your passion just by the tone in your voice when you tell me about it, Rebekah. You're a blessed woman," Betty acknowledged.

"Well, thank you, Betty. Yes, I am blessed," Rebekah said gratefully.

The next day, Andrew drove Rose and Rebekah to the bridal luncheon. Rebekah was excited, having never known there was such a thing. Her interest was heightened when she found out they were going to the Schuster Mansion in Milwaukee for High Tea.

This should be fun, she thought as they cruised down the highway.

Included in the party along with Rebekah, Rose, and Betty, were Violet's aunts, grandmothers, cousins, the four bridesmaids, and various other female friends. It was a lovely time. Rebekah made mental notes and took a few pictures of things she wanted to share with Lois when she got back to Asheville.

Betty dropped Rose and Rebekah back at the hotel room afterward. Rebekah had gotten to know Betty better at the luncheon and the dinner the night before, and thankfully, she liked her a lot as well as the rest of the family she had met.

It was three o'clock when Rebekah and Rose got back to their room where they found Andrew and James waiting for them.

"We had such a nice time," Rose shared. "I've never seen a place like that before. I almost felt we had gone back in time."

"It really was lovely, just like Violet's family and friends," Rebekah told the boys. "So did you get all measured, Andrew? I hope they don't have to do too many alterations. Where did you go for lunch? Can't wait to tell Lois about a few things that gave me some ideas for Marie Claudine's," Rebekah rambled and then saw the seriousness on her son's faces.

"Hey, Mom, come here and sit down," James gestured to the sofa, and Rebekah looked to Rose before she sat down facing the boys.

James let out a long sigh. "I got a call from Dad. He's coming to the wedding and would like to see Andrew and me before Saturday." He opened his mouth but hesitated before he proceeded. "So we're leaving around four o'clock to go meet him."

Rebekah instantly had a sick feeling in her stomach and couldn't speak. She had known this moment might be coming and told herself, *Breathe. You can get through it.*

Noticing her distress, Rose quickly got her a glass of water then sat next to her on the sofa.

"He called this morning and wants Andrew and me to come to his hotel room to visit and then take the two of us to dinner," James continued. "Up until today, I hadn't heard from him and thought maybe he wouldn't be at the wedding, but I wasn't really sure." He looked at Andrew and then back to his mother. "We're both a little nervous, since when we went at Christmastime last year, it was really uncomfortable. But you know I had to invite him and Emily, Mom," he explained.

Rebekah looked down at her hands and closed her eyes for a long while before speaking. The room may have been silent, but in her head, it felt like a freight train of thoughts was rolling through. *Will I have to sit next to him for the ceremony? Will he try to speak to me? Will I have to stand with him for pictures? Will he ask a bunch of questions? And how many questions will I have to answer from people who don't know our history? … And then there's Emily! Ugh!*

She finally spoke, "Is Emily with him?"

The boys looked at each other. James got up and sat in the empty spot on the sofa next to his mom. He took her hand in his. "We don't know, but we'll find out tonight, and then we can plan from there. Just so you know, I had to tell Violet's parents about the … situation. They understand and will do what they can to protect you. I'm going to call your brothers and tell them also. You have an army here to make sure you have minimal contact with him. I'm not inviting him to the rehearsal or the rehearsal dinner, so it will only be the wedding and reception when you see him. It's going to be okay."

Yes, it will be okay, she thought. She looked at James. This wedding was a celebration of Violet and him starting their life together, and there was no way she was going to let Ethan—or herself—ruin that. A determination came over her.

"Son, I'm fine. And I'm so sorry this has to be a cloud over your special day. I will soldier through with a smile on my face and celebrate you and Violet. And if your dad tries to make trouble, I'm sure my brothers can quietly handle him."

"No doubt about that," Andrew mumbled. He raised his eyebrows and scoffed with a grin. "And they'll do it with a smile."

Rebekah smiled at Andrew and gave a soft laugh.

"Now go see your father, and don't worry about me," Rebekah said with assuredness and then turned to Rose. "Rose and I will get our jammies on, order room service, and watch some romantic girlie movie tonight. What do you say, Rose?"

"Sounds good to me," Rose responded.

James gave his mom a big hug and a kiss on the cheek. "I'm so happy you're my mom."

"Me too," said Andrew who joined the group hug.

And in a second, Rebekah was in tears again—happy ones.

Chapter 32

When James and Andrew returned from their dinner with Ethan, they had some good news for Rebekah. Ethan had come alone. No Emily. But Rebekah now wondered why that was. Andrew must have read her mind.

"Dad said the reason Emily didn't come was because she had to work and couldn't get off, but I don't believe it. When we visited after Christmas, she seemed to be in another world. She acted like she and Dad had never been separated and like they had raised us together. Really weird. She talked to James about the wedding plans constantly. Honestly, the way she doted on us, I would have thought she'd quit her job just to come for the wedding. I'm happy she's not coming, but it doesn't make sense," Andrew said and shrugged his shoulders.

Rebekah was surprised too but reminded herself that this was actually good news. After all, Emily could be a loose cannon, and they didn't need that at the wedding.

***

The next day, Steve called to say they were on their way. It was only going to be Rebekah's brothers and their wives coming down to Milwaukee for the wedding. Her brother's sons had to run the family auto shop for the next couple of days, and the other kids couldn't get away from their school or jobs either. Now that she was a business owner, Rebekah understood the hoops you sometimes had to jump through just to get away. Everyone would check into the hotel and see them at the rehearsal dinner.

Everything was progressing smoothly, and Rebekah was getting excited—despite Ethan.

The rehearsal was fun. James and Violet were both nervous, which Rebekah found very sweet. Violet carried all the ribbons in the various colors, shapes, and sizes taken from her bridal shower gifts that had been formed into the traditional paper-plate rehearsal bouquet. Rebekah had met Violet's bridesmaids at the luncheon the day before and thought maybe Andrew would zero in on one of them. But from what she could see, he was flirting with just about every young woman there—including Rose. *He is a bit of a cad*, she thought and softly chuckled to herself. Everyone in the wedding party seemed to relax more once they got to the rehearsal dinner, Rebekah included.

Soon, Rebekah's brothers and their wives showed up at the hotel restaurant. Rebekah was talking to Violet's mom Betty when they walked in and didn't notice them until Tom tapped her on the shoulder. She turned around, and to her surprise, there was her mother on his arm.

"Mom! You decided to come," Rebekah greeted her excitedly. "I can't believe it. What made you change your mind? I'm so happy you're here!"

"I decided I just couldn't stand being left home all alone and not with all of you. Everybody loves a wedding," Ruth announced, and they all laughed—except Rebekah who was brought to tears.

Rebekah loved seeing how their family and Violet's came together. The guys were all heavy into fishing and hunting, especially since deer hunting season was just a few weeks away. And, of course, there was speculation on how well The Pack was going to do this year.

The festivities wrapped up around 8 p.m. Just before Rebekah left, Betty approached her and took her aside.

"Rebekah, I know you're probably concerned about seating for the wedding tomorrow."

Rebekah had thought of it but figured she would just have to tough it out and sit next to Ethan. She was just relieved Emily wasn't there. And her brothers, no doubt, would be behind her watching his every move.

"I just want to put your mind at ease. We did some checking on etiquette that will work for your situation, and there are several options suggested. For the ceremony, we decided Ethan will sit two rows behind you. Andrew will first escort your mother to the front row, and then James will escort you to the seat next to her on the aisle. I would suggest you pick two of your brothers to sit behind you. One to escort you from the ceremony and one to escort your mother. Ethan will then leave after you and your mother are escorted out but before everyone else leaves. At the reception, I have Ethan sitting at a table with my family. They are assigned to entertain him and keep him away from you so you can enjoy this day. It will all work out beautifully." Betty smiled and gave her a hug.

"Betty, I'm so grateful you thought of everything." Rebekah took Betty's hand. "And if you ever come to visit me in Asheville, I have a friend named Lois you absolutely must meet."

Rebekah was surprised at how animated her mom had been that evening. Maybe participating in life by spending more time with people really was the best medicine for her. Rebekah made a mental note to talk to her brothers about it. If their mother could travel this far in the car, she hoped maybe one of them *could* fly with her down to Asheville for a trip. Ruth had never flown in an airplane before, but Rebekah was starting to believe this new version of her mother could handle the trip.

After dinner, all the young people decided to go out for a drink and kindly invited Rebekah to tag along, but she politely declined. Her plan was to get ready for bed and have a good night's sleep. She was in bed by 10 p.m., never hearing Rose and Andrew arrive back.

***

Today was the big day. Rose offered to fix Rebekah's hair a little fancier than the way she usually wore it—which wasn't too hard since Rebekah almost always wore her hair down or in a ponytail. After just fifteen minutes, Rose had Rebekah's light-brown hair in what Rose called an "elegant updo." Rose handed her a mirror to see the back. Rebekah smiled. She liked the way it was twisted around here and there in ringlets on the back of her head. She felt like a princess. "Rose, I love it," she said and gave her niece a squeeze.

"Great. Next, I'm doing your makeup. We're going to have them wondering if you're the mom or the sister of the groom when I'm done." Rose giggled and went to work.

The wedding ceremony would begin at 4 p.m., but they were to be there at 2:30 for family pictures. Rebekah had anticipated Ethan would be there, and he was, but so were her brothers Steve and Ben as well as two of Betty's brothers, including Bobby Becker, the former police officer and private detective she had worked with when she was looking for Dee. They were all on it. She was well protected.

"Hey, Rebekah." It was Bobby. "How are ya?"

"Good, Bobby. I hope you're doing well too."

"Feel like I'm back on the force. My sister wants me to keep James's dad occupied. Kinda looking forward to the fun," he said and chuckled as he patted her arm. "Consider it done. You just have a good time," he said and gave Rebekah a peck on her cheek.

"Thank you, Bobby. It's good to know you're on the job."

Rebekah excused herself from Bobby and went to find Rose. As she scanned the area, she spotted Ethan talking to Violet's parents. It had been a year and a half since the day he had come to her mom's house to say goodbye, but it was in the forefront of her mind as if it were yesterday. She could feel her heart racing and wished she could slow it. Ethan looked as if he had aged some. More gray hair at his temples and the laugh lines around his eyes were deeper. He looked a little thinner also but was still the handsome man he always had been. Just then he turned, and their eyes linked. It totally unnerved her, causing her stomach to churn and her heart to race even more. She immediately turned away and went to stand by Ben.

Oh my God, can I do this? she thought as, for a moment, she struggled to take a deep breath.

Ben must have sensed her unease because he put his arm around her and said, "Sis, you are not alone. We love you and will protect you. Now, let's go get those pictures done."

Her bodyguards were true to their words. Betty's brothers stayed with Ethan, and Rebekah's brothers stayed with her.

As they wrapped up the photos, Ruth wanted to visit the restroom, so Rebekah offered to go with her. As they walked down the hallway, suddenly, there was Ethan right in front of them. She was trapped and felt helpless.

"Hello, Rebekah!" Ethan said, sounding happily surprised. He then turned to her mom. "Ruth, so good to see you."

Ruth took one look at him and let loose. "You! You ought to be ashamed of yourself. Nothing but a liar. You lied to our church, you lied to those boys, you lied to my family, and worst of all, you lied to my daughter. You call yourself a man of the cloth? More like a man of the devil. Well, let me tell you something, Mr. Devil, we have risen above your deceit and are stronger than ever." She put her hand on Rebekah's shoulder. "And my girl here is far better off than she ever was with a lying cheat like you. She is successful and happy. 'Praise God' is all I have to say. C'mon Rebekah. I can't stand the smell of someone burning in hell."

It appeared for the first time since Rebekah had known him that Ethan Hayward didn't have a comeback. He stood there, mouth flapping in the wind as Ruth waited a moment, smiled, then continued to the restroom with Rebekah close behind her, never looking back.

Yes! Now that was the mom Rebekah had grown up with. *Fire and brimstone!*

Soon it was time to be seated. The procession went just as Betty had planned it. Rebekah and her mother were escorted to their front row seats by the boys, and her brothers were seated behind them. Ethan came in after them and sat behind her brothers. James stood with the groomsmen and minister at the front as the four bridesmaids made their way down the aisle. Then the traditional "Here Comes the Bride" played, and Violet, the most beautiful bride Rebekah had ever seen, came down the aisle, arm in arm with her father. Her dress was simple but elegant—white lace with a sweetheart neckline, A-line skirt, and full-length lace sleeves—and she carried a bouquet of the faintest blush-pink and white roses.

She's stunning, Rebekah thought.

Violet met eyes with Rebekah and gave her a sweet smile just before James walked over to take his bride's hand. Good thing Rebekah had planned ahead with plenty of tissues in her bag. She already needed them.

The ceremony was about fifteen minutes long, and then they proceeded straight into the cocktail hour, followed by dinner and dancing. The mother and son dance with James was so special for Rebekah. Violet was correct: James could lead a woman around the dance floor. Rebekah couldn't get over how smoothly James steered her around the dance floor and even twirled her around at the end. Later, very sweetly, James asked his grandmother for a dance. They made some wonderful memories that day.

Violet's parents provided their daughter with a "dream-come-true" wedding. Rebekah hoped one day she could do the same for Rose when she was ready to get married.

Rebekah smiled as she watched Rose having so much fun with her newfound family, fitting in as if she had always been a part of them. She danced with each of her uncles at least once and hung around with James and Violet's friends—and Andrew—most of the evening. Rebekah loved watching Andrew and Rose dance together. They really enjoyed each other's company. Both had worked so hard to help her with the shop, and Andrew was always so serious all the time; he needed to let loose like this. She was relieved to see them dancing and laughing with people their own age.

Finally, the DJ announced he was playing the last song—a slow one. Rebekah looked up and, to her horror, spotted Ethan heading straight for her. Andrew must have seen it also because he came out of nowhere and grabbed her hand.

"Hey, you haven't danced with me all night, Mom," he said and pulled her to the dance floor.

Phew. That was close.

Ethan must have left during the last song because she didn't see him again. She couldn't lie—she wanted to know about his conversations with the boys but would not ask. It might be better not to know.

Overall, it had been an amazing day. Andrew and Rose were still visiting with people when Rebekah made the rounds to say good night to everyone and went upstairs to the hotel room. She was beat.

She went straight to her room, kicked off her shoes, then slipped out of her dress and put it neatly back on the hanger. She loved the dress and wondered when she may have a chance to wear it again. *You never know*, she figured.

After she finished getting ready for bed, she checked the clock. She thought Andrew and Rose would have been back by then, but they weren't, so she grabbed a glass of water and sat on the sofa, appreciating some alone time after being around so many people.

What a great wedding, she thought. She sure wished Lois could have been there to see it and meet Violet's mom. She and Betty were like two peas in a pod now.

Just then, she heard someone struggling with the door knob and laughing in the hallway. *Must be Rose and Andrew.* She looked through the peek hole and saw it was them. She opened the door and was greeted by their happy faces.

"Well, hellooooo, Mom! Now tell me, did you have a good time tonight?" Andrew said in a spirited tone with a toothy smile.

Rose stood right next to him, laughing uncontrollably as they barely held each other up.

"I couldn't have asked for a better time," Rebekah responded.

"Same here," agreed Rose.

"Why don't you come in before you wake up everyone on our floor?" Rebekah said, ushering them in and closing the door. *Yikes.*

They plopped on the sofa, and Rebekah sat in a chair.

"I guess you took advantage of the open bar, huh? Don't worry, I'm not going to fuss at you, Rose, because I know you're twenty-one next month. Now that I know you are safely back, I'm going to bed."

For some reason this was hilarious to Andrew and Rose who broke into a fit of giggles again.

Rebekah shook her head and stood. "Good night! I'm ready to pass out. See you in the morning," she said, walked to her room, and closed the door.

"Good night, Rebekah!" Rose sang out cheerfully.

"Good night, Mom!" Andrew said, giggling once more.

***

The next morning, Rebekah's family met at her hotel for breakfast to enjoy one last visit before they all had to head back home. Much to Rebekah's pleasure and surprise, both Andrew and Rose made it down to be with the family—although they were very subdued and teased relentlessly by their uncles.

"What a beautiful wedding, Rebekah," Ruth said. "I've never been to something so fancy before. I'll be resting all next week to recuperate, but I wouldn't have missed it for anything."

"I don't think I've ever seen you shake your booty that much before, Mom," Ben teased. "Didn't know you had it in you."

Everyone laughed.

Ruth was so flustered, she could only stammer.

"Don't worry, Mom," Steve said, "we took lots of pictures of you shaking it on the dance floor to show your friends."

The expression of shock on their mother's face had them laughing so hard, a couple of them had to wipe their eyes.

"I would like you to know," Ruth said, rather indignantly, "your father and I were *quite* the dancers back in our day. Sometimes when you kids were very small, Dad and I would even play a record and dance together. After more of you arrived and got older, we had to stop dancing at night because we were so busy and tired by that time."

Tom was sitting next to Ruth, and he picked up her hand and kissed it. "That's a great story, Mom. Thanks for sharing it with us."

"You know, Mom, if it hadn't been for that dancing, you might not have as many of us," Jake said and chuckled.

Ruth shot him the "You're in trouble" look they were all too familiar with from childhood. No explanation needed. They all broke out in laughter.

Soon it was time to say goodbye to her family, and Rebekah got a little teary-eyed as she gave each brother and sister-in-law a hug. Her brothers, as always, cracked a few jokes to help alleviate her sadness—and theirs also. They loved their little sister.

Rebekah, Rose, and Andrew did a little driving around Milwaukee in the afternoon. Andrew wanted Rose to see his old college. They stopped for a bite to eat at a little sandwich shop he had frequented.

Both Andrew and Rose were not their usual selves, still recuperating from their wedding fun the night before, so Rebekah suggested they go back to the hotel for a nap. She was tired too, thinking about how she'd need all the energy she could muster when she got back.

They got back to the hotel, and Rebekah went straight to her room to nap. When she got up a couple of hours later, she came out to the common room to find the TV on and Andrew and Rose both sound asleep on the sofa. Andrew sat slouched on one end, his head hanging back, and Rose lay curled up with her head in his lap and Andrew's hand resting on her shoulder. At first, Rebekah was a little surprised by their comfortable posture, but then shrugged, figuring it was probably more comfortable to watch TV that way.

Rebekah went back to her room to begin gathering some of her things together to make packing up in the morning a little easier. After a couple of minutes, there was a knock on the door. It was Rose.

"Hey, I need to get my stuff together too," Rose said, still looking rather sleepy. "Andrew wants to go to some restaurant he loves tonight. Are you okay with that?"

"Of course," Rebekah said, "or maybe the restaurant does take out?"

"That sounds even better to me." Rose laughed. "We can outnumber Andrew if he wants to go out."

"That's right." Rebekah was on board.

"Sounds good." Rose plopped herself on Rebekah's bed.

"You two sure were snuggled up out there," Rebekah stated.

"Were we?" Rose answered. "I didn't notice …. I'm pretty tired." She let out a big yawn. "Anyway, this has been a busy, fun week, hasn't it? But I'm ready for home."

"Me too. I've missed Asheville," Rebekah said. And then Harrison came to mind. She was looking forward to seeing him when she got home. *Home.* Yes, Asheville was her home now, and she couldn't be happier.

Chapter 33

Rebekah's phone rang as she, Andrew, and Rose were standing at the airport baggage claim the next day. It was Lois.

"Hi! Yes, we're waiting for my suitcase, and we'll be right out. Is everything okay, or did you pick the short straw to come get us? … Okay. Oh, I see my suitcase. We'll be right out. Bye." She hung up. "Listen, you two head out with your suitcases," Rebekah said, turning to Andrew and Rose. "I see mine coming. Lois is picking us up, so be watching for her car. I'll be right out."

Soon they were greeted by Lois's big hugs and loaded their suitcases in the back of her car.

"I hope everything is okay with the shop?" Rebekah asked as they pulled away from the airport.

"Everything went great. Michael is an amazing manager. You are very lucky to have him on board," Lois assured her.

It was close to 2 p.m. by the time they arrived at the shop.

"I'll take our stuff upstairs, Mom. Why don't you go ahead and find Michael and get the lowdown? I know you can't wait," Andrew said. "And I'll leave your stuff in Lois's car, Rose."

"Thanks, Andrew," Rose said and gave his back a little rub.

Everything looked just as Lois had said: perfect.

Rebekah spotted Michael at the other end of the shop and gave him a wave. He waved back and headed her way.

"Welcome back, Rebekah," he greeted her. "Have you had any lunch? How about a sandwich? I'll get someone to make you guys something."

"That would be great," Rose jumped in. "I'm starving. I know Andrew would probably like something also."

"Sara!" Michael motioned her to come over. "Would you kindly make a few club sandwiches and bring them over here for our travelers? And a pitcher of sweet tea? Thank you," he said and pointed to a table in the back of the dining area.

Rebekah walked around with Michael a little bit and then joined Rose and Andrew at the table with the sandwiches. Everything looked perfect as far as Rebekah could see.

"Michael," Andrew shook his hand, "thanks, man. Just knowing you were here allowed us to enjoy the wedding."

"It was my pleasure. I'm grateful for you guys giving me a new purpose in my life. We've got a win-win situation here I would say."

"Yes, we do," Rebekah agreed.

After they ate, they went to work. Andrew, of course, went to his office to look at the numbers, and Rebekah went to the kitchen. Everyone was happy to see her and wanted to know all about the wedding. She had a few pictures on her phone to share, and soon she felt as if she hadn't been gone at all.

Rebekah sent Rose home with Lois after they ate. She had missed some of her classes while they were gone and needed to hit the books so she would be ready for class the next morning. The rest of the day was winding down—as was Rebekah.

"Cathy, you did a great job. Looks like you and Michael work well together," Rebekah teased with a sly look when the two of them were alone.

Cathy giggled like a schoolgirl, and her cheeks turned a little pink. "Stop teasing. But you know what? We really do," she said and giggled some more.

Rebekah looked at her watch. It was almost 4:30, and the place was empty. Mondays were traditionally slow toward the end of the day.

"Cathy, why don't you and the rest of the staff tidy things up and take off early? I'm here, and so are Michael and Andrew. We can handle whatever comes up in the next half hour," Rebekah assured her.

"Are you sure?" Cathy asked.

"Yes, and I'll see you bright and early tomorrow morning."

"Okay, Rebekah. See you tomorrow." Cathy wrapped up the cookie dough she had just finished mixing and placed it in the refrigerator for the next day. Shortly after, everything else was taken care of, so she headed out the door.

No one came in, so Michael and Rebekah were able to have a little catch up meeting in the kitchen about the upcoming week and some ideas they both had. At about three minutes to five, they heard the bell jingle on the door and laughed.

"One last customer right at closing, isn't that the way it always goes?" Rebekah said to Michael with a roll of her eyes. She walked out to the counter and quickly saw it was no customer.

It was Harrison.

"Hi," Rebekah said, feeling a flutter in her chest.

"Hi. You're back!"

"I am."

"Rebekah, everything is taken care of, and I'm locking the door on my way out," Michael announced as he came walking out of the kitchen. With his back to Harrison, he winked at Rebekah. "See you tomorrow, Rebekah. Harrison, good to see you," he added, nodding his head Harrison's way with a lift of his eyebrows as he proceeded out through the front door and locked it.

"I thought I'd wait to come by at closing time, since I'm sure you had your hands full after the trip," Harrison said.

"Actually, things went very well while we were gone, and there wasn't much I had to do. Michael is a pro. I'm lucky to have him here."

"So how was your family and the wedding?" he asked.

"Let's sit down over here, and we can talk," Rebekah suggested. "How about something to drink or a sandwich?"

"A drink would be great. Do you still have that cherry lemonade?"

"We do. I'll fix one for each of us."

Just as Rebekah went to get two glasses, Andrew popped in.

"Hi, Harrison. Hey, Mom, I'm falling asleep looking at my computer. I'm heading upstairs. Tomorrow is another day." Andrew looked like he was going to fall over. "You kids have fun." He gave a little wave and headed upstairs.

"Andrew did a bit of partying at the wedding, and I don't think he's caught up yet," Rebekah whispered as she shook her head and chuckled.

"Well, you're not best man for your brother every day, are you? And besides, that's what weddings are for." Harrison chuckled also.

They went to sit down and Harrison realized he was carrying his contractor clipboard. He held it up awkwardly for Rebekah to see and they both chuckled. "I'm so used to bringing this thing with me whenever I go somewhere." He playfully bumped his forehead with his palm. "I guess I just picked it up subconsciously. Don't let me forget it when I leave. I'll need it in the morning."

They sat for a while, talking about the wedding and Rebekah's family. Harrison was an only child and said he couldn't imagine having so many people in his life. She knew Harrison probably wondered about Ethan but was sure Andrew would fill him in, which was fine with her.

Harrison told Rebekah about his latest jobs and how he didn't want to do any more out of town. His next job would be a building similar to hers just a couple blocks down. He was finding there was plenty of local work to keep him busy, and he liked the idea of working with local business owners. In fact, he was thinking about promoting one of his guys to help supervise his jobs since he'd had so many opportunities arise recently.

Harrison paused for a long time, looking down at his hands and then up before he spoke. "I've missed you this past week," he said, keeping his eyes focused on her.

"I've missed you too." Rebekah returned the gaze and felt her heart beat wildly in her chest.

"I told you before you left that I wanted to take you out to dinner, and I've been counting the days till you would be back so I could do that. I hope you haven't changed your mind."

"Oh, no. I've been looking forward to it," she said and took a sip of her lemonade, her mouth suddenly dry.

"I know you're closed on Sundays, so how does this Saturday night sound? I'm going to pick out somewhere nice and surprise you."

"This Saturday sounds perfect," she replied, feeling all warm and tingly. She extended her hand to him across the table.

Harrison tenderly covered her hand with his and held it. "Well, great," he said, seeming more relaxed and smiling. "How about I pick you up at six thirty?"

"That sounds good," she answered, feeling a little more relaxed herself, though very excited. She had never been on a date before.

They visited a little longer, and soon, her eyelids became heavy as the day caught up to her.

Harrison must have noticed. "Hey, listen. I bet you're ready to call it a day. I better let you go up to bed. Do you need any help here finishing up?" Harrison asked as he stood up.

"No, it looks like Cathy and Michael took care of everything before they left. I'll put these glasses in the kitchen, and then go upstairs. Thank you for coming by."

As she stood up, Harrison took a step forward and gently placed his hands on her shoulders, then slipped them down her back and pulled her closer. She put her head on his chest, hearing his heartbeat and feeling the heat radiating from his body. He pulled away slightly, and she looked up at him with a smile. He took his right hand, ran it through her hair, and smiled back as he let out a soft, breathy chuckle. With his other hand, he delicately lifted her chin and met her with a gentle, loving kiss.

"Do you know how long I've wanted to do this?" he said, still holding her in his arms. "Since that night I met you upstairs …. When you caught me using the bathroom." He smiled sheepishly as he pressed his forehead to hers, and they both laughed.

"I can laugh about that now, but at the time I didn't know what kind of crazy person you were or what kind of danger I was in," Rebekah shared and patted his chest teasingly.

"I can understand that. You actually scared me a little bit also. I figured you were going to pull out mace or a stun gun from your purse, and I would be lying on the floor …. Possibly wetting myself."

They both laughed hard, and after a few more tender kisses, he whispered, "I think I better go" and laughed. "You need to get some sleep."

"I do," she said quietly. "Tomorrow will be here soon."

Silently, they walked to the door, hand in hand. Harrison gave her one last kiss, paused a moment, and then turned to go. She watched for a few seconds, then locked the door behind him.

Rebekah sighed. Even though she was tired, she wasn't ready to go upstairs just yet and thought she'd sit for a moment to savor what had just happened. She hadn't thought she would ever find someone she wanted to be with again, but she liked this man and wanted to know him better. A cup of tea and a scone is what she needed to keep her company for a little while, so she heated some water, picked a decaffeinated tea since it was late in the day, and headed back to the table where she and Harrison had sat. Then she saw it. His clipboard. She gave a little laugh and shook her head. Just as she pulled out her phone to text him, there was a knock at the door. She laughed again, figuring it was Harrison coming back to get it, but when she got closer to the door, she was startled to realize it was not Harrison standing there.

It was Ethan.

"What are you doing here?" she asked.

"Rebekah, I only want to talk to you," he yelled through the glass window. "Your army of protectors made sure I didn't get near you at the wedding. I've become great friends with a guy that night named Bobby Becker. Violet's uncle. It was as if he was attached to my hip the whole night."

Rebekah chuckled. "I have nothing to say to you. Leave."

"Please, Rebekah. I only want to make things right. Please allow me to make amends," Ethan pleaded.

Rebekah considered walking away, but then she thought of James and Andrew.

"All right, but only for a few minutes." She unlocked the door and let him in.

The shop was dark with only the evening lights on as Ethan looked it over top to bottom.

"So this is *your* place? How did you ever afford to do this? Where did you get the money? I mean—"

"Ethan, you said you wanted to talk to me. Well, talk," Rebekah interjected in a voice she didn't know she had.

"Can we at least sit down?" He pointed to a table and sat down before she could respond. "I came all the way down here with the sole purpose to make things right between us—for the sake of James and Andrew and you treat me like—"

"I'll give you ten minutes, and then you're gone. Starts now." She cut him off again and looked at her watch, then back up at him. Ethan glared at her, clearly exasperated, but she didn't care.

"Rebekah … I know you are the only woman I have ever loved. Seeing you at the wedding has only reinforced that. You are the one I want to spend the rest of my life with. I don't want to be with Emily. I can divorce her, and we can be together again. We can start over here in this city where no one knows us. Emily is back in a mental facility. She's delusional. I've spoken with a lawyer, and I can get a divorce. Don't you see, Rebekah? We can have the life we always wanted. I've never stopped loving you."

Rebekah sighed and shook her head. What had she ever seen in this man? *Well, nothing really.* She had just done what her parents told her to do; she was to marry Ethan—the good man, the preacher—and that was that. She now understood how wrong they'd been. She never loved Ethan, but she did love his children—who became *her* children. She got up from her chair and pointed to the front door.

"Get out of here, Ethan. I have no love for you. You have betrayed me and so many other people—I don't know where to begin." She shook her head. "I know it's Christian to forgive, but there's no way—I can't go there with you, and I know I'll never be able to. Every day we lived together as husband and wife was a lie. I want nothing to do with you. You need to leave."

"Please don't say that, Rebekah. Give me another chance," he pleaded as his voice shook with disbelief. He was so used to getting his way. Then his face suddenly broke into a sly smile, and he said, "I hope you liked the flowers I sent for your birthday."

What? She had forgotten about the flowers. Around that time she had become so busy with getting the shop ready, she had forgotten to call the florist.

"*You* sent them? Why would you do that?" she asked, her voice breaking slightly. She was incensed.

"Because I still love you—I'll always love you," Ethan proclaimed with a demented look on his face Rebekah had never seen before.

Was he as crazy as Emily?

"I don't love you, Ethan, and I never want to see you again. I despise you. Please leave."

Suddenly, Ethan darted forward and grabbed her around the waist. As she tried to pull away, he leaned into her, and she shuffled and stumbled backward. In a matter of seconds, he had shoved her against the wall, all the while kissing and caressing her. His hold was strong, and she couldn't push him away. He had her pinned in a corner, and she was helpless. Rebekah tried to yell out, hoping to get Andrew's attention upstairs, but she couldn't catch her breath. Would Andrew even hear her? He was probably sound asleep. What could she do?

***

Harrison was beaming as he drove home. Rebekah was one of the finest women he had ever met, and Saturday seemed like forever away. As he glanced to his right before he made a turn onto his street, he realized his clipboard was missing from the seat next to him where he usually kept it. He had been so taken by Rebekah, he'd left it on the table. As he looked for a safe place to make a U-turn, he called Rebekah. There was no answer, so he called Andrew.

"Hello?" Andrew answered groggily.

"Hey. Listen, I left my clipboard in the shop when I was visiting with your mom, and I need to come back and get it. I called, but she didn't answer. Can one of you let me in?"

"Uh, yeah. I was sleeping, but I can come down." Andrew yawned and rubbed his eyes. "Hey, don't you still have a key?"

Harrison shook his head. He'd been meaning to give Rebekah his key back, but with his business being so busy, it had slipped his mind. "Yeah, as a matter of fact I do."

"Just use that. Mom must be in the shower or something. Just make sure you lock up behind you. See you later," he mumbled and hung up the phone.

Harrison parked by the front of the shop and had the key in hand when he noticed some movement inside the building and slowed his pace. Had somebody broken in? As he approached, he heard a muffled scream. What was going on? He bolted toward the door and couldn't unlock it fast enough.

***

Rebekah was fighting Ethan's advances the best she could, when all of a sudden something pulled him off her. Through her tears, she saw the silhouette of a figure swinging at Ethan. She caught her breath and focused her eyes to see Harrison pinning Ethan to the wall. Blood streamed from Ethan's nose. She ran to Harrison and grabbed his arm.

"Stop, Harrison! Please stop!" she screamed.

He was holding Ethan against the wall with one hand, ready to punch him again with the other.

Through her tears and breathlessness, she blurted, "This is Andrew and James's father. Please. Let him go." She studied Harrison's face and his look of rage and disgust, then looked to Ethan, so frightened and pitiful.

Harrison, breathing heavily, looked Rebekah in the eyes, nodded, and let go. Ethan fell to the floor.

"Rebekah?" Ethan pleaded as he looked from her to Harrison with horror in his eyes.

"Get out of here, Ethan," Rebekah said with a fire behind her voice. "I don't ever want to see you again. If I do, I'll press bigamy charges. Now I realize I was foolish to not have done it before. I've changed and will not hesitate to go after you if your face darkens my door or that of any other member of my family again. Now get out of here before I let him finish you off."

Ethan grabbed a bunch of paper napkins from a table to wipe his face. He didn't say another word, just walked, breathless, almost falling, out the front door. Rebekah quickly went and locked it, then walked to Harrison who was still breathing heavy. She put her head on his chest and crumbled as the tears fell heavily from her face.

"You came back," she whispered. Rebekah sobbed and clung to Harrison as his arms encompassed her. "What made you come back?"

Harrison took in a deep breath and exhaled before he responded with a scoff, "I ... forgot my clipboard."

Rebekah let out a laugh through her sobs.

Harrison wiped her tears with his sleeve and kissed her cheek. "I called you first and there was no answer, so then I called and woke up Andrew and he reminded me I still had a key, so I thought I would let myself in to get it." He looked down at his hands, which were bloodied from the fight. He paused for several seconds as he stared at them. "You know, I could have killed him when I saw him attacking you." Harrison looked her straight in her eyes as he confessed.

"I know. Had I the strength, I could have also."

Harrison chuckled and took her hands in his and gave each one a kiss.

"I'm sure that's the last we'll see of him. He's a pretty big coward." Rebekah leaned her face against Harrison's chest, enjoying the feeling of his arms encircled around her. She was safe.

"You have some mighty good guardian angels around you, woman," he said as he kissed the top of her head.

She smiled up at him. "Yes, it seems I do." She closed her eyes and leaned back into him. "Why don't you come upstairs and just hold me for a while? Could you do that?" Rebekah asked.

"It would be my pleasure," Harrison responded.

She pulled away to look at his face. This man was the real thing. She could feel his love and strength showering around her. There was nothing he wouldn't do for her.

They headed to the stairs, her arm around his waist, and his arm tightly around her shoulders. As Harrison pulled her closer to him, Rebekah felt a sense of belonging, one she'd never known could exist. She turned her head to look up at him, only to find him looking back down at her with a gentle smile on his face. At that moment, Rebekah knew: This was the man she had been waiting for. Was this what real love felt like? As they climbed the stairs slowly, holding on to each other, taking their time with each step, she smiled as she thought, of all the wonderful surprises that life had given her, this—by far—had been the best.

Acknowledgments

I had already started writing *Life's Surprises* before *Life's Fortune* was released and felt I was on track for a 2023 launch date, but just as life events present themselves to my characters, one managed to find its way into *my* world. My husband passed away. I thought writing would help me get through this, but it was a struggle, so I took a year off. This was a good thing for me to do because when I started back, it all felt fresh and new again, and I hoped maybe it would make me a better writer. You'll be the judge of that.

This book is dedicated to the two finest individuals I know. My daughters Elizabeth and Julianne. I may be a little biased, but they have turned out to be amazing women. Elizabeth, a pharmacist, married to a man in the military, and mother to my grandchildren. Julianne, a dedicated trauma ICU nurse who's been doing travel nursing for several years and loves what she does. The three of us are best friends and enjoy every chance we have together. I can't imagine a life without them. They have been my cheerleaders with every book I write as well as everything in life. I love you both to the moon and back.

Thank you to my publisher Mindy Kuhn and my editor Amy Ashby at Warren Publishing for all you do to help me get my books in print. You make it fun. Sue Marshall has been my lifelong friend whom I greatly appreciate along with her husband Bruce whom I drag in occasionally when I have legal questions when I'm writing. Thank you to my brothers Drew and David, Aunt Lois, sisters-in-law LeAnn, Kathy, Patti, and Cathy in addition to my cousins Pam, Katy, Sara, and Karen whose names I used for Rebekah's staff. Thought you all would like that.

I'm very grateful to all the Barnes & Noble locations who have me in for book signings; Cody Puzinski, owner of Hillcrest Pharmacy in Indian Trail, NC, for including my books in his gift area; Painted Tree Boutiques; and, last but not least, all the book clubs I've been invited to visit.

The pound cake that's referenced in this book is a tribute to my friend, Mable Topping, who gave me the recipe many years ago and told me it was the best pound cake I'll ever have. I agree and have made it so many times I can't even remember how many. I have included it at the end of this book. If you make it, let me know what you think. Mable passed away in 2010, and I have missed her very much.

My next book, and the third in the Life series, is *Life's Blessings* to be followed by the fourth and last book *Life's Journey*. I'm having so much fun creating this life for Rebekah. Make sure you check out the first book in the series *Life's Fortune* if you haven't already as well as my other series *White Lake* and its sequel *Return Home*.

Please visit my website susanamondtodd.com for more information and sign up for my newsletter.

Follow me on Facebook and Instagram at susanamondtodd.

Email me at info@susanamondtodd.com for programs and book clubs—I can do them in person or virtually—or just contact me. I'd love to hear from you.

Most importantly, thank you for reading this book.

Mabel's Pound Cake

1 tube pan
3 cups cake flour
½ teaspoon baking powder
½ teaspoon salt
2 sticks butter
½ cup shortening
3 cups sugar
5 eggs
1 cup milk with 2 teaspoons vanilla

1. Preheat oven to 325 degrees.
2. Grease a large tube pan, then lightly flour pan.
3. Cream butter and shortening in the large bowl of an electric mixer, then add sugar gradually. Beat well. Add eggs one at a time and mix well.
4. Mix all dry ingredients in a separate bowl, then add alternately with the milk-vanilla mixture to the ingredients in the mixer bowl. Beat well after each addition.
5. Pour mixed batter into the prepared tube pan, and bake for 1 hour and 30 minutes at 325 degrees.
6. Let sit 5 minutes before turning onto a plate.

Books by
Susan Amond Todd

Coastal Georgia Series
White Lake
Return Home

Life Series
Life's Fortune
Life's Surprises